THE CHRYSALIS OPTION

A KIANA AZUNNA NOVEL

ERIC COULSON

Published by Two Tails Media
213 Guthrie Avenue
Alexandria, Virginia 22305
coulsonwrites@gmail.com

Copyright © 2024 by Eric Coulson and Two Tails Media
This is a work of fiction. Names, characters, businesses, places, events, locales, and incidents are either the products of the author's imagination or used in a fictitious manner. Any resemblance to actual persons, living or dead, or actual events is purely coincidental.

Printed in the United States of America

2 4 6 8 10 9 7 5 3 1

ISBN (Paperback) 979-8-9888662-0-6
ISBN (E-book) 979-8-9888662-1-3

Cover design by Richard Ljoenes

For Karen

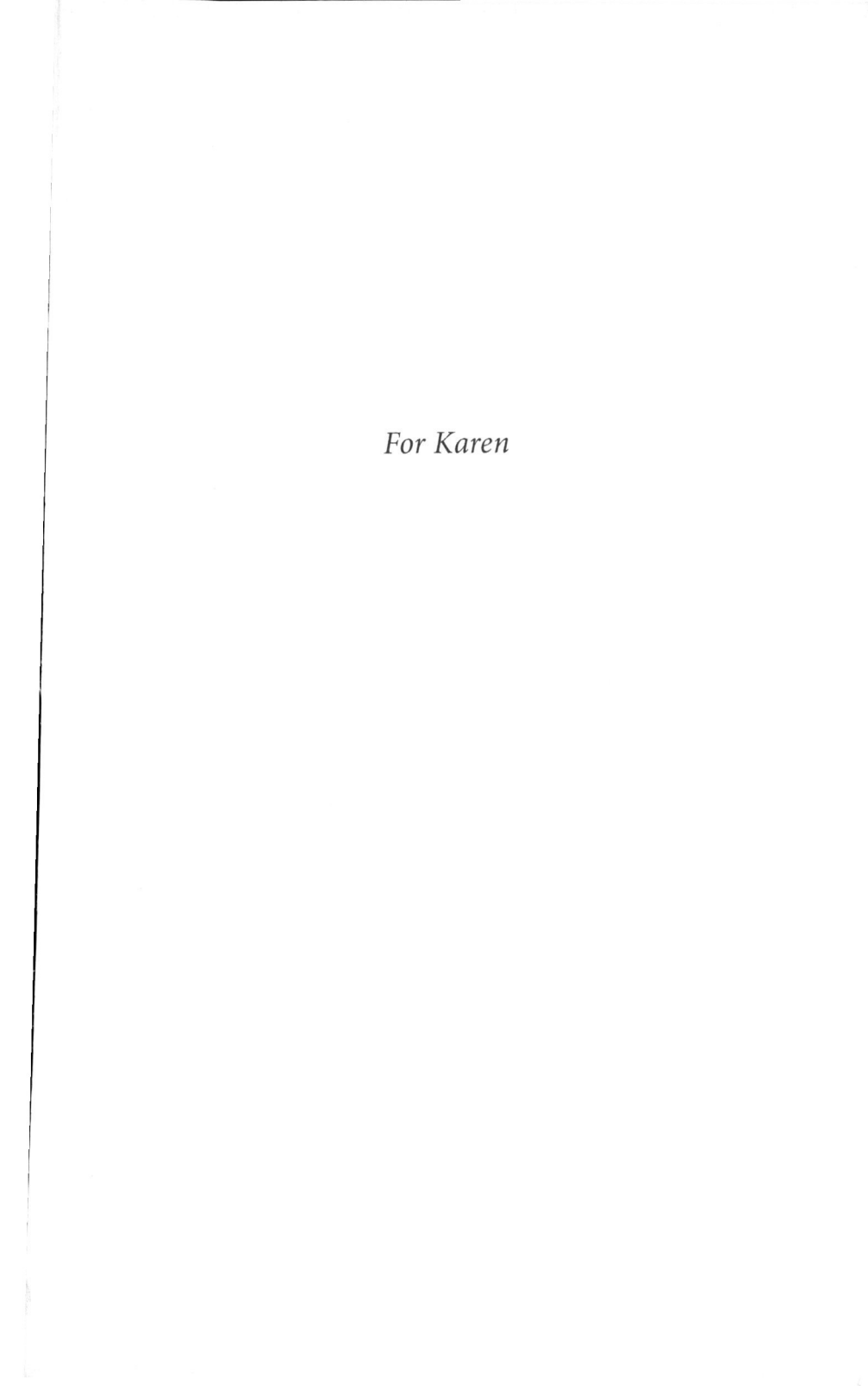

The past is never dead. It's not even past.

WILLIAM FAULKNER

Prologue

Sani Abacha's Nigeria was a difficult place merely to exist. The Biafran War had been over for twenty-seven years, but it might as well have been twenty-seven minutes. Abacha was a participant in every coup that took place during his military career and was the first soldier to rise through the ranks of the Nigerian Army to full General without passing any rank. Finally, in 1993, after years of being a mere participant, he headed up his own coup, installing himself as the military leader. He proved to be a kleptocrat and human rights violator extraordinaire.

George Azunna sat in a wrought iron chair situated on concrete slab in what passed for a garden in his family's small villa in Owerri, Nigeria. There was another chair and a table to match. George exhaled a stream of smoke from his Romeo y Julieta cigar. A bottle of 12-year-old Glenmorangie whisky sat on table as well as two empty glasses. There was a pleasant breeze that rustled the African sandalwood trees, but that breeze was a harbinger of the storm to come.

If Sani Abacha had been aware of George Azunna and his family, he would have at the very least, put them on the next plane to London. George knew that his ability to continue his relief work depended on unsavoury people, one of whom was on his way.

The tell-tale sound of his visitor's Mercedes 500 GE made his presence known over the sound of the breeze. George had instructed the underpaid doorman, errand boy, and sometime security guard to let the big man with the scar in and direct him to the side of the building where George now sat. He exhaled another stream of smoke as the big man rounded the corner of the home and spied George waiting for him. The visitor approached George and without saying a word grabbed the bottle of Scotch filling both glasses a third of the way up. He was *that* kind of man.

"George," he began as he eased into the vacant chair, "you really do have excellent taste. I don't know why you limit yourself to Scotch and cigars. Even your Range Rover is old!" The visitor let out a deep cackling laugh.

George said nothing. If the visitor's oblique reference to his family's money was meant as an insult or a taunt, it rolled off its intended victim.

"George, I know you want to help the people of the Delta, but your methods are interfering with … other things. You need to stop. Things will get better, but if you keep doing things the same way I cannot continue to guarantee your safety. You have made some powerful people very angry."

George rolled the Scotch around in his mouth. He let the peat sit on his tongue before he finally spoke to his late-night guest. "Are you threatening me?"

"Threaten? What are you talking about? Just think about the bigger picture."

George and the visitor at this clandestine nocturnal meeting were lit from the window into the principal sitting room that doubled as George's home office and the anaemic outside light that seemed to pulse with changes in the power flow.

The scar-faced man refilled his glass. "George, getting your fellow Igbo excited about reparations that aren't going to happen can only lead to violence. Talk about a new Biafran Republic makes you no friends and brings a good deal of negative attention." Despite his father having been a senior advisor to the last President of Biafra, George had not been an advocate for a new Biafra, but that hardly seemed to matter.

George continued to look at the visitor, saying nothing and the visitor returned the look, locking eyes for a time that children on a playground would have been jealous of until the visitor finally broke contact. He rose to leave.

"George, I can only hope you will heed my words." He turned on his heels and left. The only sounds George heard were the crashing of the steel gate and the roar of the big Mercedes V-8.

Chioma, George's wife, had all watched this unfold from just inside the barely lit door. "How did that go?"

"Fine." He brushed past her without another word.

The next morning George and Chioma headed to the offices of their NGO, the streets muddy from the rain that had followed the pleasant breeze. They rounded the last corner, and as they headed down the street to the modest building, it erupted into a ball of flame. George stood on the brake bringing their old Range Rover to a quick stop. Both watched wide-eyed as the building collapsed. With no office to go to they headed back to the family home.

Pulling up to the house and before George had shifted the SUV into park, Chioma rushed inside to check on the girls. They were fine.

George and Chioma had made a commitment to their work. They were people of privilege, and they knew it. Both born amid the Nigerian Civil War, their families had fled with money to London. They were well educated and could have had most any job they wanted back in the City.

"We need to go." Chioma put her foot down.

"This is how they win." George was angry, not at her, but at the idea they could be run off. "They make empty threats. They destroy things! We were meant to see that explosion; it wasn't meant to kill us!"

"You want to wait for the explosion that is meant to kill us? The kidnapping that disappears anyone of us? The unspeakable things they would do to our girls?"

A chill ran down George's spine. The thought of what they would do to his beloved family made his blood cold. He agreed that it was time to go. They would leave that night.

The family spent the day packing. Several hours before the flight out of Port Harcourt, they loaded the black Range Rover in what was now a downpour the previous night's breeze foretold. The storm was unrelenting for the next several hours, and every time there was a thunderclap George jumped just a little bit. They were all sopping wet by the time they got into the car.

George drove as fast as he could, but the rain was bad, and the traffic was worse. Chioma looked back at their two girls, ten-year old Kiana and two-year-old Ngozi. Chioma had a worried look on her face, and that look would stay with Kiana.

George and Kiana saw the bright headlights at the same time. George yanked hard on the steering wheel, but it was too late, the Range Rover slamming into an oncoming truck. If the Range Rover had been going faster, it might have resulted in the complete destruction of the vehicle, but most of it survived. Unfortunately, a metal pole the other truck had been carrying came through the windscreen and killed George instantly. Chioma, in the middle of turning back to check on her daughters, was still sitting at an odd angle when the collision occurred. Despite being belted in she was thrown forward and then back, breaking her neck.

Kiana screamed for her parents. Fortunately, someone had seen the accident. A big man with a scar across his face managed to open the rear side passenger door and retrieve the two frightened, traumatized, but otherwise unhurt children. He had the older one sit down in the steady, hard rain and then gently put the young one in her arms. He then walked away back to his own German SUV and left.

They would be soon rescued, but until then the eldest girl held her baby sister close, rocking her as the rain pelted down, making them cold while she stared into the now vacant eyes of her dead mother.

Chapter One

Captain Kiana Azunna, Royal Marines, lay on the hard ground of north-eastern Afghanistan looking through her Schmidt and Bender spotting scope. Moonrise in the far southern reaches of the Hindu Kush this hot August night was so late as to be early morning. While the moon was full, the mixed cloud cover played tricks on illumination, giving advantages to neither predator nor prey. A Taliban commander moved about what was supposed to be a little camp but looked more like a small village. After the ten-kilometre yomp from the insertion point, Azunna and her team had been in the prone position for more than an hour. Even with a lightweight pad under her body, the sharp edge in every rock seemed to make its way to her core.

Azunna had been a Royal Marine Commando for four years, having transferred from Naval Intelligence when the Ministry of Defence had finally permitted women to serve in all units. The mission of 30 Commando's Reconnaissance and Surveillance Squadron had been a natural fit for her skillset. She and her small team were on their last mission in Afghanistan. The Americans had announced a pull out by the end of the month and with it the end of the clandestine British presence as well.

Next to Azunna was her principal section sniper, Colour Sgt Tom Colley. Seventeen years in the Royal Marines, the last seven in 30 Commando, he had been around the world. Colley had been brand new to the Royal Marines during the 2003 invasion of Iraq, worked counter-piracy operations in the Gulf of Aden, led mentoring operations in West Africa, and done his own training in Belize and Brunei. An exemplary demonstration of the fortitude of Royal Marines, he was Azunna's most trusted and accurate shooter, and as her senior troop NCO advisor, both mentor and subordinate. He had eleven years of combat operations on her, and his body felt every single one of the deployments. He didn't think of himself as old, but at thirty-seven he knew combat was a young person's game.

"Any time you are ready ma'am." Colley's steel grey eyes were focused through his own Schmidt and Bender scope atop his L115A3 .338 Laupa rifle. Hours on the range outside of RM Stonehouse had allowed the rifle to become an extension of his body, rising and falling in conjunction with his breathing. The moment to press the trigger at the end of his exhale was built into him. He was ready to reach out and touch someone at over a kilometre.

"Send it," Azunna said softly.

One minute the Taliban commander was having a conversation with one of his subordinates, and the next his head disappeared in a cloud of pink mist.

"Let's move." They had a ten-kilometre yomp back to the exfil point. Their mates from 845 Naval Air Squadron would not be happy if they had to wait on the deck for them. That distance in the dark, over uneven ground was not easy, even for the fittest of people. On a night like tonight to call the yomp ahead of them a slog was making it sound like a walk at Richmond Park.

The reaction in the little encampment below them was completely predictable. Taliban riflemen looked for the threat from all around, wary of any further attack, some firing randomly into the dark. Others acting as medics quickly concluded their commander was dead and it was time to move. Some ran to Toyota Hi-Lux pickups. Out of the corner of her eye, while she shouldered her Bergen, Azunna saw something unexpected. "Hold the airstrike!"

"Ma'am, we don't have the time!" If pressed Colley would have said that Azunna had one flaw, and that was she thought she could right any injustice, save any innocent. It was an admirable flaw to be sure. Colley did not think of himself as a cynic, just a realist. The world of possession and privilege was a cruel one, and Colley was just trying to do the best he could. In the middle of the chaos, two little girls had emerged from a small building that seemed at the centre of the camp and Colley knew his commander well.

Azunna was already on the move, M4 up, peering through her night vision scope, pressing toward the girls. If she could get to them, the Marines could carry them to the exfil point. She had no idea what would happen if she showed up in Kandahar with two orphaned girls, but she'd worry about that later.

"Everybody stand-by and get ready to move! I'm going with the gaffer!" shouted Colley. *Fuuuuck. I can't believe she is doing this. No. Of course I can.* He set off in pursuit of Azunna, M4 up, ready to engage.

Azunna put two 5.56mm rounds into one Taliban soldier and kept moving. A machine gun opened up, 12.7mm rounds stitching the ground behind her. She dove for cover behind a large rock quickly followed by Colley.

"Ma'am, there's no time! We need to move, the strike aircraft and our ride are both inbound."

"The intel said this was strictly military, we are not killing innocent kids. Come or stay, I don't care, but I am getting them." Azunna was diligent about her duties to Queen and country, and also to the ideals she had. Little girls weren't going to be killed because she had given the strike order. She hadn't allowed a combined eight years in the Royal Navy and Marines, with four combat deployments to Afghanistan to change her to that degree.

And with that, she was off again, Colley in hot pursuit, and they entered a raging gun battle with a group of Taliban. The 7.62x39mm rounds of the enemy AKs bounced off the rocks, sending little chips of stone their way. Azunna and Colley replied with the 5.56x45mm rounds of their M4s. She could see other Taliban getting in their Hi-Luxes and Land Cruisers and racing off. They dove behind another large boulder.

"Captain! We're blown. We need to move to the exfil site!" Colley screamed.

Azunna had lost sight of the girls and so looked up above the rock just enough see the camp. The human eye does amazingly well in the dark. If there is a full moon, it can be almost as good as daylight. The firing had slowed down and the flurry of activity that had been below them was almost all gone. Azunna rolled out from around the rock, rifle up, moving forward. Colley still right behind her.

Then she saw them, standing in the open, illuminated by the headlights of the Land Cruiser bearing down on them. The vehicle stopped, and a rough-looking man exited the passenger side of the SUV, picked up the girls and pushed them into the front seat, climbing back in after them. The driver must have had the truck in gear because the vehicle was already backing up as fast before they had even shut the door.

The grey darkness was about to turn to bright light. The roar of the RAF Typhoon strike fighters was upon them before they knew it, each one releasing a Paveway IV laser-guided 500-lb bomb that landed in the middle of the encampment. The combined 1000 lbs of high explosives did three things: it turned night into day, even if only for a couple of seconds; it destroyed everything in the little encampment; and it sent the two Royal Marines flying, blowing them off their feet and onto their backs.

The lethal radius of the Paveway IV 500-lb bomb is about 80 x 30 metres. Azunna and Colley had been about 200 metres from the point of impact, but that did not mean they were safe.

It was impossible to tell how far the Land Cruiser had been able to move in the fifteen seconds between when it pulled away, and the bombs detonated. Theoretically, it should only take six seconds to move far enough. Theoretically.

Azunna was out for who knows how long, later she would figure that it had probably been less than a minute, but as she came around, she felt as if it could have been hours. Her ears were ringing and her vision a mess. She shook her head trying to get a sense of time and place. Both freezing cold and burning hot, she quickly triaged herself, from head to foot, by quickly being in touch with her body. *Thank goodness for all that yoga.* Her right knee was in a great deal of pain, but other than that she appeared to be alright.

She struggled to sit up, finally using her left side to leverage her body into a more upritight position. Looking around she searched for Colley. After her vision returned to normal, she saw him, about two metres to her right. He lay motionless in the early morning grey light. His head was titled in her direction, eyes open, vacant. She tried to get up to go to him, but her knee completely failed, shooting even more sharp pain to every part of her body.

"Sergeant Colley, get up!" Her cry was almost an order, a command. It was as if her authority as an officer with a Queen's Commission, would solve this problem. Just looking at him, not moving, those open, vacant eyes, the injuries started to overcome her, and she eased herself back to the ground. And Azunna was jolted back in the pouring rain on that Nigerian roadside, holding Ngozi in her arms, staring into the vacant eyes of her mother.

Chapter Two

Azunna was going into shock. As she was about to pass out, the rest of the section arrived. There were just four of them on the mission, one Marine made a quick evaluation of Colley. He looked at Smyth, the second most senior NCO in the section, and shook his head while Smyth attended Azunna's knee. It had been shattered by the explosion.

"Ma'am, the evac team is inbound. Just hold on." Smyth had radioed the exfil flight and told them they now had a Medevac. The minutes seemed like hours. Even wrapped in the emergency blanket, Azunna was cold despite the warm ambient temperature, and she was fading in and out of consciousness. Most of the Taliban had fled or been killed, but the occasional random shot pinged off the rocks around the team.

Finally, the two Merlin HC4s of 845 Naval Air Squadron arrived. One flared as it landed, the three Rolls Royce Turbomeca RTM 322s that powered the enormous carbon and glass honeycomb blades adjusting blade pitch as it did so. Four medics came off the rear ramp and ran towards the team while the other aircraft, with Lt Cdr Phoebe Sparrow, Azunna's best mate and running buddy, in command, took up a security position orbiting the evac site, watching for enemy movement. Gunners on each side of the aircraft had FN MAG General Purpose Machine Guns ready for troops in the open.

Two of the medics reached Colley, quickly deploying a body bag which they expertly slid him into. With two Marines holding his shoulders and one lifting his legs, they moved as quickly as they could towards the Merlin. They approached the rear of the helicopter at a 45-degree angle from the tail with the aircrewman guiding them in to avoid the tail rotor. As they reached the ramp the aircrewman helped them load Colley's body into the helicopter.

The two medics then returned to Azunna. Smyth and the other two medics had deployed a litter and one had started an IV.

"On three, lads!" Smyth counted, "One...two...threeeee!" Together they lifted her onto the litter. One of the medics checked that the IV bag was tucked safely in the emergency blanket. "Again, lads! Same approach to the bird. One...two...threeeee! Move! Let's go!"

Fading in an out of consciousness Azunna sensed being lifted, she knew she should have been warmer, but what she really was numb. A hundred images seemed to crash across her mind's eye like shattered glass. She could see Ngozi laughing the last time they had dinner, before this deployment; a rainy dark stretch of road where she was blinded by both rain and bright lights; and of the first time she had tried whisky with her drinking and running sidekick, Phoebe, Lt Cdr Sparrow in helicopter orbiting above.

Once again, the five Royal Marines approached the Merlin's ramp at a 45-degree angle. On board, they strapped the litter down. The aircrewman raised the ramp and gave the pilot the signal to go.

The pilot applied full pitch on the blades and the Rolls Royce engines did their thing, raising the huge helicopter in the air. Pulling up on the collective, dust and rock started to fly everywhere once more, this time impacting no one. As the engine reached maximum power, the Merlin started to lift in the high thin air of the Hindu Kush where even normal helicopter operations became high adventure. After twenty-plus years of war, the downright dangerous had become routine.

Rising above the stubby tree line, the Merlin continued to gain altitude and speed as it headed for Kandahar airbase. The Merlin that had been pulling security and exchanging gunfire with random Talib shooters on the ground, came in trail and off to the left side of the lead aircraft. Both helos continued to gain altitude. There was a sudden flash from a below. Some bright spark had finally figured out how to fire an RPG.

The RPG is an impact weapon, not designed as an anti-air system, but helicopters are vulnerable targets, and this RPG warhead managed to impact the tail of the second Merlin just as the rocket was losing its forward momentum. The resulting explosion ended up damaging the tail rotor, the one that kept the aircraft from counter-rotating against the main rotor thus creating forward momentum. Losing the tail rotor would result in a loss of the aircraft.

Inside the now lead aircraft, call sign Junglie 2, Azunna continued to drift in and out of consciousness. The medics had already changed one IV, she had become very dehydrated, but did not appear to have lost a good deal of blood. She should be stable enough back to Kandahar. She was vaguely aware of the body bag on the cabin floor across from her.

Meanwhile, in the now second aircraft, Junglie 1, Lt Cdr Sparrow, knew her aircraft was in serious trouble. The anti-torque pedals were not responding as they should and seemed to be failing more with every minor adjustment she tried to make. Every alarm system was going on in the cockpit; red flashing lights and sirens wailing.

What she did not and could not know was that the main shaft leading back to the rear rotor had been practically severed by the shrapnel from the RPG. It was simply a race against time, and she needed to set the helicopter down to prevent a crash. Standard operating procedure would be to set the helicopter down now, but this was not a normal operation.

As the tail rotor did its job, pushing against the thin cold air to keep the Merlin from counter-rotating and allowing it to maintain forward progress, it also pushed against the main shaft in the tail, causing the partial break to increase in size.

Fifteen kilometres outside of Kandahar the last little bit of the shaft split open and before Sparrow, with hundreds of hours of combat experience, could do anything, the Merlin went into a wild spin as the rear tail rotor suddenly stopped functioning. She had time to send out one "Mayday" before the Royal Navy Special Operations Merlin impacted the Afghan earth at 200 kph, in a ball of fire killing Azunna's best friend and long-time confidant, as well as everyone else on board.

Hearing the mayday call, the pilot of Junglie 2 had banked right to see if there was some way to help, so they saw it when the aircraft exploded onto the ground. Junglie 2 orbited the crash site and prepared to set down, but even a casual inspection revealed what everyone already knew to be true.

"Kandahar Tower, this is Junglie 2, Junglie 1 is down. You need to get a recovery mission out here." The instinct was to still set down, but they had a wounded Marine who needed attention and there was nothing they could do for their teammates in Junglie 1.

"Roger, Junglie 2."

As Junglie 2 set down five minutes later, the special operations Merlin again sent dust and rock flying just as they had on the mountainside, but this time on the medical helipad.

Two teams were waiting, one ready to grab Azunna and get her into proper medical care, and the other a team from the morgue. Adjusting the blade pitch, the pilot kept the engine going to keep all in preparation for moving the helicopter to the other side of the base. The aircrewman lowered the ramp the hospital team pulled the litter out and onto a gurney.

Smyth made sure the latest IV was properly tucked in. Azunna was only half conscious, completely oblivious to the loss of Junglie 1 and her friend Phoebe. Although Azunna had sensed their movement, mentally and emotionally she was still on the mountainside. "The doc's going to take care of you, ma'am." Smyth was trying to whisper in her ear but with all the commotion and the three Rolls Royce engines at low throttle, the sound was almost deafening and Azunna could hear almost nothing other than the helicopter engine. The team rolled Azunna away from the Merlin. There was a waiting ambulance, an old Land Rover Defender 110, with flat khaki paint and a giant Red Cross on the side.

As Azunna was loaded into the ambulance, the morgue team was repeating the scene with the body of Colour Sgt Tom Colley. This time a team of six Royal Marines approached the helicopter in the same fashion. The body bearer team leader produced a Union Jack, seemingly from nowhere and covered the body bag. This team had done this many times before, too many times, and knew they had to hold the flag tightly to the bag, lest it fly away in the rotor wash.

Keeping their heads down and doing something halfway between a crouched jog and a formal march, the team moved Colley's body away from the Merlin. The pilots, needing to focus on operating the idling helicopter tried to sit up a little straighter, looking straight ahead, mimicking somewhat the position of attention. The crew chief still wired into the aircraft communications system stood at attention and rendered a salute. Once the team was clear of the rotor wash, they stopped, came to full attention, and then marched to the rear of a second waiting Defender, this one a pickup. The tailgate was down, the team centre-faced, and eased the Union Jack-covered body of Tom Colley into the vehicle for his last journey home.

Chapter Three

Azunna stood quietly in the front of the St. Ermin Hotel where she had been in residence for almost a week. Dressed for a summer run in black Lululemon running shorts, a grey tank top, and OC running shoes in a mix of colours, grey ankle socks just peeking out. Even in late London summer, one can go running at 0530 with plenty sunlight and no one on the street. She barely needed her alarm, having been an early riser for years. She was up, dressed, out of her room, and ready to resume her habit of a daily run.

This was the first leave she had been granted since her return from Afghanistan. Every other absence had been a part of her rehab. This run was only the second time she had left her room since checking in. Deliveroo and room service had kept her fed. It had been an agonizing ten months. There were the multiple surgeries, then the physical rehab, her relief from command and assignment to the nearly meaningless staff job. And of course, the funerals. It had been blow after blow.

Azunna turned right onto Caxton Street at a brisk pace and worked her way through the side streets of Whitehall until she emerged at the Birdcage. The weather was perfect for a run like this, not too warm, moderate humidity. Turning right again, she ran past St. James Park until she emerged in Parliament Square. She was building up a sweat, the months of rehab were paying off. Her knee was feeling good, several surgeries and the long days with the physical therapist as well as time in the gym had put her almost back at full strength. Azunna favoured Hollywood action movie soundtracks for her runs because they were all written at 160-180 beats per minute and helped keep her heart rate up. She was listening to whatever Thomas Newman had composed for the latest shoot-em up. She turned left on Parliament Street and drifted to the middle of the famous boulevard.

She had attended the funerals on crutches in her Number 1B Lovat Dress uniform. Colley's husband and their children had been anguished at a future without him and Sparrow's parents inconsolable at the loss of their only daughter. As the mission had been top secret neither family knew any of the details. They could hardly blame her. But, of course, she blamed herself.

Her pace picked up as she ran past the Cenotaph, the Memorial to Women in War, and Ten Downing Street. She checked her running app. She was running at a good pace, just short of five minutes per kilometre, but still not where she wanted to be. At least she was finally free from the knee pain, for the most part.

Her principle job since the Afghan withdrawal had been physical rehabilitation with some minor and what she thought of as meaningless staff work thrown in. But her two loves had long been running and drinking. She had met Phoebe when she arrived at Cambridge in the fall of 2006, and they had shared living quarters. Phoebe came from money and among her family's many investments was a whisky distillery. At eighteen, Phoebe's father had taken both of them on numerous whisky-tasting trips around the country. It was a revelation. Azunna loved the smokiness and the smooth burn.

As she reached Trafalgar Square, she was now fully at the pace she had wanted to achieve. Sweat was gathering in her lower back and on her forehead, and she turned south again towards the Thames. Now able to maintain her pace, her mind wandered to her younger sister Ngozi. Finally, out of sixth form at Elizabeth Garret Anderson School, she was a student at SOAS University of London studying for her LLB. She had chosen SOAS because it had a comparative law program and a focus on international law. Like her older sister, she wanted to make the world a better place.

Now on the pathway along the Thames, Azunna was in full stride, her long, lean-muscled legs carrying her as fast as she could go. Construction on Queen Elizabeth II Tower, the home of Big Ben, sent her left onto Westminster Bridge and the south bank of the Thames. Continuing west towards Vauxhall Cross she reached Lambeth Bridge, turned right and was back on the north side of the Thames.

They had their monthly dinner the night before, Ngozi and Azunna. Since her last return from Afghanistan, she had made monthly trips to London as part of her rehab. They ate at their favourite restaurants, and Azunna went to see her psychologist in Marylebone. These monthly meetings were strictly off books, but she did not find the support she was being offered by the MOD to be of any great benefit.

Back in Parliament Square she turned left, but just as she arrived at the Birdcage, she turned hard right onto Horse Guards Drive and ran until she turned left onto the Mall. She could see Buckingham Palace at the end of the drive. A long straight boulevard, the scene of many famous and even infamous parades, she gave it all she had. One fast stride after the other. Arms pumping. Music thumping. And then she was there, the Victoria Memorial, the gate to Buckingham Palace, the Royal Standard flying in the summer breeze, the RAF Queen's Colour Squadron mounting the palace guard. The death of HRH The Prince Phillip the previous year made her idly wonder how long the guards would hold that title.

Being relieved from duty with 30 Commando was not necessarily career-killing. She had been a small-unit leader, not even in full command, but she was loath to spend the rest of her military career doing staff work. It wasn't just the need to be where the action was, it was to make a difference. That's why her summons to London had been so mysterious and intriguing.

As Azunna slowed to a walk, she hit the pause button and then the save run option on her fitness app. She looked at the data. She smiled; she was nearly back on form. She was dripping with sweat, and it ran off her close-cropped hair. Her top was two shades of grey darker. She put her hands on her hips and walked up to the gate of the Palace. She had never actually seen the changing of the guard here, and she had participated in enough military parades she couldn't see the attraction. Still, she thought, maybe she should put it on the to-do list. Satisfied that she had acknowledged her surroundings sufficiently, she made the short walk back to the St. Ermin.

***

Using her smartphone with the hotel's mobile key system, Azunna went in a side entrance and took the stairs two at a time to her fourth-floor suite. She felt the right knee a little more than the other, but it did not quite hurt anymore.

In the room she rang down for breakfast and popped BBC Breakfast on the telly, and grinned at the thought that Naga Munchetty was sure to inflame old white men again today.

Stripping off her running gear, she hopped in the shower for her usual four minutes of steaming hot water followed by the one-minute blast of ice-cold. Today, she took the time for one extra minute of heat to help alleviate the lingering knee soreness.

She towelled off in front of the full-length mirror. Despite the year plus off from real running, she had managed to maintain the toned, but not too muscular look she had developed over the years. She dragged the towel quickly across her hair, worn close to the scalp, a look she could carry off and still exude both femininity and toughness.

Putting on the hotel robe just in time for breakfast to arrive.

She opened the door and admitted the steward. As an orphan who grew up in boarding schools, Azunna took ridiculous pleasure in her food and drink as an adult. It was always a tricky balancing act of trying to eat healthily and luxuriously.

Shirred eggs and wheat toast were complimented by black Vietnamese coffee from Whittard of Chelsea, two turmeric shots, and a large bowl of fresh fruit. As her meeting was not until noon, she took her time enjoying the food in the sitting room portion of her suite.

She thoroughly enjoyed this level of comfort. The suite was two rooms. The bedroom had a king-sized bed, with matching bedside tables and lights as well as a good-sized writing desk. The window looked out over a little side street. There was a TV on the wall between the windows. The sitting room provided a sofa and a club chair with a low coffee table and another TV. The entire place was decorated to be very comfortable and on the verge of luxury, but not *quite* there. It suited Azunna just fine.

Scrolling through Twitter on her phone it was obvious that the world was not becoming more transparent, it was opaquer. The electronic space was interesting because everyone could enter it. Ten Downing Street could be in the same space as the Taliban leadership. Political, military, or personal foes could face off on a virtual playground. And of course, sub-text was completely missing in all of this.

The fallout from the mission in Afghanistan had been less than expected, of course, that was mainly due to the coverage of the American withdrawal writ large. There was never even a press release about the mission's success, or the deaths. Her

Majesties' then-current Government lied so much, the fact that UK Special Operations Forces had been conducting non-training missions up to the point of the American closure of operation had barely raised an eyebrow, much less trended on Twitter. It had barely rated a fourth page bit in *The Times*.

Naga's usual incisive questioning of Tory ministers had given way to the more sobering news that the Queen's virtual meeting with the Privy Council had been cancelled. Given that there was a new Prime Minister, this seemed highly irregular. Azunna decided it was time to get dressed.

She matched a French blue Emma Willis linen blouse to some cream-colored linen trousers with flared legs and an unstructured saffron linen blazer. She considered pumps, however, in a concession to walking and mobility to she chose some off-white Cariuma trainers. If they were good enough for Dame Helen Mirren, they were good enough for her. After all, it was Mirren who had told women they needed to spend more time telling the world to fuck off. Finally, her Bremont S302 GMT, stainless steel with a black face and 40mm case. Nothing beat a good automatic watch. It was still mid-morning, so she had time to kill. She ordered another pot of coffee and decided to work on the crossword in *The Times*, figuring that would kill most of the hour until her lunch appointment. Finally, it was time to summon a cab.

Chapter Four

Azunna arrived at the corner of Maiden Lane and Southampton Street promptly at 1145, the London black cab having taken the most direct route. They still beat Uber when it came to service, and she regarded good service as money well spent. As the cab drove off, she took a step back simply to acquaint herself with her surroundings. A BBC news alert also let her know the senior members of the Royal Family were all on their way to Balmoral where the Queen had been spending her later summer holiday.

Azunna then proceeded down Maiden Lane on the left side of the street. Two minutes later she was in front of Rules, the oldest restaurant in London. The doorman touched his hand to his hat as he opened the door for her.

"I am meeting someone here at noon," she started with the maitre'd, "Mills, I believe."

It was early for lunch in London, but in a place like Rules, one became accustomed to people with habits that might not be the expected. He checked the list, "Ah, yes. They are not here yet. Would you like a table?"

"No thank you, I'll wait in the bar."

Finding a place where she could easily see the front door, Azunna turned to the barman. "An espresso and a sparkling water please." She'd considered champagne but decided to hold off... for now.

"Certainly, madam." He drew the water from a tap and placed the glass in front of her and then started the process of making the very small shot of very intense Italian coffee. He placed the demitasse cup in front of her, it had cube of sugar and small slice of lemon peel on the plate. She twisted the lemon peel to express the oils and dropped it in the hot brew, taking a sip.

At noon on the dot, a party of two approached the maitre'd, a middle-aged, non-descript white man and a younger, fit black woman. Intriguing. The way they were dressed and carried themselves did not look like they would know each other socially. The maitre'd led them off into the dining room.

Sixty seconds later he appeared in front of her, "Madam, your party is here. Follow me please." She finished her espresso in one shot and followed him. The two people she had observed entering were sitting side-by-side at a table. They did not look romantic. As Azunna approached they both stood. The middle-aged man was in the uniform of an aspiring Whitehall mandarin, charcoal grey suit, single-breasted, with charcoal stripes, white shirt with cocktail cuffs, and a burgundy tie. Not clearly Regimental so she assumed it was associated with his school, as were the cufflinks. The woman on the other hand looked both professional and fashionable. Her dress came to her knees, was sleeveless, and had a round collar. It was wheat coloured and contrasting with her dark green pumps – just enough to catch the eye without being off-putting to those who would be shocked by anything out of the norm.

"William Tickner," the man said, extending his hand. Azunna shook it. It was firm. He was reserved but was taking her seriously. *Good*. She was tired of tough sells.

"Erica Mills," the woman said, doing the same.

"Have a seat. How are you on this beautiful London summer day?" asked Tickner, not really caring about the answer.

"Fine, although the news concerning the Queen is disquieting, if perhaps inevitable."

"Indeed." They all paused to give the news some respect. Tickner continued, "I suppose you are wondering why we wanted to meet with you."

"A little. I was told to meet a 'Senior Defence Ministry official' here at noon today."

The waiter brought menus. "Give us a few minutes," directed Mills.

They slid their cards across the table to her.

They read *William Tickner, Chief of Staff, Secret Intelligence Service.* And *Erica Mills, Associate Director for Field Operations, Secret Intelligence Service.*

"So, what can I do for you two?" Azunna barely lifted a brow but was quietly impressed. She didn't want them to know that, though.

The waiter approached. "One more minute please," said Mills. Her tone was not one of patience. "We'd like to talk about your future Captain Azunna."

"Sure, why not. I was not sure I had one."

Mills motioned the waiter finally. "Order whatever you like, it's on the Service."

The Rules menu was the typical heavy English roasts and game meats. Something that Azunna would normally appreciate, but today she felt the need to be light.

"Would it be possible to scramble some eggs and serve them with the Beetroot and Carrot salad?" asked Azunna.

"Of course, Madam."

"Oh, and a glass of the rose Veuve Cliquot."

Tanner and Mills placed similarly light orders and the waiter receded into the wall.

"So, tell us about Afghanistan," began Tickner.

"Here? I don't think I need to tell you this, but all that work is highly classified. I'm not sure this is the place."

"Is it us, or the place? Because if it is the place, we can assure you that this establishment has a long history of working with the Service and other agencies with HMG that need quiet, semi-secure places, that are a bit more relaxed than Vauxhall Cross."

"Fine. But what's there to tell? I am sure you have read all the reports. I was leading a Marine Commando unit on a capture or kill mission, with a high preference towards the latter, and blew it all up. I failed. Is that what you want to hear? Why does the SIS give a damn about a washed-up Royal Marine captain?"

"Washed up? Hardly, from what we hear," Tickner chortled.

Mills piped in. "We've read the official reports. We've read your statements. What we want to know is what were you thinking. That's not rhetorical or dismissive. We want to understand your decision-making process."

This irritated Azunna, but she decided to play. The formal inquiries had their military structure to them, but this felt personal. And everybody deep down wants to tell their story.

"The intelligence indicated this was a camp, training facility, or operational centre of a semi-temporary nature. The senior operations officer for the Haqqani network was supposed to be there. We were to capture or kill him, again with a preference towards the latter, and then call in an airstrike to destroy the camp. In my mind, the directives were clear to kill him, but the rest were less important. We were trying to degrade their operational capability, not commit murder. When these two little girls ran out of the hut, my calculus was that killing innocents was morally wrong, against the law of armed conflict, and counter to our aims in Afghanistan. I decided to try and get them out of harm's way."

She paused, remembering the brief flicker in which she had seen herself and her sister as children. She decided to forgo that detail. She took a long sip of champagne, then continued.

"Yes, ostensibly we were in Afghanistan merely as a training partner to the Afghan Special Operations Forces. Yes, I was aware that Whitehall had promised the British public that we were no longer in combat operations in Afghanistan. Yes, I know they were 'sensitive' to British casualties, whatever that means. Colour Sgt Tom Colley was my responsibility and my mate. I was the one who spoke to his husband and explained what had happened." She sighed. "I just thought Her Majesty would prefer us to not kill little girls. At least if we could avoid it."

Azunna hoped her white-hot rage came across as cool professionalism. There was a pause as they all took a drink and considered what had transpired. Mills and Tickner looked at each other. Tickner raised an eyebrow and Mills just smiled.

Tickner began. "As an aside, did you conduct any training for the Afghan special ops blokes?" Again, Azunna was irritated. Why had she come to London to tell these two things they could read in a report?

"Yes, we did. It was mostly logistical work. They had quite good, almost intuitive field craft. We were trying to get them to use and understand modern logistical support."

"How did they take to a woman leading that training?" Tickner's question was both sincere and tone-deaf. Azunna paused. Maniacal laughter raged inside her. *White guys never get it do they?*

She leaned forward. Tickner moved just slightly, but noticeably back. The floor was hers. "About as well as a bunch of white boys at Lympstone. Maybe even better."

The silence was such that Azunna had time to sit back and really notice the room. Rules was like the dining room of a London private club. Hunting prints on the wall, heavy wood, red leather. Very much of its time and place, almost a time vault of decades past.

"Mr. Tickner, you seem to believe that because someone makes a policy, that changes everything and the world continues as if the old way of doing things never existed. I am going to give you the courtesy of assuming that is mere naïveté. Let me assure you the change, while welcome, does not erase memories or institutional practices overnight. While Whitehall might have changed the policy regarding women serving in the Royal Marines, it is up to me and people like me to change hearts and minds. Although why that burden rests on those of us who simply want to participate is beyond me."

More silence as they all took a drink. Azunna felt good, it was not that she was saying things that had been bottled up, it's that she was able to say them to a person who had benefited from the system for so long that they were blind to how it impacted everyone else. But Tickner looked a little impressed. Mills even more so.

"It's just like those politicians in Whitehall. They thought that they could put two 500-lb bombs on a target in Afghanistan and no one would notice. And, to some extent I guess they were correct. The Americans deciding to end their effort was probably just a coincidence, but it certainly made our small operation not even register as a blip on the radar. After all was said and done, the bombing, Colley's death, the little girls, and the true nature the British Armed Forces mission in Afghanistan, the British public just went on. None of it even trended on Twitter."

Just then the food came. As the servers presented the dishes, all three of their phones buzzed with BBC news alerts.

The senior members of the Royal Family were all enroute to Balmoral to be by the Queen's side.

But as the food was being served and the news about Her Majesty digested, Mills leaned back and focused on her more immediate task. A smile on her face. She liked working with Tickner, he was a good colleague and well-intentioned. But like every man was a prisoner of his own experiences. She enjoyed watching him get an education in what the world was like for other people.

"I made a judgement call," continued Azunna putting the first bite of luscious egg into her mouth. "That's what I was trained and paid to do. And I would do it again. Despite everything." The feelings of loss inside here tremendous, but publicly airing those were of no purpose as far as Azunna could tell.

The professional conversation took a pause as they enjoyed the excellent meal and speculated about the what the news from Scotland might mean in the short and long term. Everything had to come to an end at some point. The longest reigning monarch in British history was ninety-six years old, after all.

After thirty minutes of enjoying the food and some more causal banter, Mills leaned forward and returned to the matter at hand. "Captain Azunna, would you be interested in continuing this conversation at a future time?" They had set aside an hour for lunch and that time was rapidly coming to a close.

"Sure, why not? My time in physical rehabilitation is up and my next assignment is still unknown."

Mills continued, "Would you be interested in continuing your career along similar lines?"

"Yes, of course, but that seems unlikely now."

Tickner signalled for the bill. The waiter brought it forthwith and he quickly signed off on it and rose with Mills.

"It was a pleasure, Captain Azunna," Tickner said, once again extending his hand.

She shook it.

"I look forward to our next meeting." Mills shook her hand, and they were gone.

Chapter Five

Azunna remained at the table. In truth, she was a little shocked at herself, but pleased, nonetheless. That Tickner bloke seemed nice enough, but he had a lot to learn about how the real world worked. Mills had not said much during the entire encounter, but Azunna sensed she would have an ally there if this actually turned into something.

She nursed what was left of her champagne. Here she was in London for a few days and the one reason she had come was complete. She thought for a few minutes about what she wanted to do, soaking in the clubby atmosphere, and decided on hitting Jermyn Street for some new shoes, and then maybe popping up to Regent Street for some window shopping. In addition to whisky, Phoebe had also introduced Azunna to the concept of well-made clothing and shoes, and shopping made her feel close to her friend still.

The first stop was Crockett and Jones, the bigger store close to Regents Street, not the smaller one down near the Davidoff store at St. James. Eight years in the Royal Marines made her fond of combat boots, but she wanted something a tad more stylish. The Jane model, 8-eyelets, lug commando sole, and black cavalry calf skin would do nicely.

"Can I help you, madam?" The sales associate was the epitome of English upper-crust service. As a well-dressed adult in a multicultural city, she was always greeted with the same civility as any other would-be customer. She could remember a day growing up in Brixton that was less so.

"Yes, I'm interested in a Jane. Black calf, size 9."

"If you have a seat, I will see if we have that." The chairs were wood with green leather details. Elegant. The sales associate returned two minutes later with a selection of boots.

"Here is the Jane, as you asked for. I also bought a pair in the Dark Brown Burnished Calf with the Danite Sole, and the Molly. It's like the Jane but taller with a strap at the top."

She tried them all on. The strap on the top of the latter model seemed a bit of a nuisance, but the Northampton shoemaker lived up to their reputation. They fit like a custom glove from the get-go.

"I will take both of the Janes."

"Excellent choice." She presented her card, and the sales associate took it to the register, putting each big box into its own solid-green bag carrying the company's emblem and noting they were also official suppliers to the Prince of Wales.

Five minutes later she was back on Jermyn Street headed to Emma Willis. The sun was shining and having started off her day with a good run, and an excellent breakfast, followed by a very intriguing lunch, Azunna was in as good a mood as she remembered being in a long time.

Azunna wasn't rich, but she was certainly comfortable. Family money combined with her salary had been kind to her.. People complaining about the price of Made in England goods, and then also complaining about their own wages confused and angered her. She was no nationalist but certainly wanted her fellow countryman to have good-paying jobs. If one was not willing to pay the price for good paying jobs, don't complain they don't exist. And plenty of deployments to places around the world had allowed her to save up a good bit of money.

Many of the women in her line of work would have avoided the pink. Too feminine they would say. Just as Azunna revelled in her toughness and capability, she revelled in her femininity. What was tougher than being a woman? Women's bodies were routinely put through hell – pregnancy was a risky event even the most developed world. It seemed like half the time women's bodies were trying to kill them. She loved the way pink looked against her mahogany skin. And she could kill enemies of the Crown while looking good.

Next stop, Belstaff for a new motorcycle jacket.

After running and whisky, Azunna's other passion was motorcycles. Her daily ride was a modern Triumph Street Scrambler with the twin exhaust. A modern-day take on the cafe racer and adventure bike of old.

Crossing Piccadilly, she headed up Albemarle Street, right onto Grafton, and then left onto New Bond Street. On New

Bond Street she briefly looked in the window at Chanel. Her mother had favoured the iconic Chanel No.5. Maybe because the scent so reminded her of her mother, it was something Azunna avoided personally. Azunna would be found usually wearing the citrus floral of Floris No. 127. She smiled at the happy memory of her mother and moved on.

Right on Conduit Street that would take her up to Regents Street and the Belstaff store. Steeped in tradition, but as a purveyor of motorcycle clothing, the staff at Belstaff was both eclectic and traditional. Characteristics seemingly at odds with each but creating just the right vibe.

"What can I help you with today?" The heavily inked salesclerk was perky, too perky by half, but she had a distinctly American accent. Maybe that explained it. The number of Americans who had appeared in these jobs around London always surprised her. She seemed helpful though, and after all who was Azunna to bring someone else down.

"I need a new waxed cotton motorcycle jacket. One for serious riding."

"Splendid."

"Well, we have four models that might suit you. The Fieldmaster is of course the icon."

Not rejecting it outright Azunna asked, "Anything a little less boxy?"

The clerk pulled out a Navy-blue jacket with brass buttons crossing diagonally.

"This is the Brady. It will sit on the hips and then flair just lightly. What size do you normally wear?"

"What is this? Italian sizing? Maybe a 50?" She slid out of her saffron blazer and into the jacket. In the mirror, she could see it fit perfectly over her blouse. She was concerned though about layering. Riding a motorbike around the English countryside was almost never a warm experience. "Maybe I should try a 52 for layering."

"One minute."

The salesclerk quickly returned with a 52 in the deep navy. Azunna slid it on. It did not quite give her the trim look that was on trend, but this was not a fashion statement. Or at least not totally a fashion statement. She could wear a warm jumper under this.

"This will do nicely. I'll take it."

"Anything else today?"

"No. I think that will do."

Payment made, email given, Azunna was back on the street in five more minutes looking for a cab back to the St. Ermin.

Chapter Six

Promptly at five o'clock, the black cab deposited Azunna in front of the St. Ermin. She was pleased with herself. The original home of the World War II Special Operations Executive seemed like the perfect place for her to stay when in London. The hotel played up its cloak-and-dagger history with the house bar, the Caxton Grill, serving a flight of cocktails named after the Cambridge Five. She went to the front desk, loaded with her purchases of the day.

"Good afternoon. Any messages?"

"There is a gentleman waiting for you in the bar, madam."

"Really?"

"Yes, maybe thirty minutes."

"Thank you."

Seeing she was loaded down with packages; the clerk summoned the bell captain. "I will have these packages taken to your suite, if you'd like, Ms. Azunna."

"Yes, thank you."

Keeping her saddle bag purse but leaving her purchases with the bell captain she started towards the bar. She had chosen the hotel herself and had not told anyone where she was staying.

She walked through the bar area, a few people having quiet drinks and then into the next chamber, a little more private. An older gentleman rose and extended his hand. He was fit and taller than average, almost certainly ex-forces. He wore a deep charcoal double-breasted suit with a French blue shirt, a regimental tie, she did not quite recognize, and brown suede loafers.

"Captain Azunna. Welcome. Pleasure to meet you. Please . . . have a seat."

He gestured to the wingback across from him. He seemed terribly sure of who she was even though she had said nothing to confirm that for him. His cockiness struck her as different to the normal sort she ran into every day in this line of work, so she sat. The barman approached.

"Can I get you anything?" The gentleman had been drinking what looked like water up to this point.

Azunna looked at the flight of cocktails.

"I'll have a Hicks aka Guy Burgess." The mixture of Champagne and St. Germain Elderflower sounded refreshing.

"The same for me."

"Very good. I will bring those right up."

"I'm afraid you have me at a disadvantage, sir."

"That is rude of me." He slid a calling card across the small table. It gave a name and said Director-General, Secret Intelligence Service. "You can call me C."

"Nice to meet you." Her true feelings were more mixed.

It was nice to have people interested in her work. Conversely there was a good deal of discussion about an incident she would rather forget.

"The pleasure is all mine. Did you enjoy your lunch with my colleagues?"

"It was very interesting, although I am not sure exactly what the point was. And how did you know I was staying here?"

He simply smiled and pointed at his title on the card.

"Oh, right."

"Clearly you have a sense of history and adventure. Why else would you have chosen to stay here? A coincidence? I think not. There are better located and frankly more luxurious places to stay for the money."

She said nothing. They looked at each other appraisingly. Azunna was intrigued, he wasn't your normal bureaucrat. Had he been, he would not have been meeting a prospective intelligence officer in a hotel bar. She knew that much.

"My colleagues were intrigued by something you said today. It was something akin to, 'the British public did not want to be involved in combat anymore, but also did not want to be killing children.' Is that an accurate summary?"

"Yes. I would say it is. We are a democracy; we have a duty to those we are sworn to protect. And that duty includes not killing innocents in their name."

Their drinks arrived. Almost simultaneously their phones both buzzed, a BBC News Alert. All it said was *Queen Elizabeth II has died.* They both looked at each other and instinctively picked up their glasses and raised them in a silent toast.

Then, "Long live the King." It was simultaneous from the two of them.

This was one of those strange times where you would always remember where you were, where a person felt like everything should stop for an appropriate amount of time. But how long was that? Who decided? But as the cliché says, life goes on.

Following what seemed like a decent interval C continued, "I quite agree with your previous point. Clearly, I am going to need to return to work. There will be other things I need to do with the news we just received, so I'll come right to the point," C began. "I would like you to come work with us. You have just the right skill set and more importantly, the attitude we need in this organization."

"Doing what?" All she could imagine was writing reports and giving briefings to pols. She despised the notion. She'd imagined this all was just a further second-guessing of her decisions in the field, although to what end she could not possibly imagine. She had not thought this was a job interview.

"A trouble-shooter. The Service has a small team of trouble-shooters to deal with tricky situations. I think you'd be perfect. You would operate in the field, outside of Britain. Much like you have done in the Royal Marines. Just more discretely. You have the judgement and nerve to operate independently."

"Afghanistan was not very discrete."

"No, it was not. And that is the whole point. You understand that bombing anything was not discrete. The people who made the mistaken assumption about discretion were here in London. Not you in the field. Called them on their game. I like that."

Without another word he rose and handed her another calling card. It had nothing but a number on it.

"Think about it. We can talk further of course, but I don't think you need that. Call me, day, or night, 24/7, at that number. Please let me know either way. Good evening, Captain Azunna." And he was gone.

Azunna, sat there for a couple of minutes sort of numb. The barman approached.

"Something else, Madam? The gentlemen paid the bill and said that if you wanted anything else just to let me know."

"Right," she paused, "no thank you. That will be quite enough."

Coming back to the present, she left the bar and went up to her suite. She looked at her watch. Nearly six. Her sister had an ensemble part in a play at the university. It was supposed to begin at half seven.

Contemplating seeing her sister again, she decided that she was hungry. Lunch had been small and many hours ago. She rang down to the restaurant.

"Ms. Azunna, good evening, how can I help?"

"May I have a grilled rib-eye, rare, a green salad, a bottle of the Goldeneye Pinot Noir, and a bottle of Glenmorangie?" Maybe it was because Glenmorangie was the most popular single malt Scotch in the UK, but without knowing it Azunna's preferred choice of Scotch was the same as her father.

"Certainly. That should all be up there in thirty minutes."

"Thank you."

Stripping off her clothes, Azunna went into the spa-like shower, and unlike her usual morning routine, let the warm water roll over her body without counting the minutes. Steam filled the room. She tried to relax. Some, but not all the tension began to leave her shoulders and neck, and as the warm water flowed over her knee, the final bits of physical pain from Afghanistan began to leave.

She towelled off, pulling on black Lululemon running shorts, black sports bra, and olive-green ribbed tank. She put her watch back on and just as she entered the living room the doorbell rang. Azunna looked through the eyehole, dinner was here.

"Good evening Ms. Azunna. Where would you like it?"

She gestured to the big chair near the window.

"Very good, just ring down when you want us to pick it up. And if you could just sign here."

"Thank you."

"Have a good evening, Ms. Azunna."

She turned on the BBC World News and listened to Karin Giannone deliver the day's events which were all, of course, about the death of Her Majesty Queen Elizabeth II. The Forces would be quite busy for the next few days as the nation mourned her passing.

The steak was done to perfection, the high-quality British beef melting in her mouth. The summer brought excellent fresh vegetables and thus the green salad was farm-to-table at its best. The wine a good table red, and she could finish the bottle tomorrow. As she came to the end of dinner, she looked at her watch. The time for the play had well passed. She opened the Glenmorangie and poured the light amber Scotch into the heavy crystal tumbler.

"Sorry, Ngozi. Maybe next time," she said to the empty room.

She, like many across the world, felt compelled to watch the news, as if it were a communal way of grieving the loss of the most enduring and central figure in British culture. The news covered everything from what happened next to historical reviews of her reign. Not drinking a lot, but at a steady pace. She thought about Colley dying in Afghanistan, the long, cold flight from Afghanistan back to the UK. Commando training, cold, dirty, and wet. Cambridge, and the bloody Socratic method where a bunch of prigs thought they could put her on the spot.

She thought about that day twenty years ago. She was ten years old, her sister barely two, looking into her mother's vacant eyes, holding her sister, and getting wetter by the minute. Since that day, Ngozi and the Royal Marines had been the only real family she knew. And when the Squadron Commander relieved her, it felt like her parents dying all over again.

She looked at her watch again. It was midnight, she had consumed a quarter of the bottle of scotch. A doctor or physical trainer would certainly disapprove. She picked up the card with the number on it, turning it over in her hand several times. She picked up her phone and dialled the number.

"Yes?"

"I'm in."

Chapter Seven

Late summer had already given way to early fall when Azunna arrived at Vauxhall Cross on a Monday morning a few weeks later. She had travelled from Sandstone in Plymouth on Sunday. Once again checking into the St. Ermin, which was quickly becoming her favourite hotel in London. The location was great, the history intriguing, and she still had to get through the Cambridge Five cocktails.

It was raining, and Azunna debated between rush hour on the Tube or a taxi while standing on the front landing of the St. Ermin. She was wearing her traditional Burberry over a more stylish and modern sheath dress in blue, paired with some taupe kitten-heeled sling-backs. Looking at the weather she decided a black cab was in order. It was, after all, the first day of a new job.

The bell captain hailed one for her using a phone or an app, she wasn't quite sure. The way things changed these days everyone was old enough to remember a time things were done differently. Things were moving so fast that it was just not possible to keep up.

As a hotel staff member held the door, she stepped into the black cab.

"Good morning miss, where to?"

"Vauxhall Cross please."

"You want the station?" The driver seemed a little confused.

"No. Thank you. If you could drop me off at the corner of Vauxhall Cross and the Albert Embankment that would be brilliant."

"Ah, I see." A glimmer of recognition in the driver's eye.

Twelve minutes later Azunna was exiting the cab in front of the building at SE1 7TP. When seen from the other side of the Thames, it was the world-famous headquarters of the British Intelligence Service. Completed in 1994 it was an architectural masterpiece that integrated well with other pieces along the banks of the Thames such as the Battersea Power station.

The rain had eased a bit, but Azunna opened her umbrella and clutched her bag as she decided what to do next. The reporting instructions hadn't been particularly clear. To her right was what looked like the main entrance. To her left, fencing and a moat, then the sidewalk back to Vauxhall Bridge. Or at least so it seemed.

"Hiya!" Mills had snuck up on her. Just as she had decided to try the main entrance.

"Hello. Sorry if I am a bit behind. The instructions I received were maddeningly vague." She was not reflecting Mills' cheery demeanour.

"You aren't late and sometimes the vagueness is intentional. Come with me." They walked towards the Albert Embankment, past what appeared to be the main entrance. After they had seemingly passed the building, they turned left into a small gate and down some stairs, at the bottom of which was a plain door that looked like a service door to some subterranean utility. Mills swiped her card in an access point, and they were in. There was a guard with an M4 at the ready standing just inside, with another behind a bulletproof glass window. Azunna presented her passport and Royal Marine ID for comparison against the pre-vetted list. She was granted entrance and given a visitor's badge.

"Just until we get your normal badge. And we try not to have those of us who work in Chrysalis come in the main entrance. There is a car park below and your numberplate gets you in. Or you can always come this way."

Azunna hoped she would not be spending too much time in the office either way. That sounded like a fate worse than death.

They walked through subterranean tunnels, concrete-lined, high ceilinged. The building was not hermetically sealed but did have an over-pressure system that would thwart any attack with gas or biological agents. There was plush red carpet that seemed incongruous next to the rest of the brutalist decor.

"We are headed up to C's suite of offices. That's where I work. Tickner too. Chrysalis is small, and we try to keep it that way, for everyone's benefit."

Now they were in the elevator. Mills pressed a series of buttons so quickly Azunna couldn't have told you the sequence., but clearly it was some sort of access code.

"That's the second time you have mentioned 'Chrysalis.' What is that?"

"It's the section you will be working in. C will explain it in more detail."

With that, the elevator opened. They emerged into a main hall that was lightly travelled. At the end of the hallway, there was a large glass door with glass panels on either side. The panels each had the symbol of the SIS on them. One door had the letter 'C' emblazoned on it, the other the word 'Suite.' Someone had had a bit of cheek when putting that all together.

Through the glass doors, Azunna found herself in a reception area, the glass behind the receptionist's desk revealing what appeared to be C's office. She could see him looking at his computer, holding a phone to his ear. All the openness, the light and the sky coming through seemed so incongruous to a highly secretive organization. Azunna supposed there were technological solutions to those challenges though.

As if reading her mind, Mills commented, "At the push of a button the glass can go from transparent to opaque. Also, small vibrations are electrically transmitted through the glass, so any audio surveillance is defeated. The glass is protective enough that one would need a small rocket or naval gun at short range to penetrate."

C wrapped up his phone call and signalled for them to come in.

He grabbed his suit jacket and put it on as he went to open the door. Mills escorted Azunna in.

"Pleasure to see you again, Major." He extended his hand, and they shook. It was also her first indication that her pending secondment to the Service might have had something to do with her unexpected and unplanned for promotion.

"Thank you. Pleasure to see you as well. Clearly you were convincing."

He gestured to the walnut-brown leather couch and matching chairs. There was already coffee service on the table.

"I will leave you two." With that Mills withdrew, touching the button that took them from a clear glass box to one that was opaque. Instant frosted glass.

And now it was just them seated across from each other in deep leather chairs with a small coffee table between them.

C began. "We have a special section in mind for you. But let me give you a broad overview first. We have field intelligence officers around the world. That is really no secret to anyone. Everyone does it to some extent. Some of them are embedded in embassies. Depending on the nation they are working in they may be declared. That is, the local government knows what they are doing. We generally declare our agents in Washington, and they declare their agents here. In some countries, they are not declared, but they are still protected by diplomatic immunity. If there are caught engaging in irregular activities, they are almost always immediately PNG'ed by the local government. In the world of intelligence and espionage, that is all routine. You follow?"

"Yes, quite." She had had experience in both Iraq and Afghanistan with the local intelligence officers out of the embassies, so this was nothing new to her. She did imagine it was a tad more difficult in places that were not an actual war zone. In an increasingly untrusting world, every Brit was going to be assumed be working and reporting for the government.

"Good. After that, we have people working long-term in other countries under non-official cover, also known as NOCs. The intelligence officers all gather information first-hand, but more often act as case officers for agents they or others working for the Service have recruited in the past. Because their cover is unofficial, and they are not protected by diplomatic immunity, a country can and will arrest them. If they are UK citizens, we of course offer our diplomatic good offices and work to free them. Nonetheless, it can be a bit dicey. Still, it is a part of the normal course of intelligence operations. Still all make sense?"

"Still tracking all of this, C."

"Good. Now all these sections function pretty much in mirror to the Foreign Office. Political desks, economic intelligence, military manoeuvres, etcetera. Much of that work is done on the up and up through open sources. While a lot of that is secret, for the most part, the broad outlines are known to other governments and the public. But sometimes the work calls for something a little less public, and a little more, shall we say direct. That's the sort of work I want you to do."

"I see. Tell me more."

"Sometimes problems exist where at least part of the solution is the elimination of certain people and problems. Chrysalis exists to solve those problems. We maintain a list that is unanimously approved by the PM, the Foreign Minister, and the defence minister of people whose elimination would solve a range of problems. That list is reviewed by them quarterly on a brief from me. Once on that list, no further action is needed to approve a mission. When we decide to commence an operation against someone on that list, we notify the Principals Committee that an operation is underway. And, of course, if a crisis arises, the Principals Committee can approve other specific targets."

"So, you want me to be an assassin?" She did not hate the idea. There were plenty of very bad people out there.

"I prefer the term 'trouble-shooter.' In almost every case, other methods have been tried to deter the person from whatever course of action they are on. No one on that list would be shocked to find themselves there. They know exactly what they are doing. But we need people who can do this quietly, with minimal fuss, and precision."

"Then why me? The Afghanistan operation was loud, fussy, and anything but precise."

"Ah, yes. But that had almost nothing to do with you. The Government wanted it both ways, they wanted the benefits of the mission yet none of the blowback. You made a judgement call. Do you regret it?"

"We've been over this before. I certainly regret the deaths of my mates. Colley was my responsibility and Sparrow was my best mate. I will carry that with me the rest of my life. Every run I think of Sparrow, and every time I look at my uniform, I remember Colley. So, I certainly regret that part of the decision. I also have no idea how I could have made any other decision."

"Quite. Your instinct was to not kill unnecessary targets. An understanding that 'collateral damage,' as our American cousins say, should be limited, and after twenty years of war I am glad we are still producing people like you who understand that."

"So, what is next?"

"We don't select people who don't already have the skillset we need. There is no formal training program. Rather we conduct an Onboarding and Assessment Program. The principle purpose is to help you learn how to operate completely on your own. Ex-forces people like yourself and field intelligence officers from the more regular side of operations have enormous amounts of support in the field. Working in Chrysalis requires a good deal more independence." He paused.

"After that, you will be on a probationary status until you have terminated any two people on the list. Unless a specific target comes up due to a crisis. Once you have accomplished those two missions, and upon my review, you will be designated a Chrysalis Officer. You will be read in on more high-level intelligence and given the authority to solve these problems."

Azunna was still soaking this all in. C continued.

"Mills is my Associate Director for Field Operations. She runs Chrysalis missions and the Onboarding and Assessment Program, as well as recruiting. She spotted you herself. She will help you with all the details." He stood up, which Azunna took to mean the meeting was complete.

"Good luck, Maj Azunna. I look forward to seeing you again in about six weeks."

Chapter Eight

───────────

The Land Rover Defender 90 was delivered precisely at 0830 as promised. The valet had rung Azunna's room to advise her of the drop-off and she requested bell service at the same time. The history of espionage at the St. Ermin made the staff a little more accustomed to the idea of secret rendezvous and mystery deliveries, even if the history was long ago and sometimes mixed with fiction. Who wouldn't want their own little role in a spy novel?

Mills had walked Azunna through all the administrivia of joining a government bureaucracy. The intelligence world was not much different from any other government agency that collated and acted on data. They simply did it in the shadows and against people who were not being particularly cooperative or friendly. From email, salary deposits, expense accounts, laptops, and phones, it was all quite ordinary. When it came time to select a company car, Mills had recommended the Defender. "It's not like you are going to get an Aston Martin," Mills commented sardonically.

The vehicle was Tasman blue, with white metal wheels, and a white roof. Beautiful in how basic it was. The interior was a medium British khaki. Azunna looked at the odometer and it had less than 1000 miles on it. She quickly familiarized herself with the controls and then set the Sat Nav for Penderyn. It was not exactly where she needed to go, but the possibility of a quick visit to a whisky distillery as part of work seemed like a splendid idea.

The sun was breaking through the early morning clouds, and it appeared as if it was going to be a rather glorious fall day in the south of England. She adjusted her sunglasses and eased out of the St. Ermin's parking area. Azunna was excited, a wry smile on her normally taciturn to face. She was back on mission, on a new adventure.

She turned right on Caxton Street and worked her way through the side streets till she was on the Birdcage again, turned left onto Horse Guards Drive, left again onto the Mall where she could see Buckingham Palace. Sometimes these roads were inexplicably and inconveniently blocked off but, not today.

She rounded the circle in front of the Palace and headed towards Hyde Park. The tourists were still relatively thin on the ground at this hour but increasing by the minute. Floods of commuters were arriving at Green Park Tube station and walking through the park to the various offices and shops in the area. London was bustling as always.

Passing Hyde Park, Azunna turned right onto Oxford Street and then an almost immediate left onto Orchard Street at the flagship Marks & Spencer. From there it was several stoplights and a name change to Baker Street before she arrived at Marylebone Road, just short of the famous fictional detective's home. Left would take her back into Central London, but she turned right onto the A501, which turned quickly into the A40 to take her out near Heathrow.

Azunna was now in the counterflow to the daily commute. As much as she enjoyed the city, this day she was glad to be on the way out of it. The weather seemed like it was going to cooperate, so she opened the driver's side window to let in the early autumn air and enjoy the rare bit of sunshine.

Once on the M4, Azunna maintained a steady at 70 mph, the national speed limit. These new Defenders did not strain the way the originals did and were certainly more comfortable. Seventy was easy, and Defenders were popular enough she blended right in.

And that was one of the goals of the training mission: to blend in and operate in such a way as to evade official detection. So as much as her observation of the speed limit would annoy some fellow drivers, she set it there and was in the far-left lane, only coming moving right to pass the lorries or the occasional caravanner. As wonderful as the Defender was, it was not going to receive unwanted attention.

After numerous bits of reconstruction, the M4, the only motorway into and out of Wales, was nice and smooth. The instructions for this five-week assessment had been frustratingly thin. She knew where she was to stay, and she had methods of communication on her mobile and her laptop. And she had been told she was going to receive instructions to accomplish tasks and acquire information. That was about it. But she was determined to make the most of it.

Azunna was alone in her thoughts, and the monotony of the motorway permitted her to reflect on how she had gotten to this point, of events far and recent. Born and raised in Peckham to Nigerian immigrant parents, her journey to this trip to Wales had been long and improbable. Sheer grit and determination had sent her to Cambridge passing out in 4 years with degrees in Diplomatic History and Middle Eastern Studies. Her parents' estate footed the bill with some left over. Fluent in English and Igbo from a young age, she added French at Elizabeth Garret Anderson and Arabic at Cambridge.

Kiana and Phoebe had made the decision to join the Forces together. Phoebe's father had served in the Royal Navy and encouraged the young women to do the same. They reasoned they were more likely to see much of the world with the Royal Navy than other branches. After completing Royal Naval College at Portsmouth, Phoebe was off to the Fleet Air Arm and Azunna was off to join Royal Navy Intelligence. Her language skills gave her early entrée to the world of Royal Marine Commandos and a leg up when that was finally opened up to women later.

As part of her intelligence training, she was put through the combat swimmer course, where she completed one lesson so quickly that the evaluators assumed she had cheated. Only after she walked them through her tactics did they realize her tactic was completely original. It was immediately adapted as the principal Technique, Tactic, and Procedure for the installation of limpet mines.

As a Navy Human Intelligence Collector and later as a section leader in in 30 Commando's Reconnaissance and Surveillance Squadron, Azunna led missions to Afghanistan, Nigeria, and Jamaica. While ostensibly training for local forces, these missions were in fact for intelligence collection and reconnaissance. They even resulted in the elimination of Taliban, Boko Haram, and drug cartel operatives. Azunna had been deeply involved with the detailed planning of these operations, demonstrating her cool reliability to close with and kill an enemy operative. When the Commando Forces finally opened to women, Phoebe had been the first to encourage Azunna to apply.

All this culminated in *that* day, now over a year ago, in the mountains of central Afghanistan. The truth was she cared not one whit about the fact that continued British participation in the war in Afghanistan had been publicly revealed. The pols and prigs who wanted it kept secret were not doing so because it was deceiving an enemy, but because it was politically expedient. The death of her trusted NCO and the crew of Junglie 1, including her friend Phoebe, weighed on her mind, but second-guessing combat was a fool's errand. She'd dealt with enough survivor's guilt over the years, it was just another thing to process. And even as her relief from command had been upheld on investigation, she had been cleared of any specific wrongdoing.

What really bothered her on this day as she drove in the early fall English sunshine was what it had all been for. Phoebe and Colley? Did their deaths mean anything? Why was she in this business if she was not going to make a difference? She had chosen the Forces over an NGO or even the Foreign Office because she wanted to be able to make positive change. Ten years after making that decision she might admit that it had been a choice that was not fully informed, but she still felt that she could be that agent of protection and change and she trusted her instincts.

Which brought her to her sister, Ngozi, who was just finishing up her law degree. She had not seen Ngozi much over the previous eight years. Oh, they communicated regularly with texts and emails, the occasional letter or package through the post. Their parents' estate had provided them with plenty of money. It had covered school fees, helped by the fact that they had both earned academic scholarships.

That was the personal war raging inside Kiana Azunna. How to be effectual for herself, her younger sister, and every other disempowered person out there. It felt both overly ambitious and not ambitious enough.

By the time the Land Rover started to cross over the Prince of Wales Bridge, Azunna was clear that she still wanted to accomplish many things, but that maybe she had a thing or two to learn and was determined to take advantage of this opportunity.

Just east of Newport, she turned off the M4 to the A449. The Brecon Beacons, where she was headed, was a place favoured by adventurers around the UK for its rugged and beautiful landscape. Pen-Y-Fan, one of the more challenging hikes, or tabs as they said in the Army and yomps in the Royal Marines, was famed for being the location of selection for the Special Air Service, Britain's most well-known Special Operations Force, but in truth, anyone wanting to serve in some form of Britain's elite soldiers, sailors, marines, or airman was going to yomp Pen-Y-Fan.

Now she was heading north, the road changing from four-lane to two-lane and then back again, seemingly randomly. Even as the sunny day continued, the rains had kept the hills of Wales a vibrant green. Azunna loved Wales. It was a place to get lost, with a surprise around every corner. From outdoor adventures to history, to cheese, to whisky she could always find something new and interesting in Wales. She was glad to be able to spend some time here.

After she passed through Crickhowell, she was firmly on two-lane roads. Most of the population of Wales lives in the south along the coasts, so each mile further north took her further away from large groups of people. By the time she reached the A470, population clusters had started to disappear. As she approached the Llwyn-on Reservoir, she decided to find a lay bye and pull over to get her bearings. She pulled over to the right when she found a place on the north end of the reservoir.

Clouds were gathering like an iron-grey building in the sky, replacing the bright sunshine she had for much of the trip. *Storm's coming*, she thought. She clicked the button that closed the sunroof and took off her sunglasses, grabbed her phone and got out of the Defender. Her Belstaff jacket, Rag-n-Bone jeans, and brown Crocket and Jones boots were enough against the wind that was coming up, but she was glad that she had packed the full range of layers for this this adventure.

She took a good look around, the gravel under her feet making that crunching sound only gravel does. The reservoir was to her right and the occasional cars whizzed by to her left. Across the reservoir, the hills rose dramatically, covered in green; across the road it levelled out and then rose slightly before dipping again, denying one any expansive view of the horizon. With her eyes closed, Azunna turned her face towards the sun just as it began to finally disappear behind the clouds, took a deep, almost yoga-like breath, held it, and then exhaled, expelling every bit of air from her lungs. Here she was. A woman. On her own. Opening her eyes, she pulled out her phone, opened the satnav app, and made a final plan for approach.

It was late afternoon before she finally arrived at her destination. She had made a quick detour to the Penderyn distillery where she picked up a couple of bottles of their fine single malt, including one of her favourites finished in a Madeira cask.

She was heading north still when she spotted what she was sure was her destination. Azunna turned on her signal and slowed to allow two lorries, the only traffic she had seen for the last 20 minutes, to pass. She entered through an iron gate that was left open and attached to unusually high stone walls. One could still barely see over them.

One might have described the building as a carriage house although Azunna was sure that was wrong. The building looked to be over 100 years old in parts., with a hodgepodge of styles showing where additions had been made. It was long, two levels for the first two-thirds, and then four levels at the far right. Towards the far left, there was a small passageway, room enough for a vehicle through which Azunna pulled the Land Rover into a small car park capable of hosting ten to twelve normal-size cars. There was a little garden behind that with a few tables and chairs, evidently for visitors, but he beyond that was the oddly tall stone wall and the wild green of Wales.

There was only one other car in the parking lot. It was a late model Vauxhall Insignia in a British racing green. Nice but not particularly flashy. Azunna parked the Land Rover at the far end and got out.

Feet on gravel again, she looked around for any sign of another person, other than the car. There was a door to the right of the passageway and Azunna started to make her way towards it when it opened.

"You must be Kiana! Welcome to Wales." A petite brunette with contrasting skin that was too perfect, emerged. She had a familiar look. "I'm Lewis, Elisa Lewis. Pleasure to meet you." She extended her hand in greeting and Azunna took it.

"Kiana Azunna. Pleasure."

"Let's get your bags, shall we?" They both returned to the vehicle as Azunna used the remote to open the tailgate.

Together they grabbed the three duffels and one rucksack, with Azunna also taking the time to grab one of the bottles of whisky from the front seat.

"Ah, a fan of our local single malt, eh?"

"You might say that. I have had enough trips to this part of the UK that, while it is not home, I am quite familiar with its charms."

"Hmm. Quite right. Well, let's get this in the building." The two women brought everything Azunna thought she would need for the next five weeks into a little foyer.

"Why don't we leave this here and have some coffee before I show you around the place and to your quarters."

"Thank you, I'd love a brew."

"The kitchenette is this way."

They walked down a short hallway. The floors were hardwood with wide planks, the colour of dark chocolate, with plenty of scratches, while the walls were a fading pale blue covered with a dozen framed pictures of people. Some individuals, and some small groups of mostly men, with the occasional woman appearing.

They emerged into a kitchenette with a farm sink, deep with a strong-looking faucet, a few cabinets, and a stove top, but no oven. A medium-sized farm kitchen table, the sort of thing that looks like a modified butcher's block, sat in the middle of the room with six round-back chairs around it. The walls were the same pale blue and the photo motif continued. On the table was a large Chemex pour-over coffee carafe, with the filter and coffee already in it; two proper mugs, as well a cream and sugar service. A kettle was about to come to a full boil on the stove.

"Yes, yes. I shouldn't've walked away from the stove with something on it. We all take a little risk now and then," Elisa said cheekily. "Have a seat."

Azunna looked around the kitchen. There was a door at the far end leading to another room. She peered into what looked like an office, but one with wide windows, as if it used to be a sunroom. As that part of the building was generally oriented to the north, there must have been glorious days of long sunshine at the height of the Welsh summer. Satisfied, Azunna sat.

"What is this place?" Azunna's curiosity was finally piqued.

"Oh, sort of a school, sort of a respite. People can learn all sorts of things about themselves here." Elisa was being coy, too coy by half.

"Well, I guess that is what I am here to do: Learn. And I suppose one does not always need to know or have a plan as to what one is about to learn, eh?"

Elisa was pouring the boiled water over the coffee. She created the coffee bloom and waited the recommended 30 seconds before adding more water. The women both watched as the brown liquid dripped slowly but steadily from the cone, as if reverent silence was a required part of the ritual of making coffee in this manner. The only sound in the room being the drip or the occasional car passing by. Azunna would have sworn that she could hear the movement of her Bremont.

"Who is your preferred roaster?" Azunna asked after Elisa returned the kettle to the stove. She figured she might as well gather some information.

"Oh, I switch back and forth between Union Roasters and Whittard of Chelsea."

"Lovely."

People that are intimately familiar, like long-term partners, can sit together in silence for hours. Likewise, people can sit next to each other in an airport lounge for hours and not exchange a word. But when two people meet for the first time in some sort of meeting or introduction, silence becomes unnatural and awkward at some point. Even the most well-trained and disciplined person is going to want to fill the space, either eliciting information or providing information. Here it became somewhat of a test of wills.

The coffee was ready, and Elisa poured out two mugs, offering the cream and sugar service to which Azunna demurred. Azunna put the mug to her lips waiting for the comforting flavour to touch her tongue.

Elisa considered her new visitor and sipped her coffee as well. Then their eyes met.

"Kiana," she paused. "May I call you Kiana?"

"Of course." Azunna was certainly one not to be hung up on ceremony or formality.

"I have been working for C and the Service for a good ten years now. I have kept this place running. It's a place of respite, training, learning. New officers come here to get acclimated to the Firm. Sometimes people come here as a getaway after missions. You can get the comfort of decent lodging, a kitchen, without all the attention that can be overwhelming at other establishments."

"So, I am here for acclimatization?"

"Are you? Chrysalis only tells me you are coming. I don't receive the details. I can help you though, but I need to know what sort of help you need."

Both continued to sip their coffee.

"You want some of this Penderyn in your coffee?"

"Why don't we show you around, get your gear to your room, and then have a proper drink before dinner?"

"That's an even better idea!"

The sun was setting behind the cloud cover. The lighter grey had faded to dark gunmetal, and the sunroom had grown dim, with the lights in the kitchen starker. They returned to the hall for the bags. A door Azunna had not noticed on the way in led to a small set of backstairs, narrow and relatively low. The steps were the same dark brown wide planks, and they looked a little out of place in such a small space. They headed up them and emerged on the next floor into a more normal-sized hallway with the same motif, pale blue walls adorned with random pictures, and the dark brown floor. To the right was a series of rooms that Azunna would later learn were for meetings, training, or just small sitting areas. To the left were windows looking out over the car park and the gardens.

After passing five or six of those rooms, they emerged in a landing area. This was clearly an addition. The floors were newer, and the woodwork looked fresh. But the pale blue paint was the same, the photos more recent.

"This is the central staircase. There are four *en suites* on each floor. I have put you in the far back corner on the top floor to give you a maximum amount of privacy since no one is here and I am not expecting anyone for all least several weeks." They hauled the gear to the fourth floor.

On the residence floors, there were installed carpet runners in a dark British racing green, to limit the creaks and squeaks of the wood. There was a skylight in the middle of the small tower to bring some natural light in and on each floor, there were four rooms, with doors in the centre of the wall. As they finally arrived at the top level, Azunna saw the number on the first room was 40, she looked around the one to the left was 41, Elisa turned right and took her to room 43. One of the many photos stood out as they drew near the door. The photo must have been twenty years old but the good-looking young man with piercing blue eyes still stood out.

Elisa dropped the bags. "Each suite is accessed by a code. Room 43's default code is 4343." She punched the number in, and the bolt slid back with a heavy thud. "This card will tell you how to change the code so you can have your own secure space."

Azunna took the card and appreciated the appearance of privacy, but she knew there was no possibility the Service would allow her or anyone to completely cut off access.

The suite looked comfortable but hardly luxurious. The TV hung on the wall, and there was the expansive bathroom.

"Make yourself at home. Why don't we meet downstairs in say, forty-five minutes for a drink and some dinner?"

"Sounds great."

"Oh, and don't forget the Penderyn." Elisa winked as she left, and Azunna was alone again. The pale blue had given way to more of an eggshell paint. The artwork in the room was less personal, British landscapes and history. There was even a print of The Fighting Temeraire, which according to a 2005 BBC 4 poll was Britain's favourite painting. She went to explore the bathroom.

Nothing remarkable about the toilet or the bidet, but she was happy to see a large bath and a separate shower and to feel the warmth from a heated floor flood her body.

Azunna was not a big nester. Years in the Royal Marines had made her ready to move quickly, but as she knew that she was going to be here for a few weeks she quickly unpacked. Her folded garments, underwear, workout gear, and jumpers went into the dresser; trousers and shirts into the closet; and her footwear – mostly boots and running shoes – were lined up on the closet floor. She left her small rucksack untouched but pulled out her laptop and quickly connected to the Wi-Fi network. The room felt stuffy, so even though the early autumn the temperatures could easily get down to 5 Celsius, she decided to open the windows for a little fresh air. One last look at her phone showed no recent emails from work so she pocketed it, grabbed the whisky, and headed for the door.

At the last second, she backtracked to grab the instructions on changing the code and took two minutes doing so. *No reason to make it too easy,* she thought. And then she headed down to the ground floor.

In the formal dining room, one end of the long table had a small dinner service laid out. Off to the side were two heavy crystal tumblers, emblazoned with the crest of the Prince of Wales. Azunna cracked the Penderyn and poured two fingers worth into each glass. She could hear someone moving about in the large kitchen, so she took the whiskies and followed the sound.

"Ah, you are here. Great. And you remembered the whisky, not that I doubted you would," Elisa said as she graciously took the tumbler offered.

"Cheers." They clinked their glasses.

"Right now, I have a chicken roasting. There will be plenty leftover to make a take-away lunch. There are also plenty of breakfast items. I don't normally make meals but given your late arrival and lack of lodgers, I have whipped something up. If there is something special you want, I have a clipboard over there with a running list, just put it on there."

"Wow. Well, that's comprehensive."

Elisa picked up her phone and looked at the timers. "Ah, the chicken should be just about done." She went to one of the ovens and pulled out a small roasting pan. Azunna could see a perfectly roasted Welsh chicken that was the perfect golden colour that merges into brown and just the right places. Azunna supposed there *were* people who did not like a well-roasted chicken, but she didn't know any of them. Using a Thermapen Elisa checked the internal temperature of the bird. "Perfect. We can let that rest."

Elisa pulled a tossed salad out of one of the refrigerators and a small bowl that turned out to be a vinaigrette dressing. She also produced a baguette, a brick of butter, and a Beaujolais wine. By the time Elias produced plates, cutlery, glasses, and uncorked the wine, the chicken was ready for carving. They both helped themselves to the offerings and headed to the dining room. Azunna poured the ruby wine, filling the glasses well above a standard restaurant pour.

The meal was perfectly pleasant, and conversation was kept light, but by 2100 the wine was bottle was empty and Azunna was ready to wind down. "I need to get some rest, and who knows when I will get a tasking. Any thoughts on that process?"

"Well, I do know this, as much as you might be called to action, to exercise that discretion, to pull the trigger, this is a cerebral process. You said you were a Royal Marine officer? They know you know how to do things under pressure. It's about learning the right information, using your judgement, and taking your ego out of the equation. The people who do well here are the ones who are willing to learn, mostly about themselves, and to be patient. I know enough to be aware that when you are in the field, sometimes the only way to achieve your mission objective is to take a slower more thoughtful approach." And with that Azunna thanked Elisa for the meal and retired for the evening.

Back in her room, Azunna finally looked at her phone. Several BBC news alerts, Twitter of course, and her personal emails. As she was scrolling, another one appeared.

> *From: Mills, Erica (MillsE@sis.gov.uk)*
> *Cc: C (Director_General_C@sis.gov.uk)*
> *To: Azunna, Kiana (AzunnaK@sis.gov.uk)*
> *Subject: Mission Tasking*
>
> *You need to meet your contact at the top of the Pen-Y-Fan at 1000 tomorrow. Charles will be wearing a blue beanie and have an orange rucksack. Learn as much as you can from him and find your next tasking. Confirmation code is Snowdonia.*

Chapter Nine

Azunna was on the road at 0700. It was less than five miles to the start point of the trail, the famous red phone booth, and even if she was very leisurely it was going to take her no more than two hours to get to the top of the hill, which was more a plateau anyway. This was not the climb of Ben Nevis, Scafell Pike, or Snowdonia. SAS selection took place here because it was challenging enough, but it was not the path itself that was the main challenge, it was the time spent and the weight they were carrying. Fortunately, that was not a concern of hers today.

At this hour the sun was just beginning to come up behind the cloud cover, but the odds of seeing much of it today were going to be limited. She had prepared accordingly, wet weather gear, insulating layers that would still work when wet, and, of course, many pairs of socks.

She rounded the last corner coming from the south and the road was heading up the mountain. On her right, she could see the red telephone booth and the Storey Arms. To her left was a narrow car park with some concessions selling sandwiches and instant coffee. She was glad she'd had time for a properly brewed coffee before she left the lodge.

She pulled off the road to park in the last lay-by before the car park. *No need to get caught up in that with a bunch of other people coming off the mountain if that happens.*

It couldn't have been any more than seven degrees, with high humidity that was going to threaten rain throughout the day. Azunna had on her trusted yomping boots – she had probably worn them only once or twice since that day in Afghanistan – some charcoal grey Prana Zion hiking trousers, and a blue wool commando jumper. She pulled out her blue 36-liter Osprey pack that had two litres of water in the side pockets. Inside she had two more pairs of socks, never underestimate the restorative power of clean dry socks on a yomp, she had learned; she left another pair waiting in the Defender, if needed at the end of the day. Also, she had a light Rab puffer jacket and a red waterproof shell. She added another litre of water to the bag, along with the chicken sandwich she had thrown together from the night before leftovers. A couple of apples completed the load out.

There were very few other people out at this hour and there were only two other cars parked up. Azunna's goal was to be on the top a good half hour before the rendezvous time, so she set off.

This was Azunna's fourth time here. She'd been here for own assessment, the time she had been an assessor, and for a recreational hike with her mates from the SBS. There is a certain masochistic quality to foot soldiers and marines where they like to relive times of physical challenge that felt, at the time, like they were being pushed too far. They can spend the rest of their life chasing that adrenaline high of overcoming tremendous mental and physical obstacles.

Today though Azunna had plenty of time for her tasked mission on her own timeline, the weight she was carrying was minimal, and she was in fine shape. Even though the humidity had made it seem colder than the air temperature, she resisted putting on the puffer jacket, instead relying on the fact her body was about to start working very hard and that would warm her a bit. Her only further concessions to the cold were an olive-green beanie and some hiking gloves.

Azunna walked up to the Storey Arms and the jog-trotted across the road, angling up toward the red phone booth and the trailhead. She felt mentally prepared for this, but the nagging question in the back of her mind was how her body would handle it. All through rehab, she tabbed a bit on flat ground but nothing remotely like real hiking. She wasn't even going to do the full route, the Fan Dance, at least that was not her plan but still, the human memory wants to believe it could do what once did.

After she passed through the gate she was on a narrow sharply ascending trail, to her right a fence and a grove of trees, to her a left a green uneven and rocky field. Later in the winter the cold weather would turn a good deal of the vegetation brown, but for now the effects of long days of sunshine combined with plenty of rain kept it all a wonderful green.

***

The first part of the path was a steep climb. It was enough to keep the not-very-serious from even beginning this hike and for the special operations candidates who tackle it with gusto enough to tax them early on enough that they are going to be looking for their mental reserves quicker than normal. Azunna's breathing hardly changed as she moved, her aerobic conditioning was such that this part of the climb was nothing. But after five strides, her quads and hamstrings were instantly awake, being used in a manner they had not been in quite a while. This first part of the trail couldn't be more than two hundred metres, but it was a daunting way to start a trek.

At the top of the first section, Azunna stopped after she went through the gate designed to keep livestock on one side or the other. The increase in elevation had already changed the view of grey rocks and greenery. The only obstruction was the low cloud cover and the fog in the distance. She remembered doing this on clearer days when the walk was against the clock. She'd had time for a mere glance then, but it still seemed to carry on forever. Today her vision was blocked by the clouds, but maybe later she would be able to see more.

From here the incline would be less steep, it was merely about getting on with it. Experience taught Azunna that the next mental challenge was the descent to cross a creek.

Azunna assumed that whoever or whatever committee had chosen this route for special operations assessment had done it because there are two mental challenges right away. First, the ascent from the phone booth, and now the descent to cross the creek. All that work to "get up the mountain" can feel wasted, because one looks across to the other side sees that they need to do that climb again. And who knows what lies beyond that?

Azunna looked at her Bremont. She was doing just fine on time, and she continued to descend to the creek, giving her quads a break but engaging her calves and hip flexors as they controlled her descent. The real test was the increased pressure on her left knee, and it seemed to be holding steady. She was convinced that whoever had developed the saying "it's all downhill from here" had never done any serious hiking. Controlling a descent could be just as hard as the climb up.

The trail is well marked on Pen-Y-Fan, but that does not mean it is always in great shape, and there are plenty of places the walker needs to be careful of their footfall lest they roll an ankle. Azunna was being particularly careful, her knee seemed to be doing just fine and she wanted to keep it that way. She made it to the creek. There was no bridge, just rocks and water. And it's not as if the water was particularly deep, but the walker, if given a choice, would always prefer dry boots to wet ones. There was going to be enough sweat in the socks anyway, no reason to give blisters and cold and added advantage.

Carefully choosing the flattest stones, Azunna worked her way across the creek, briefly pausing on the other side to look at where she had come from and grab her first gulp of water.

Even in the cold weather sweat had formed on her forehead and lower back, the body heat she had generated with her effort clashing with the cold Welsh air. She moved on.

Even at the bottom of the creek bed, to Azunna, the hardest part was passed. Now it was a steady ascent to the top of the Pen-Y-Fan and her rendezvous. She was not exactly on autopilot, still watching her footfall, but her mind was starting to generate questions for her contact. She was also thinking back about her vague instructions. There was no Program of Instruction for these five weeks, which she had also been led to believe could either be truncated or extended. Mills had told her to be patient. To watch things, develop, and then as necessary, act. This was harder than it sounded. One might have thought that laying in sniper hides would have prepared her for this but compared to this five-week, open-ended . . . she did not even know what to call it. Mission? Tasking? Training? She chose to stick with the preferred Service nomenclature, Assessment – those times in sniper hides were quite compressed timelines.

Still trying to understand what this was all about, she arrived at an outcropping of rocks called Corn Du. It was approaching 0900. She had over an hour till the rendezvous, and she wanted to be there early. Not because she was afraid of holding her contact up, but her instincts said she needed to scout the area and be prepared when she met this "Charles."

***

At 883 metres, Pen-Y-Fan is one of the highest peaks in Wales, but people don't walk it specifically for that, they walk it for its connection to British military history. Peak, Azunna felt implied the top of a triangle, one last little bit of rock reaching towards the sky. At least in the United Kingdom, the top of a mountain did not necessarily resemble the image of an Alpine or Himalayan peak. Rather, at Pen-Y-Fan it is an oval-shaped area that was the rounded top of the mountain. In what would be the northeast corner the ground rose slightly and some bright spark, in an example of British exactitude, had measured and marked the highest point on the plateau ensuring walkers could know, in fact, they had made it.

In the direction Azunna was coming from two approaches were possible, a sweeping curve to the west and then south, finally turning back to the east, or straight across a small ravine. Azunna chose the ravine both because it was shorter and deposited her at the peak which allowed her to "summit" and then get about her business. "Summiting" was not so much a necessity at this point, but merely a reflexive action.

The weather had not improved. One could only tell the sun was fully up because the dark iron-grey sky at sunrise had given way to the dove grey of day. The cloud cover was lower now at the top but the view, and while it did not seem rain was imminent, one never could tell.

She walked down the small slope towards the southwestern side of the top, found a rock she could reasonably sit on and dropped her rucksack. Now that she had stopped working so hard to climb, she was starting to get cold. The perspiration no longer cooling her inner core and settling on her skin began the chilling effect, moisture wicking top and wool sweater notwithstanding. She pulled out her puffer jacket and put it on, zipping to the top and instantly feeling warmer. She grabbed one of the apples and the half drank litre of water, sat on the flat part of the rock she had identified as a makeshift chair, and then began to wait.

Alone in her thoughts was a difficult place for Azunna to be. She'd spent a lifetime running from them. To be alone with them was to feel out of place, both abandoned and as if she was unreliable, that she could not do enough. She wanted, needed, to fix everything for everyone. At Cambridge, she had wanted to belong but failed to ever really fit in. The Royal Marines advertised themselves as a family, as so many militaries try to do, but that word has all sorts of complicated connotations and in the end, they were not a family, not really. But that – family, a sense of belonging – was something Azunna felt like she needed to have.

The wind had picked up and the clouds seemed lower. Being an autumn weekday meant the walkers were fewer, but there were still plenty of people up to the challenge. Azunna finished the apple and used her best cricket throw to send it over the edge. She finished the bottle of water and put the empty container at the bottom of her rucksack. She stood up to stretch her legs. Even with the puffer jacket on she had gotten a bit of a chill. She looked at her Bremont again, it was five to ten.

At ten after ten, Azunna shouldered her rucksack and began a careful walk around the top to the mountain. There were three trailed approaches, and someone could do something crazy and scale the rocks, but that was unlikely. She thought maybe he had decided to wait off one of the approaches.

She rounded the crest again then descended into the ravine from which she had come, climbed back on to the trail and then reproached the top from the pathway she had avoided earlier. Nothing. Her phone pinged. It was Mills.

SITREP.

Azunna put the phone back in her pocket for a few moments. It was now half ten. Thirty minutes late. She looked at her phone again and scrolled up to make sure she had understood the instructions. Another ping.

REPORT.

Azunna quickly typed, *No Joy*. Using the pilot slang for no contact that had been adopted by so many in the military.

Finally, Azunna decided to make a brief walk down the opposite path to see if she could see anything. She walked for about ten minutes, before she decided to return to the top.

It was now past 11. He was over an hour late. She pulled out her phone.

> Please confirm rendezvous was
> 1000 this date
> summit of Pen-Y-Fan, Wales.

Three dots then they disappeared. Then three dots again.

Confirmed.

> I have checked all approaches.
> No sign of subject.

Roger.

Request further instruction.

She waited. Nothing from London. Not three dots. Nothing. Azunna was growing frustrated. Her first "training" mission was going sideways, and she had no idea why. Finally, three dots appeared.

Stand by.

Great. Stand by? What was she waiting for?

While waiting for London to pull its collective head out of its ass, she selected a different set of rocks where she could rest and where she could better observe all the approaches. She sat on the ground this time and leaned forward to stretch her low back. Then she leaned back against the rock, got another bottle of water out, and pulled out the chicken sandwich for an early lunch. *Should've put more salt on the chicken.*

Most people who were walking the trail did not stay on the summit very long, so no one noticed that she was closing in on two hours on top. The weather had not become noticeably worse, though rain seemed more imminent. Finally, her phone pinged again.

Your call.

Azunna made a face. Pursing her lips. *Of course,* she thought. She decided to ignore the text for the moment. She finished off the last of the sandwich and put the water back into the side pocket of her rucksack. She still had a litre and a half of water. No real problem if she ran out, but she could still end up dehydrated by the end of the journey.

Azunna looked at her watch again. Approaching half twelve. *Well, this day is not going as I had thought it would.* With the rain pending she shed her puffer jacket and wrapped it back up, pulling the waterproof shell out.

Walking back down the last trail she had come on curved around till she came to the cut off back through the ravine and to the summit. Nothing. Nobody.

To make sure did not miss anything, she had decided to return via the opposite route. She crossed the plateau and began her descent. This route was longer, but it was a gentle slope down, and no matter how well her knee was holding up, mentally she appreciated the less strain on the joint. She knew this route would have her walking back up the A470 to the Defender, and that had not been her original plan but as she well knew the plan rarely survived first contact. Still, she was frustrated. She had thought she would get to shine on her first test. It felt like a bust at best, a failure at worst.

It started to rain. She pulled the beanie off and pulled her hood up. It was more than a sprinkle but less than a deluge, and she was grateful that the path was gravelled for the most part. On the other hand, the bigger pieces of rock could be quite slick. It was a pick-your-poison sort of situation.

The people passing her on the way up had slowed to a trickle, and no one passed her on the way down. It was one of those situations that made ex-forces types remember long days in the field in shitty weather, almost as a fond memory because they had endured it, but also as one that made them glad to know they would spend the night in a bed.

By the time she had been walking for 90 minutes, she was back at the A470 at the Coed Owen Bunkhouse. From here it was less than four miles to the Defender. Even going uphill, she was going to be able to cover that in less than an hour. She was finishing off her last little bit of water, the heaviest thing she was carrying with her, so her load had decreased.

She was tempted to walk along the inside track closet to the mountain and against traffic, that "should" be the safest route. But with any vehicles making inside turns she was concerned they would not see her. Where she was, she would be highlighted against the grey sky and her bright shell would at least make her a little more visible. She also hated to waste what view there was.

The steady rain had increased, and she was glad she was at least on the road instead of the steep path. Even as her heart pumped more blood with every step of exertion, she was starting to get colder. Pausing to put the puffer jacket on would mean getting wetter and colder. She was less than two miles from the Landie, so she pressed on, lorries going past splashing just enough water to be annoying. The occasional car driving way too fast for the wet conditions. Finally, the blue SUV came into sight.

When she was within ten metres, Azunna used the remote to pop the tail gate. It rose slowly and by the time she was there she slid under it and was finally given a respite from the unceasing rain. Unshouldering her rucksack, she placed it in the hold and opened it, pulling out her puffer jacket. She took off the shell and donned the puffer, immediately warming even as the rain splashed against her. She grabbed a spare bottle of water from the back of the car, hit the button that closed the tailgate, and dashed around to get in with minimal soaking.

In the driver's seat, she took a big breath, locked the car, and took a big gulp of water. The litre bottle was already half empty. Soaking wet, ever the Commando Azunna decided to get of her wettest clothes. Alighting from the Landy she popped the boot hatch, seeking a bit of shelter and dug out some dry socks, trousers, and underwear. Returning to the driver's side and overlooking the valley that gave her a wee bit of privacy, she quickly changed, saving the socks for when she was back in the warm SUV. She then started the car, turned up the heat and turned the wipers on.

Back in the lay-by, Azunna took a moment to just breath. The rain intensified. The word deluge was not an exaggeration at this point. She pulled out her phone. And opened her secure messaging app.

She quickly typed out *No contact. End of mission.* And then hit send.

Three dots appeared. And then disappeared.

Finally, though a response came.

Roger. Send AAR within 24. E

Mills at least singed off with the friendly use of her first initial. Azunna turned on the right blinker, looked in her mirror and then pulled back on to the A470 heading for Brecon a mere twelve miles further on up the road.

Chapter Ten

By now it was late afternoon, the dove grey sky pre-rain had given way to the charcoal of the storm and, as the rain started to ease, was turning to the inky blue-black of night-time even though it was barely approaching 1700. The low temperatures, while not literally freezing, felt like they might as well be. But Azunna was not quite ready to go and enjoy the warmth of her shower and her lodgings; that would feel like giving up on the day as a whole, not just the incomplete mission.

Azunna drove into Brecon from the east meaning she ran into mostly row houses with the odd business. One needs to pass all of that, past Christ College Brecon on Bridge Street and across the River Usk before one gets to something that resembles a proper high street.

Crossing the river, the B4601 turns from Bridge Street into Ship Street and then turns right. The road goes past Wheat Street and The Rourke's Drift, one of many pubs and restaurants int the town that are tributes to the common foot soldier. It was just past where Ship becomes High Street, and Azunna was lucky, she found an open parking place.

The rain had finally stopped and Azunna was warm again. She was also hungry. She had burned plenty of calories on this walk and had gone light on the food. She was pretty sure she remembered a good Nepalese restaurant in town. The odd visitor might have found Brecon a strange place for such an exotic cuisine from a relatively small country, but the Gurkhas had been in service to the Crown since at least 1815, first as part of an armed force for the British East India Company, then as part of the British Indian Army, and now in today's modern British Army. That long history of infantry service had culminated in a small but vibrant Nepali community here in Wales.

Parking up, Azunna walked down the High Street until she arrived at Glamorgan Street and turned right. There it was, The Gurkha Corner, just like she remembered. Nepalese food in unfussy environs.

She entered through the low red door, ducking her head and waving to the host. She took her seat with her back to the wall where she could see whoever was approaching.

"Would you like anything to drink?"

"Yes, please. A litre of sparkling water and a Kathmandu Lager. A pint, please."

"Very good, ma'am."

Azunna perused the menu and reflected on her previous meals here, spicy, tasty well made. Much like her lodging, this place was lined with photos of small groups of people, again mostly men, but with some women in the more modern photos. Clusters on mountainsides, jungles, beaches. Photos of military exercises or recreational romps in the sea. The walls were painted in a fading eggshell, and the restaurant was low-lit, not so much in a romantic fashion, but one that hinted toward privacy, reflection, and maybe a hint of intrigue. Traditional Nepalese decorations hung from the walls around the pictures.

"Your water and your pint. Are you ready to order?"

"I am. I'd like the lamb chop appetizer, please." Azunna's mouth already watered at the idea of high-quality Welsh lamb seared with Nepalese spice. "Then the Masu Ru Bhat with the chicken and . . ." she paused. "The Bhuteko Bhat." The rice fried with mustard seed and onion sounded intriguing.

"Is that everything?"

"Another beer, please, uh, when the appetizer is ready. Thanks."

It was still early for dinner, but other people had started to trickle in. She imagined their stories. A couple in their 70s, him long since retired from the forces, and her as the dutiful partner who had stuck by him through it all. Must be going on 40 years plus of marriage. The two young men, short hair, serious, maybe training themselves in the Brecons. The family of four, giving mum a break from the kitchen on a weeknight. A nice-looking gentleman eating solo as well. He looked fit but he was clearly not from a family long from Brecon. His complexion gave that away. She suspected he was ex-forces as well. Reliving adventures? Remembering accomplishments? Mourning the dead?

The screen on her phone lit up with a text. It was Mills.

Good job today.

What was she talking about? The contact hadn't shown, or she had failed to see him. Nothing about it felt like a "good job."

Setting her phone aside she turned her gaze towards the gentleman sitting across the room. It had been a long time since she had seen anyone romantically.

She drained her beer and as she did, so the lamb and the second beer arrived. Simultaneously, she and the other single made eye contact. They smiled at each other, locking their eyes before looking away.

Three little lamb chops, perfectly seared on the outside, she picked up her knife and sliced into the thin, delicate meat. A bright pink with the juices running perfectly. The distinctive flavour of the lamb mixed with spices filled her mouth, she felt the warmth from the fire used to prepare it run through her. She closed her eyes for just a moment. It had been ages since she had had lamb, and after a day like today, it was all the more delicious.

Each chop could not have been more than three bites, so even as she tried to savour them, they were gone relatively quickly. As soon as she lay the knife across the top of the small plate, she sensed the waiter approaching to remove it. She looked up, but instead of the waiter, it was the gentlemen she had made eye contact with.

"May I join you?"

She considered it a moment. He was very good-looking, John Boyega good-looking.

"Sure, why not. Have a seat."

They looked at each for a second, and in that moment both felt a spark.

"Sam Khumalo," he said by way of introduction. He extended his hand to her.

"Charmed, Mr. Khumalo. Kiana Azunna."

"Call me Sam. What brings you to Brecon?"

Azunna eyed him carefully, taking another sip of her beer while she considered him further.

"You know, exercise and reminiscing." It was halfway true anyway. Every foot soldier, marine, airman, and sailor had trekked through the verdant mountains of Wales at some point. Even though she had been on mission today, it's not like the memories of her time here had not come flowing back. "You?"

"Much the same. I'm a Ghurkhas officer," he began. "I guess I should say former. Not really sure what my technical status is now. I am completing the Army leavers program, trying to decide what is next. I came out here for relaxation and reflection. I find the cool air and the landscape soul filling."

Azunna's first thought was, "who talks like that?" But at the same time, it was nice to hear someone speak clearly from the heart.

"I knew we had something in common. I was a Royal Marine Commando officer." She had not meant to impress him with that remark, but whatever he was expecting her back story to be, that was not it. She could see it on his face.

"What? Do I not look like I could be a Royal Marine Commando?" She wondered if she had already misjudged him.

"No, that's not it. I just did not know what one looked like. Now I think about it, you look exactly like I might have imagined one may look." She was not sure that he was telling the truth.

"Nice save there," Azunna smirked.

The waiter noticed that he had moved and since they ordered at similar times their food arrived together at Azunna's table.

"How did you end up in the Royal Marines?" Even though Kiana did not think of herself as one, she was a pioneer. She was one of the first women to complete the commando training course and certainly the first in the Special Boat Service. It was a natural question to someone that had blazed a trail that new.

"My best mate from uni, Phoebe, had wanted to fly helicopters for the Navy. I had no really good idea about what to do, but I had a good language background, and the Navy was more than willing to take me. I soon realized that life aboard ship was probably not for me, and I was considering intelligence when the Commandos opened up to women. I jumped at the chance to do something completely new. How about you?"

"Oh, you know, every regiment comes to Sandhurst pitching themselves. It's rather a humorous dance. Some people of course are determined to go into a particular regiment, either because it is their home regiment or it's got a family connection. Some are looking for technical jobs, Engineers or Signals." He paused for a bite. Wiping his mouth with his napkin, he continued. "I was pretty sure I wanted to be an infantry officer. I wanted the challenge, and I wanted the experience of leading people.

I was quite keen on the Ghurkhas but played hard to get, told them I was from the Duke of Lancaster Regimental area. Many cadets express interest in the Ghurkhas but then baulk at the six months of Nepali language or postings to Brunei. Both sounded interesting to me, although I was sceptical of my ability to master the language. In the end though when they posted the assignments, there I was."

Chapter Eleven

The dinner had gone well and Azunna wanted to spend more time with Sam. Azunna's armour was strong, and she was not sure he had broken through. She could see him mulling over the next step. They lingered over coffee, stretching out their evening together. Finally, he asked, "Would you like to come back to my place?"

Azunna was loath to admit it to herself, but the conversation and the man had made her feel alive in ways she hadn't felt for some time. "Yes, yes I would." The words came out before she thought of them. Her voice higher and more excited than she ever remembered it being. "We can take my car."

It was a proper Welsh down pour outside and neither of them were really dressed for it, so they jogged their way to her Defender. They were soaking wet by the time they were in the car.

"Once I was, working with the Americans," said Sam once they were safely in the car, "and one said, 'If it ain't rainin', we ain't trainin'." They both laughed as his northern accent attempted to mimic a southern good ol' boy from the US, and the universal understanding of veteran field soldiers that it could always be worse.

Sam gave her quick directions. His hotel was less than a mile away on the road exiting Brecon. He had her pull around back to see if there was a parking space.

Sam used the code on the five-button lock and they eased into the staircase of the old pub. It felt like a race to the room, trying both to be quiet, but now quite anxious to be with each other. "I don't think all the rooms are taken, so we probably aren't disturbing anyone." Still, the last thing they wanted was to have their soon-to-be amorous affair interrupted by a light early sleeper.

The room was a small, almost dingy affair, but it was also cheap. As Sam was not on a luxury vacation and had not planned to spend much time in the room, it made perfect sense.

Azunna took little time to contemplate all that as her lips locked with Sam's.

Hurriedly they worked at taking off each other's clothes. Rain parkas and wool jumpers came off easily, but as they can to undo each other's trousers they both realized they had heavy boots on that could not be kicked off like trainers. Laughing at themselves, they both sat down on the edge of the bed and removed them as quickly as their cold fingers could move on the laces. Back in a lip lock, they continued removing each other's clothing, soon they were down to next to nothing. Azunna was in a black sports bra, and boy shorts designed to wick the sweat away and not entice lovers, but she had never felt sexier.

They rolled onto the bed. The anaemic space heater couldn't keep up with the Welsh weather, but the cool dampness of the room was starkly contrasted by the heat the lovers were generating in their closeness. As Sam removed Azunna's sports bra she shivered, partly due to the abrupt chill against her bare back and partly from her excitement of the moment. He lowered his head to her neck, and she arched her back, leaning into him. Beads of sweat formed between her breasts as he lowered her gently to the bed. The two were in sync with electricity, and their lovemaking was a spontaneously perfect dance.

Azunna's carefully cultivated armour was melting, and all of a sudden she felt as if she was making up for lost time.

It had been a long and exhausting day for both of them before they had even met, and so it did not take long before they were both spent. The room became quiet, with only the sound of the weak heater, Azunna rolled over, Sam placing his strong arm across her body, and they both fell asleep.

Chapter Twelve

Azunna was awakened by her phone with its constant vibrations of text messages. She looked at her Bremont that she had not bothered to take off, it was 0730, and she had slept well past her habitual 0500. It must have been the hike and the sex with Sam. She looked over at him in the double bed, lying on his side, his back to her, still sound asleep. She looked at her phone. It was Mills and Lewis.

Where are you?

Are you OK?

Report!

This whole thing was bullshit she thought. An experienced Royal Marine Commando being sent for an assessment that had her hiking up the Pen-Y-Fan for no reason other than to be blown off. Two could play at that game. She checked her email.

There was an email similar to the one that had sent her up the Pen-Y-Fan, some nonsense about a rendezvous. No mention of yesterday's fiasco. That's the only thing she could call it. She turned her attention back towards Sam. She could see the scar on his upper back, which must have been from the shrapnel wound he told her about. Ignoring her phone, she got out of bed and headed to the shower. It was small and cramped; Sam was here on a budget clearly. But she still managed to get a decent four minutes of hot water, before her one minute of cold.

As Azunna emerged from the bathroom Sam had begun to stir.

"Good morning." He rubbed the sleep out of his eyes and then stretched.

"Same to you."

"I suppose you need to get on your way. Back to whatever you are doing out here. Another long walk to nowhere?"

She wondered if she had said too much. "No. I was thinking we should drive out to the beach." Azunna looked at her phone again. More of the same.

Sam looked out the window. The sky was dark and it was not from lack of sunlight. It was going to be another wet rainy day. "Does this look like beach weather to you?"

She laughed. "It's Wales. It's almost by definition dreary!" It amused her that a former Infantry officer might be put off by a little bad weather.

"Sure," he said with a grin. "Let's go to the beach."

Her clothing had dried, for the most part, and she had more clean, dry socks in the Defender. She'd swap those out when they left. He got dressed quickly, and in ten minutes they exited the small pub and were in the Defender heading for the High Street and coffee to accompany them on their trip.

Soon they were on the A4215 that runs north and west through the countryside. The rains of the autumn had turned the landscape a brilliant green, and the intensifying downpour was going to make the countryside even greener.

"So, tell me," Azunna started, "you are out of the army. What's next?"

"Oh, you know. The usual. Other Government work."

It was just mid-morning, but gun-metal grey seemed too light a colour to describe the sky. A let up of rain was unlikely for remainder of the day. As Azunna and Khumalo rounded a bend on the A4215 they were suddenly blinded by the high beams of a large vehicle. Azunna slammed on the brakes and the Defender came to a screeching halt. Three shadowy figures wearing balaclavas exited the truck now blocking the road. Azunna slammed the vehicle into reverse only to be stopped by the blinding light of another SUV with another three menacing figures all armed with sub-machine carbines approaching the Defender.

Azunna instinctively locked the doors even though they were already locked.

"What the fuck is going on?" She threw an accusatory look at her passenger.

"I don't know!" Khumalo appeared just as confused as Azunna.

As combat arms professional, Azunna recognized this was no ordinary banditry on the highway. By his demeanor, she saw Khumalo knew it as well. Before either could take any action, the toughs were at their door side windows pointing their carbines at their heads.

"Get out! Get the fuck out, NOW!" the figure shouted from outside Azunna's Riverside door.

"What should we do?" Khumalo's voice was rising even as he tried to contain his panic.

Azunna looked for room to manoeuvre the Defender, but they were simply too closed in, forward or reverse, she would simply hit the other SUV's and then give these unknown assailants reason to open fire. Since they had not done so yet, she reasoned their principal purpose was not to kill them. Reluctantly she said, "Comply."

As soon as Azunna pushed the unlock button, the assailants yanked open the doors and pulled them onto the wet tarmac in the heavy rain. Azunna's mind went elsewhere; another rainy, dark day, pulled from a different SUV, not knowing what was happening or what her future would hold. For a moment, she was that scared little girl again. Then she was back in the present.

The assailants pushed their targets prone on the tarmac and zip-tied their hands behind their backs. Black cloth bags were put over their heads. Azunna was pulled up under her shoulders and shoved into the SUV in front of the Defender.

The SUV holding Azunna reversed, made a quick U-turn. She could hear the other SUV take off and fade away. They were taking her north, and Khumalo wasn't with her.

Chapter Thirteen

Twenty minutes later Khumalo was dropped off in front of the pub where he was staying. The attackers pulled him out of the SUV, cut off the zip ties, and pulled the bag off his head.

"Don't call the police, don't tell anyone what just happened." The person who Khumalo took to be in charge, at least of this part of the assault team's voice was low and direct, and full of menace. "If you do, we will know. Not only will we kill her, but we will be back for you as well. Understand?"

Without waiting for an answer, the assault team was back in the SUV and on their way with Khumalo standing in the pouring rain on the street, with no idea what to do or where Kiana was. Or even why this had happened.

***

The ambush on the road was less than three minutes, but the ride in the assault team's SUV had been almost an hour. The bag over Azunna's head had completely disoriented her, and the movement of the vehicle on the twisty country roads was making her mildly nauseous. Every time she started to speak; she was told to shut up. The accents of the group all seemed to be British.

The rain had not let up and the vehicle came to a sudden halt. Azunna heard all four doors open, she was roughly pulled out and marched into a building. Once inside she heard a door slide closed behind them. Her escorts stopped and spun her around. She felt her kidnappers remove her jacket and jumper. They pushed her into a rickety wooden chair with a damaged rattan seat. They pulled off her boots, socks, and trousers. Finally, they removed her hood. She was on an uncomfortable chair, in her underwear and shirt, cold, wet, and not just a little afraid.

"What were you doing?" demanded one of the assailants.

The scene was coming into Azunna's focus. The building was made of field stone with old timber supports. She supposed it was or had been part of a farm, whether a shelter for animals or storage of harvest she did not know, but now it was clearly an interrogation centre. She was staring at a table of at three people with three more behind them. They all were still masked and the three-standing held what appeared to be some AK carbine variants. Three O-ring lights were turned on her at what seemed to be their brightest setting.

The lead interrogator asked again, "What were you doing?"

None of this made any sense. By manner of dress, these kidnappers seemed like old-school IRA, but that was crazy. Even if the IRA were active again, Azunna was unknown and a nobody. Some sort of al-Qaeda offshoot? Possible. But why her? And what had happened to Sam?

"Who are you working for?"

"I'm . . . I'm a Royal Marine officer on leave . . . I'm just having an outdoor holiday," Azunna stuttered. She had no cover story and knew enough to not try to invent one on the fly. That was the fastest way to be trapped in a lie.

The room was dank and made more so by the weather. There were no windows that she could see, but she had to assume they were in a very isolated place in northern Wales. No one was coming to help. Maybe she should not have ignored all those texts.

Azunna was frightened, of course. But she was also very confused. She knew the most important thing was to survive, and by harnessing those emotions she should be able to do that, much like she had done in combat so many times. She decided that she could reveal most everything except that she worked for the SIS, what had le Carré called it? The Circus?

The lead interrogator started again. "Major Azunna, we know who you work for. What were you doing? What sort of mission were you on?" Clearly she was the target of the ambush and kidnapping. This was no random criminal event.

"You seem to know who I am. Major Kiana Azunna of the Royal Marines. I am based at RM Poole. I am here on holiday."

That answer did not impress the panel of masked interrogators.

"You want to play a hard game? Fine. Put her in the hole."

Two of the bigger toughs grabbed her by the arms, pulled

her out of the chair, and drag-carried her to an open door behind her. She saw a glimpse of a table and the lights. They threw her in.

This new room was small, though she might be able to lie down in it. A small window near the ceiling let in some light. The rain seemed to have finally stopped. The room was of the same field stone construction, and the door was a heavy wooden one with iron hinges. She had heard metal pieces clank when they closed the door; she tried to open it but confirmed it was locked.

It was getting cold; she was still wet. There were two thin, old, wool military-style blankets and some hay on the floor. The blankets did not seem particularly damp, so she fastened one around her waist. She gathered up as much of the straw as she could, it was far wetter, but created a small cushion in the corner. She hoped the blanket would counter the wetness. She pulled the other blanket around her shoulder and settled down into the corner to think and to wait.

Back in Brecon Sam had found the local constabulary and was trying to make a report. It was not going well. He had precious little information to give them. He had her name, and the type of vehicle they had been travelling in, but he did not know where she was staying, and they had not even traded phone numbers yet, so there was no way to track down her cell phone. He had finally persuaded the police to go with him to the spot the abduction had happened. The problem was there was nothing there. No weapons had been fired, so there were no shell casings. There were so many different skid marks that no one could be sure if they related to this incident or another, and despite how prevalent CCTV was in the UK, this country road was not under that type of watch.

After almost an hour on the scene, the police had returned to Brecon, dropping Sam off at his quarters. The constable in charge told Sam they would file a report, but there was little else they could do. It was not that they did not believe him, there was simply nothing other than his testimony and that was very little to go on.

Azunna decided to try to sleep, or at least rest with her eyes closed. She was not particularly tired but knew that rest would be important in whatever was to come. Finally, after what seemed like forever the door open. As she heard the metal-on-metal sound, she got to her feet expecting to be dragged again to the interrogation chair. This time though, there was only one person. Head to toe in black still but taking a different approach.

"Come on." The voice was firm and commanding, yet slightly higher. So, there were women on this team. As Azunna existed the small cell, the woman gripped her upper arm and escorted her back to the interrogation chair. "Tell us what we want to know." The voice was calm, not shouting, but very much in control. "This can all be over with; you can get back to your holiday." She sat Azunna back in the same rickety wooden and rattan chair.

"Who was that you were with when we found you?"

"Just a guy I met last night. We had dinner and went back to his place."

"Open your phone." There were many reasons Azunna did not want to do that. Her texts would among other things reveal she was not on holiday. It was also the general principle. The woman who had escorted her to the chair tossed her the phone.

"I . . . I . . ." Azunna stuttered because she had no idea how she was going to avoid doing this.

"You what? You can't? Look besides your password, I am sure you have fingerprint and face recognition on this phone. Open the fucking phone."

Still Azunna hesitated. The team leader nodded at the two big guys, and they grabbed her by the arms and head. The woman who had so far seemed to be relatively calm grabbed the phone and turned it to Azunna's face.

"Come on Kiana," she almost cooed. "Look at me, look at the phone."

She grabbed Azunna by the chin, and as one of the toughs behind her rotated her head so that it was straight on. Azunna saw the phone unlock and blink to life.

"We don't need to do this the hard way." The woman sounded aggravated as she handed the phone to the chief interrogator.

He started going through the text messages and emails.

"Who is Erica Mills?"

"Just someone I work with."

"She seems to have expected that you would be heading to Cardiff today. Why did you tell us you were going to the beach? Why were you heading west?" He continued scrolling through the phone. Azunna was silent.

"Looks like you were not reading your work messages or email." He shook his head and made a disapproving sound. "You need to do a better job staying in touch with your office."

Azunna had no words. *Could this be part of the "training"?*

She had been so irritated by yesterday's seemingly pointless mission, though clearly ignoring Mills had been a mistake. But that still did not explain who these people were. Or how she was going to get out of this.

"So tell me again what you are doing out here in Wales."

"I told you I am on holiday. I hiked Pen-Y-Fan yesterday, the Fan Dance route."

"Fancy yourself an SAS-type?" The sarcasm was dripping from his voice, but Azunna expected that.

"Special Boat Service actually. Led troops in Afghanistan." Azunna had decided that self-confidence might be the best way out of this at this point. She wasn't sure what was going on, but while they had given her rough treatment, they had not tortured her and did not seem inclined to do so. Mill's last words before she left London started to come back to her. "Stay in touch and follow your directions."

"Take her back to the cell." The two big men grabbed her by the biceps and drag-carried her back to the cell.

The sun was well done now, so the cell was almost completely dark. Just a little bit of light crept in from the small sliver of moonlight that had peaked through the clouds. She resumed her position in the corner of the cell. Mill's words still echoed in her ears. *Would Mills really authorize this? Of course she would.* Azunna was being brought on board to kill people. This was nothing. She decided to try and sleep.

Chapter Fourteen

Azunna was awakened by the metal-on-metal sliding open. She stayed huddled in the corner, maintaining the warmth she had accumulated, expecting them to grab her as they had done before.

"Come on," one of the guards ordered, but more softly than previously. "Come on out."

Slowly, partially because she was coming out of a deep sleep and partially out of trepidation, she got up and walked towards the cell door.

"Over there." The guard indicated the same, solitary chair where she had been interrogated hours earlier. *Now what do they want to know?*

"Get dressed." To her surprise, next to the chair, Azunna found her clothing neatly folded and now dry. There was also a military-issue puffer jacket that she had not brought with her, she pulled it on over her clothes.

"My phone, my watch, wallet?"

"Right here," the team leader said indicating towards a small bag on the table. "Nice watch. You will get these back soon. Don't worry about those."

Now fully dressed, the bag was placed on her head and she was escorted to the SUV. They placed her back in the middle of the rear seat and the SUV took off, driving at a more leisurely pace than when they had arrived.

After about ninety minutes, the vehicle made a sharp turn, hit gravel, and stopped suddenly. The guard helped Azunna out of the car. With the bag still over her head, she felt a small strap being placed behind her neck and then suddenly a small weight in front of her.

"Your phone, watch, and wallet are in the bag around your neck. Wait at least sixty seconds after you hear the vehicle leave before you take the bag off your head. And please, learn to follow instructions."

With that, he was gone. She heard the SUV leave the gravel and return to the tarmac. Heeding his last words, she counted to sixty before removing the bag. She adjusted her eyes and looked around. She was back at the lodge. Opening the bag she found all her items as promised, put her watch back on and looked at the time. It was 0200. She made her way into the lodge and up to her room. She wondered what had happened to Sam. *Where is he? Is he OK?* But she was too exhausted to do anything about that now, she needed rest if she was going to do anything else. Understanding she was finally safe, she stripped off her clothes, crawled into bed and went straight to sleep.

Chapter Fifteen

Azunna had been back in London for two days. She'd spent another four weeks in Brecon after her kidnapping completing various training missions. She never ignored a text after that night. And never saw Khumalo again; they hadn't exchanged numbers before they were abducted, and she was reluctant to go down an emotional rabbit hole looking for him.

She was staying at the St. Ermin again. She supposed at some point she would need to consider moving to London, but the Service was happy to pay the St. Ermin bill for now, and she liked her flat in Poole. Dorset suited her just fine. She checked in with Mills on Monday and spent the rest of the day and Tuesday doing administrivia even Intelligence Officers have to do. Late on Tuesday, she received a text.

Meeting with C tomorrow. Ten sharp.

That was why she was now in the opaque glass cube and sitting in front of the large naval desk. It was cold in his office. She was glad she had matched a jumper to her fashionable dress.

"Captagon. You know it?" C began without preamble.

"Drug, I think. Some sort of highly addictive amphetamine, if I recall correctly."

"Precisely. And the Syrian Government is the world's largest manufacturer of it. The mess in Syria has created a narco-state on the Mediterranean. Right next door to Greece and Turkey, which means right next door to us." He paused. "It's not even as if there is a large market for the drug here, but drug smuggling and terrorism go hand-in-glove these days. A bunch of rich Saudi and gulf kids doing drugs will eventually blow back on us." Another pause. "Ever do any operations in Syria?"

"Nothing quite like Afghanistan. I did one rotation through during the 'Defeat ISIS Campaign,' working with the YPJ and YPG. Kurds were great fighters, and well-organized. Downright feminists for that part of the world." She had spent a good ninety days in Syria coaching some of the women who were fighting ISIS, Syria, Turkey, Iran, and anyone who was not for an independent Kurdish state.

"Maher-al Assad. Heard of him?"

Who hadn't? After that explosion on Canada Wharf and the insane chase down the Thames, there wasn't a person in the UK who did not know what the TLSN was, at least superficially.

"Wasn't their operational head killed in that shoot-out? I was in Afghanistan at the time. Not sure of their status now. I imagine that like most organizations, even when someone so seemingly important is removed, they have continued to operate. And their name implies a large reach. Of course, it's not like the Red Brigades ever fielded such a large organization. I would assume that names like that come out of the megalomania of their founders."

"Quite right, Azunna," C jumped in. "Quite right. The sanctions regime has really squeezed the Syrian elites. Not that they were unlike organized crime before the war, but now they have all the indicia of a Mafia organization. Make *Peaky Blinders* look downright friendly. It seems the Assads have linked their survival to this organization. Near at least as we can figure."

The reference to the popular British TV show made Azunna laugh out loud.

"What?"

"*Peaky Blinders*? The thought of you sitting at home watching any popular entertainment just seems mad."

C pursed his lips. "Never mind that. The Assads have turned Syria into a narco-state. Captagon is produced in huge quantities in regime-controlled territories. What was once a respectable pharmaceutical industry has been completely converted into the illicit drug trade. And while it has not become popular here, being favoured mostly by the children of rich Saudis and other Gulfies, the attendant problems of the drug trade are affecting us. More directly though is that Major General Maher al-Assad, Commander of the Syrian Arab Army's elite 4th Armoured Division, and younger brother to Bashir al-Assad is the head of all drug operations in regime-controlled Syria."

C tossed a red file folder on the desk marked "Eyes Only" with a thin khaki tape around it. Here is the down-and-dirty on Maher. Azunna put her hand on it, but she kept her eyes on C.

"Your mission is to track him down . . . and kill him." Azunna, this is your first mission here, but not your first – as our American cousins would say – rodeo. You are probationary in the section for your first missions until you have met the standards operationally, but I have every confidence in you. It won't be easy, but you will be up to the task." C rose, indicating the meeting was wrapping up.

"Thank you, sir," Azunna said, swiftly tucking the folder under her arm as she stood.

"Connect with Mills," C ordered quickly crossing the room to the door. "As you know, she runs Chrysalis, she will connect you with logistics for your kit. That's all."

"Sir."

She closed the glass door behind her, and it went from opaque to clear. The secretary's desk was empty. He must have been out getting coffee or something. Azunna turned left and went back down the hall where she and Mills had talked those weeks before. Azunna knocked.

"Can I come in?"

Mills looked up. "Of course." Extending her hand as she rose. They shook hands and Mills gestured to the table with two chairs.

"Coffee, tea, water, something else?"

"Coffee would be lovely."

Mills pushed a button. "Two coffees, black, side of milk to Executive Suite please."

"Right away," came a disembodied voice.

"We didn't talk much the other day. How was Wales? Learn much?"

"Well, you know, this and that." Azunna was still trying to understand this relationship. She would have been surprised to find that Mills was in the same quandary. Not peers, but still two high-achieving women in a man's world, and of course, Mills monitoring Azunna in action on a potentially deadly worldwide battlefield. Distance felt safer.

"Happy to be here. And be working again."

"I'm quite sure. So, you spoke with C? You have the rundown on the Assads?"

"Apparently all right there," she said placing the red folio on Mill's desk. "I'm guessing you could connect with logistics for my kit."

The coffee arrived.

"That's right. I'll text you the details. Logistics can be funny about how they do things. And when I say Logistics, I mean – the Head of Logistic Operations. He was C's protege. You know C ran Logistics for the Service at one point?"

"Yeah, I heard. And aren't all of us who work in the shadows a little quirky?" Azunna said with a wry smile.

"Fair play to you on that score. Any questions before you pop off?" Mills's face looked like it was more of a rhetorical question.

"Not that I can think of."

"Well, you can just leave that file with me when you are done. Good luck. And do be careful."

"Always."

Chapter Sixteen

Turkish Airlines Flight 2230 from Istanbul to Gaziantep touched down at precisely 1125. Azunna had flown to Istanbul the day before and spent the night. Since she had to clear customs and gather her bags anyway, she thought a good night's sleep before she met a contact in the field for the first time was in order.

Now, as she emerged into the bright sunlight of Gaziantep, Turkey, Azunna donned her Barton Pereira sunglasses and took stock of the situation. Her luggage – one leather and canvas duffel and an anonymous roller-bag carried by every business traveller between here and Oslo – made her arrival unremarkable. Being so close to what was still ostensibly the border between Syria and Turkey, combined with the general busyness of any modern mid-sized city, meant that the arrival hall was teeming with people. Everyone had some business to do somewhere. It might as well be here.

Azunna got her bearings and looked around for her ride. She wanted to avoid eye contact with the many taxi drivers, official and unofficial – she did not have the time to waive them all off – but she also didn't want to be there too long. Clearly not a local, she started to attract unwanted attention from would be taxi-drivers, venders, and hawkers, or even the less savoury characters points of transit always seemed to attract.

"Taxi, madam?" An older gentleman was speaking to her. *Guess I can't avoid all of them*, she thought.

"No, thank you."

"I have a nice van. You should really try the pistachios of Turkey."

Azunna stopped and looked at the man again. She really needed a better way of sorting through the all the noise of who her contact might appear to be. "I hear the olives are good too."

He put out his hand. "Kemal, at your service." She had imagined a taller more rakish figure. Instead, he fit in with all the taxi drivers of Gaziantep, slightly unkempt, rumpled trousers, worn black leather jacket, and by the discoloration on his hands, a chain smoker.

"Kiana Azunna." They shook hands and he grabbed her duffel bag.

"Follow me" She took his lead, her anonymous roller bag in tow. The curbs and gravel making the task of rolling it that much harder. After a few steps, she decided just to pick it up.

They walked across the small airport carpark and out the back side of it. The airport may have been decent sized, but the size of the carpark reflected the fact that most people in this part of the world don't own a car, and if they did, they were certainly not going to pay the cost of parking or trust the vagaries of developing world public security. This wasn't Heathrow, or even a small place in the Midlands.

They emerged on a side street, still on the airport grounds, where they found a blue Fiat Ducato panel van that had certainly seen better days. Being dirty was a given, but the panels were dinged, the paint faded, and there was some rust around the wheel wells. It would not attract any attention.

"I thought you said you had a nice van."

"I lied." He paused. "Actually, I didn't lie. It's just that this is not the nice van." He laughed. Azunna was less convinced. She just hoped it would get them where they were going. Being stranded on the side of the road was never much fun, much less when you were a non-declared intelligence officer on a mission to terminate a known drug supplier. Kemal opened the back and they put her bags in, while she kept her messenger musette bag.

"Let's get out of here. You can see a little bit of the city and then we can get to our compound."

"Sounds good."

Being in the field for the first time since Afghanistan was both thrilling and a little nerve wracking. On commando missions, helicopter evacuation or resupply was a mere radio call and short wait away. True, response was not instantaneous, but it was more than she had here. Now she was on her own with whoever she could decide to trust.

The traffic was chaos. People creating lanes where none existed, jockeying for some perceived advantage to try and inch around a donkey cart. Venders selling vegetables, bread, or street food taking up space along the edges of the road. All the commotion meant the trip through town was not going to be a fast one.

"So how long have you been doing this?" she asked. It was cool outside, but the sun here heated the metal van quickly and she was getting warm. Rolling down the windows though did not seem like a good idea, either from the security or air quality perspectives.

"What? Picking people up at airports?" he laughed. Kemal's efforts at being obtuse came across as lame attempts at humour, and Azunna was not sure what to make of him. For the moment, though, she decided maybe face value was best.

"A bit more than that I should think." Azunna was at her best when she was serious. Carrying a sense of lightness about her, especially given the stakes, was not something she ever imagined herself wanting to do. This was going to be challenging relationship.

He laughed and threw a few pistachios into his mouth.

"British Intelligence? My whole life. My grandfather started the 'family business' during the war. Helping British intelligence know what the Axis were doing as well as what the Soviets had in mind. My father and his brothers inherited the operation as Turkey turned into a convenient Cold War place of operations. And now as the shadows are alternately darker and lighter, Turkey is and always will be a key player in the Great Game. You can't change geography. Egypt will be important if the Suez Canal is important, so too Turkey will be important as long as people need to transit from Europe to

Asia and Asia to Europe." He grabbed another pistachio. "You want some?"

"Not right now. You are from here?"

He looked at her with a side eye. One she clearly got.

"No. Istanbul. Southern Turkey has great food and lovely weather, but I prefer a more cosmopolitan life. I am down here at least once a quarter checking our operation or providing this sort of support, but live? No way. Hard to get a decent martini down here," he laughed and gave Azunna a cheeky smile.

They finally moved passed whatever the bottle neck was, and they were moving along at a decent speed turning down a series of streets that brought them into a quieter neighbourhood.

The battered van pulled up to a walled compound, no different from the other compounds on the block. Although the sun was high, the trees and taller building cast enough shade to make it feel cooler. Kemal hit a button and the gates opened. The gates, solid metal and faded green, creaked as they opened into the property. The inner courtyard revealed a small parking area with two other nondescript vehicles, although Azunna took a liking to the old Land Rover 110 immediately. The courtyard was dry, dusty, and plain, with a fountain that had not seen water in years in the middle. It looked plenty secure.

Pulling the van into a spot next to the Land Rover, Kemal put the van in park and got out. Opening the back of the van, he began to give her the rundown. "Welcome to our little oasis here in Gaziantep. There are several rooms here for people to stay and we have prepared one for you. They are all *en suite*, steel doors with triple locks as well as secure storage. You and the gear are perfectly safe."

"Thanks." Azunna was taking it all in – the building, the layout, the area. She was not one hundred percent convinced she could find the safe house in the dark, but certainly during the daylight.

They entered the building through a main door that aligned with the fountain. She imagined that at one time a moderately well-to-do family had lived here. It seems that, and this is always the case, that as cities and towns grow, the wealthier move to the outskirts and suburbs in the effort to enjoy what the city has to offer and a more bucolic setting. Although, of course, cities like London had seen a resurgence of people moving into the city, hence the astronomical prices to live there. Urban Gaziantep was a few steps behind in that regard.

The floors were marble, aging, but in good shape, a kitchen off to the right and dining room to the left. She could see what appeared to be a great room that probably linked the dining room. The walls were concrete block, painted a faded white and sparsely decorated. Kemal led her upstairs, and to the end of the hall where he opened a door.

"Here's your room. I trust you will find it satisfactory."

"Quite."

"I'll leave you to get settled in." He handed her a card that accessed the electronic lock.

Azunna planned on having this entire mission complete within the next five days, so comfort was less a concern than security. Nevertheless, the room was comfortable enough but stopping short of luxurious. Better than the hard ground of Afghanistan, but not the St. Ermin either. The rear-facing widow looked out onto the courtyard, and she could see with a ten-foot wall shutting off the compound from the rest of the world. She tapped the glass lightly – it was clearly bombproof.

Since she did not plan on being in Turkey all that long, she elected to not unpack. She stowed the H&K and her Thuraya X5-Touch Satellite Smartphone in the safe, set her own combination and had a seat. She needed to stretch her legs and catch her breath. The two days of travel from London to here had not been particularly exhausting, especially with the night of sleep in Istanbul, but she wanted to make sure she was on top of her game. Once she was in Syria, she needed to have all her focus on the mission. After taking a bit of time to collect herself she went downstairs and met Kemal in the foyer.

"Coffee?"

In the coffee-tea wars she was clearly on the side of coffee and glad to learn Kemal was as well.

"Sure."

"I know a great coffee shop, best Turkish coffee in town. Not the newest or the flashiest, but definitely traditional. You game for an adventure on the streets of town?"

"Sure, why not?" Azunna mustered as much fake enthusiasm for going back out into the madness of the Gaziantep traffic as possible.

Ditching the Fiat, they hopped into a smaller, newer, but equally nondescript Renault sedan. As they exited the compound, they turned back the way they came. Azunna took her time assessing the area so that if she needed to, she could find the compound. Having good egress routes was as important as being able to find one's way home.

They headed into town to the one of the larger boulevards of Gaziantep, navigating the vendors, cars, and donkeys. They hit no major traffic snarls, and so twenty minutes after they left the compound, Kemal found a spot large enough for the Renault and parked on a side street. Kemal knew exactly where he was going so once out of the car it was a straight walk to the main street, something that would pass for a High Street in the UK, a left turn and down half a block. He was greeted warmly, and they were escorted to a discreet table. They ordered two Turkish coffees, very black, some sparkling water, and some baklava.

Kemal pulled out a pack of cigarettes and offered her one.

"No, thank you."

He took a drag on the cigarette, and they both looked out the window onto the chaos of the street, the table being situated such that everyone could have their back to the wall. The vague unidentifiable smells of fruit aging in the sun, donkey excrement, and diesel exhaust were soon replaced with the aroma of coffee and Turkish tobacco.

"How long have you been doing this?" he asked. He blew smoke rings toward the ceiling.

"Long enough." Her eyes were penetrating and remained focused on him. She was not sure if she appeared new or he was just making conversation. While she might have a bit to learn, especially from people like Kemal, she was not going to appear too eager. After all they were Turks working for her government, not the other way around. He was going to need to come to her with information.

The order arrived. She opened the water and poured two glasses. Her boots were now coated in dust and the restaurant was not exactly the cleanest one she had ever been in. The tiled floor and walls had seen better days, now faded due to time, sun, and dirt making less a bright white and more a dirty cream. But the coffee was strong, and the baklava looked a delight with the honey glistening on it.

"The shipment arrived from London, so we have all the equipment that was asked for. The list was very specific, so I assume it was drawn up at least in part by you." Earlier Azunna would have categorized Kemal as non-descript, but here in the cafe he became a more distinct person. His hair was black and short. A salt and pepper beard that was kept equally well trimmed, a scar about his left eye.

"What do we think about this place?" She inclined her head indicating the coffee house. Conversations about secret things held in public places was a new experience for her. She had taken off her blue Belstaff jacket to feel more at ease, and a little cooler, but the whole idea that they were discussing the logistics of a plan to a kill an Assad while in a public place seemed absurd.

"I have been coming here for years. Turkey is crawling with spies, double agents, con men, mercenaries, and every other sort of bad actor you can think of. Could someone hear us and compromise the whole bloody thing? Of course, but the chances of that are slim." He seemed impatient with what he clearly thought of as excessive caution. Kemal appeared to be one of those people who had incorporated so much risk into his life, that he as almost unaware of its existence.

Azunna on the other hand had been making risk assessments for most of her life. It kept her alive, and sane. She recalibrated. For anyone to have the remotest sense of why she was here or what they were discussing would have meant the organization here and in London had been deeply penetrated. Highly unlikely she thought, and they'd have bigger problems if that was the case. She glanced down. The amount of dust on her boots was suddenly, inexplicably annoying. She decided to return to the topic at hand.

"I had some very specific requirements, yes." She appreciated the logistical support, but the customization of her kit was entirely her affair, and she had no reason to justify it. She picked up her coffee and took another sip. It was excellent. She would need to take some back to London.

"Yes, and the more generic items were picked up here. They are all in the lock-up on the compound."

The post-lunch coffee crowd was thinning out a little bit and the late-morning breakfast on the plane no longer satisfied her. "Can we get something more to eat? Maybe a shawarma?"

"I know just the place." Like a switch, Kemal had changed from the judgemental logistical manager to the convivial host. "Follow me." He threw two five lira notes on the table, and they grabbed their things. Azunna pulled her jacket back on and as they exited and adjusted her sunglasses.

They started walking against the direction of most of the crowd, but, Azunna thought, that may just be her perception. There were shops selling everything from rugs to homeware, every space possible for display used. Vegetable carts on the street were covered in a thick layer of dust. In a town that was home to hundreds of NGOs, journalists, and the other hangers-on that come with living next to a war zone, Azunna's presence was just part of the scenery and remained unremarked. Finally, they arrived at a shawarma cart on the street.

"Ah, here we are." Kemal ordered two lamb shawarmas in Turkish, and Azunna studied the vendor slicing thin layers off the meat that was slowly turning in the vertical spit. The aroma was tantalizing and making her salivate. The heat radiated off spit enough to touch Azunna, and even in the warm sunshine, she felt the increase in temperature. Using a fork, he laid the tender meat in the flatbread, topped it with tahini, threw in some onions and tomato and wrapped the whole thing in thin brown paper. The five-lire note Kemal handed the shawarma chef was a fifty per cent tip. They continued wandering at a more leisurely pace, in the same direction they had been headed, slowly enjoying their sandwiches.

"When do you want to go over?" This time Kemal seemed more casual, as if he was having a regular conversation. He had seemed overly earnest in the coffee shop. Maybe it was he who needed to relax.

Azunna looked around, mostly taking the experience in, although situational awareness was second nature to her at this point. They had reached a major intersection. "I was thinking tomorrow night."

They turned left and walked parallel to the street on which they had left the car. The shops seemed to be on an endless loop. Homeware, rugs, clothing, shoes, bakery, pharmacy, rinse, repeat. The crowd remained the same. People going about the daily business of survival.

"Why don't we push it to Friday night. The middle of the weekend for the Syrians. Their guard will be down a little. That way we have plenty of time to go over all the kit and get properly set up."

Azunna's bias towards action wanted her to get the mission underway now, but she thought back to her time in Wales. She was getting new information, time to absorb that and readjust her plan. "Makes sense. I agree."

They were at another major intersection, and they turned left again. "We are almost back to the car. Let me take you back to the compound. You can relax while I do some other errands. That's the problem with having a cover business, you end up doing two jobs!" He laughed sardonically.

Another left turn and they were on the side street they had parked on. Smaller more specialized shops and a few small homes dotted the street. She saw the car, the layer of dust thicker than when they had left it.

Chapter Seventeen

Azunna rose the next morning at her habitual 0500. The safe house had a small room in the basement with a treadmill and kettlebells. *How Turkish, she thought.* She liked using kettlebells, but they immediately called to mind the image of Turkish weightlifters engaging in demonstrations of strength.

The ceiling was lower than she would have liked. Unlike the small gym in Wales that had been purpose-built, this was clearly a retrofitted basement that was barely tall enough to stand on the treadmill. Of course, she had worked out in more stark gyms in Afghanistan and on her other deployments. On board some of the smaller ships she served on as a Royal Marine, one's head was constantly competing with overhead piping for room. At least here she was not about to bang her head on something. She would do a three-mile run, some stretching, and lightweight exercises to keep her limber and ready, but not exhausted.

After the workout she took the stairs two at a time, returning to her second-floor bedroom. She took a quick shower and threw on some prana Alana pants in bark, a deep brown, a grey t-shirt from the same brand, and some black gum Cariuma trainers. She should be spending the whole day on the compound, and she wanted to be relaxed. If all went well, she would be back here by next Monday, en route to London.

At 0700 she entered to the expansive kitchen to find a young woman getting the coffee going.

"Good morning?" Azunna half-phrased the greeting as a question.

"Ah, good morning, Ms. Azunna. I am Ceylan, Kemal's oldest child. Pleasure to meet you."

Ceylan was striking. Thick dark hair, that if it was not back in a ponytail, would have framed her angular nose and high cheekbones well. It was not hard to imagine her in a fashion magazine, but today she was in jeans, a white tank top, a black hoodie, and white trainers. She was casually all business.

"Nice to meet you as well. Do you do the meal prep here?" She paused and continued. "I'm sorry, that was a poor presumption on my part." Azunna was embarrassed by her own preconceived notions of people's roles, especially given she was so often the target of the practice. People could only process so much information, the brain naturally made assumptions.

"It was, but that's fine. If anyone is going to do the meal prep, I am the last one you really want to do it. My younger brother, Hamza, is a much better cook. He will be by later, around lunch and dinner." She paused, "No, I am here to help do the technical inspections and equipment prep for your mission. We can do the load out tomorrow afternoon. But first I need a cup of coffee. Care for one?"

"Please."

Ceylan had a kettle going, and at first, Azunna thought she was going to be the victim of Nescafe, the ubiquitous coffee of developing world hotels, which would have surprised her in Turkey, but Ceylan was just getting started. She pulled out a large Chemex and put in the filter. A high-speed electric coffee grinder was next and then she retrieved a bag of coffee beans from the freezer. After apportioning enough to make a strong brew for two, she began the grinding process, and the kitchen was filled with the rich smell of the beans.

"There should be food in the refrigerator. Help yourself."

Azunna opened the French doors of the stainless-steel refrigerator and rummaged up some yoghurt, butter, figs, and dates. There was a loaf of whole grain bread on the counter that appeared to be fresh. She dished up the yoghurt, put some figs, dates and almonds in it, sliced some bread, buttered it, and sat down at the counter.

Ceylan brought some coffee over. "Enjoy."

"Thanks. So, what do you do here?"

"Well, Ms. Azunna . . ."

"Call me Kiana."

"Wonderful, please call me Ceylan. It means antelope. I can run very fast." She giggled at that, a surprise to them both because she didn't seem like a giggler.

Azunna dug into the food. It was delicious. The coffee was in a proper white stoneware mug. She held it in both hands and listened.

"Officially, I am the Vice President of Operations for Turkish International Exports. What that means, in practicality, is that I have carte blanche to travel all over Turkey checking on our warehouses and offices. With the situation as it has been in Syria since 2011, our business has been thriving. We have similar facilities at cities up and down the border."

One quick summary had blown Azunna's earlier assumptions away. Young, but a self-possessed woman, she could clearly work anywhere she chose to. Azunna was suitably impressed.

"And how long have you been doing this?"

"Me? Since I was a child. I was pulled into the family business from the beginning, although I did not understand it for the most part. Save four years at the London School of Economics, this is what I have been doing."

All of a sudden, the British education and the four-plus years in London became evident. Azunna worked on the food a bit more, enjoying the freshly baked bread in particular. They both sipped their coffee. The only sounds were the quiet hum of the refrigerator and some birds chirping outside.

"And you Kiana? How long have you been doing this sort of thing? The questions seemed to hang in the air, at least for Azunna.

"What sort of thing?" Azunna played coy.

"You know, running around, solving problems for now-King and country." Azunna wasn't sure if the tone in her voice was sarcasm or ironic detachment. It was hard to be in this line of work without some level of scepticism and cynicism. Even when you believed in something, the hard truth of the world was always much more complicated.

"Well, I've served for three years in the Royal Marines, six in the Royal Navy before that. This is sort of a secondment. Of course, I've had specialized training, operations in the Middle East and Africa and a few other places. Now I am here. An old hand at field work really. Just a different scale." Azunna took another sip of coffee without looking away at Ceylan's face, trying to read it. If Ceylan was to help with the prep work, Azunna needed to be sure of her.

"I've been working on logistics issues here in Turkey for years. But I am hoping to get closer to the tip of the spear on this one." Ceylan seemed highly motivated, and she appeared utterly capable, if somewhat inexperienced. While she emanated a certain confidence, that was made even more impressive by what appeared to be an innate candour. Smart, capable, and truthful always made for a good team member. Azunna wanted Ceylan on her team.

"Well, I'm not sure how Kemal sees this all playing out, but I think we should work closely together."

They clinked coffee glasses. It felt odd toasting with coffee at an early morning hour, but Azunna felt like she had found a kindred spirit. They finished their coffee in silence as they checked emails and scanned the news.

Chapter Eighteen

Azunna headed outside twenty minutes later. The size of a three-car garage just to the right of the villa, the outer building served well as a workshop and prep area. It was painted a fading grey over the concrete block construction, and the steel doors were of a similar, but bluer, hue. The garage doors opened out in the middle and would certainly not have been up to scratch in Kent. Nonetheless, when they were closed, they sealed up nicely and were quite lockable. The sun was well up, but the other buildings and walls created enough shade that there was not a shadow to be seen.

Ceylan was already in the garage, preparing to unpack the big wooden crate and the two Pelican boxes. She had several crowbars and hammers littering the broken concrete floor in preparation for opening the wooden crate. Azunna surveyed the scene, arms crossed against the slight morning chill.

The garage itself was not overly neat but wasn't a mess either. Clearly, things happened here on a regular basis. Azunna liked that. It meant she was working with professionals, not a fly-by-night set of amateurs. She had made that assessment of them in person, but it was good to see evidence confirming her judgement.

The markings on the wooden crate were nondescript. They indicated a destination, Gaziantep, and an air freight carrier, DHL. Nothing hinted as to the contents – the seals were intact. A bill of lading was attached, but no one had bothered to open it, and Azunna felt no need to do so either. She knew what was supposed to be in the crate. She could look later if there was a discrepancy.

"Give me a hand." Ceylan swept her ponytail back and handed Azunna a crowbar. "You get the right side, I'll do left."

"Right."

Sliding the crowbars between the gaps in the wood, the women both pushed and pulled, pushed, and pulled, until the first nail popped out, at least to the point where they could use the big carpenter hammers to pound the wood, slowly pushing all the nails on the short side of the crate out. It took a good fifteen minutes just to get one side of the crate open, but at least she was well warmed up by the time the first part of the crate was off.

They then repeated the effort on the top of the crate. Because it was narrow only one person could hit the top of the crate from underneath and Ceylan took the honour. Once that end was separated enough from the main part of the crate, each woman was able to work their way along opposite sides with a crowbar. They worked as a team because as each nail emerged from the wood, the pressure changed allowing the next one to come out just a little easier. There were at least seven 8-cm nails along each side of the top panel and, finally, they got to the last one on each side and the whole panel came free easily. Azunna noted that they worked well as a team, even with minimal communication.

They lifted off the middle of the top panel, being careful of the long-exposed nails, and lent it against the wall, nails sticking out. Without saying a word to each other they worked on getting the nails out to avoid injuring themselves inadvertently later.

"Whew. A little more work that I thought it would be." Ceylan had worked up a sweat as well, although she seemed like she felt comfortable with the work. "Whoever drove those nails in London, certainly did a thorough job." They finished opening the crate.

Once open, the crate revealed a nearly new Triumph Scrambler 1200 XC in a khaki green. Azunna had put it through its paces for almost 200 miles in the wilds of Wales to ensure it was solid and she was familiar with it. At the time she had no inclination that the motorbike would be part of this mission. It had been one of those things that she did not see the point of at the time, but it was part of the familiarization program. Now it was slowly beginning to make sense.

The Scrambler was stock except for the new knobby tires and the extended range gas tank that the technicians had installed, taking the normal fifteen -litre tank to twenty-two, extending the range by 100 miles. The motorbike was designed with serious off-roading in mind. It had handled Wales just fine, and Azunna had no doubt that it would be up to the task of the Syrian desert as well. They stripped the plastic sheeting that had been placed around the vehicle to protect it from moisture to reveal the motorbike in full.

"She's a beauty," commented Ceylan. Azunna had not expected Ceylan to have an opinion about motorbikes.

"You ride?" Azunna asked.

"Smaller ones, mainly out of convenience in Istanbul. Never ridden anything this big before." Azunna could see both envy and trepidation in Ceylan's eyes as she contemplated riding a motorbike with an engine that big.

"It's a nice-looking bike." Azunna ran her hand down the length of the bike in admiration. "Like my own motorbike at home, but a bit beefier. I've put this one through its paces. Should do the job nicely."

Azunna noticed the zip ties and pulled out her knife. It was a Benchmade Bugout. With its locking back it would be strictly illegal in the streets of the UK, but it was part of her official kit so she could carry it on official duties, and it's not like she was going to carry it as part of tourist run through Buckingham Palace.

Now free of the final attachments, they moved the blocks of Styrofoam and bits of plastic out of the way, Azunna engaged the clutch, and with Ceylan pushing from the rear they freed the Scrambler from its cage, rolling it to the other side of the garage. Azunna put the kickstand in place and turned the handlebars to better balance the motorbike as they prepared it for the mission.

"Petrol?" Azunna asked. The first thing to do was makes sure the fluids were at the correct level and the engine was still in working order.

"Over here." Ceylan walked over to some five-gallon cans of petrol. Azunna had not noticed the four metal Jerry cans in the corner. Ceylan dragged one over and together they filled the tank.

Checking the fluid levels and the electronics Azunna noted that it all looked good.

"Let's fire it up." She pushed the electronic ignition. The roar of 1200cc of British engineering filled the space. At first, the noise was such that Ceylan and Azunna could barely hear themselves think much less each hear each other, and with each turn of the throttle, Azunna made the noise a little louder, smiling at Ceylan and enjoying the sudden change to the atmosphere. She let it run for a good five minutes, ensuring that nothing had changed since she had last used the bike. All appeared to be in order, and nothing indicated it was anything other than in tip-top shape, ready to be tested to the maximum of its capabilities. She then shut it down. Silence suddenly returned to the garage.

"Bike is in good shape, not that I expected otherwise. Let's open the first case," Azunna pointed to the black Pelican case labelled #1.

Ceylan pulled out her own knife and sliced through the customs seals on the case labelled with a stencilled "1" on the box. There were latches on three sides of the big case, not only securing the contents from would-be thieves, but also from unwanted water and air. Azunna produced a set of keys, and they undid the locks and the latches. Inside were all the things to finish kitting out the bike.

Even though it came with an inventory list Azunna rattle it off from memory.

"Arai XD-4 helmet, matte black, extra battery pack?
"Check."
"Go Pro Hero 10 camera, with satellite uplink?"
"Check."
"Garmin Foretell 610 GPS wrist unit?"
"Check."
"MP7A1 personnel defence weapon?"
"Here."
"Suppressor?"
"Check."
"Night vision optic?"
"Yep."
"Three 30-round magazines?"
"Uh-huh."
"One hundred rounds, 4.6x30mm ammunition?"
"And check."

"Let's get started. I'm going to boot the GPS and GoPro Satellite and give it a few minutes to locate itself, and make sure it is fully charged." Azunna grabbed the units and held the button till the screens came to life. The screens flashed, searching, then 64% charged for the GPS and 53% charged for the GoPro. Azunna plugged it into the chargers on the table and let it do its thing.

"What do you want me to do?" queried Ceylan.

"Could you attach the extra fuel can, the luggage pannier, and then the tank bag?"

"Got it."

Turning her attention to the MP7 she pulled it out of the Pelican case. She performed a functions check, mostly of out habit rather than necessity. She was there at the packing and sealing of the shipping containers and there was no reason to think anything had changed. The bolt pulled back easily and slid forward the same. A pull of the trigger confirmed it was a fully functioning firearm.

Azunna sat down on a small stool and broke open the two boxes of ammunition. Grabbing the three magazines she began slotting the ammunition into them.

"So where are you from?" Ceylan was looking at her with intense curiosity.

"Born in Peckham. Pretty much raised there and in Nigeria until I was twelve."

"You?"

"Oh, Istanbul mostly. Apart from uni in London that is. I loved it there."

"It is a marvellous city." She thought of Ngozi back there, working on her law degree back home.

"What else?" Ceylan was trying to probe without seeming too nosey.

"When I was at sixth form, Michelle Obama came to my college. I was at Elizabeth Garret Anderson School when she came to visit."

"Oh, that must have been exciting!"

Azunna was never quite sure how to explain her feelings about that visit. She had been one of a handful of girls who had been able to shake hands with the then-First Lady of the United States, but it's not like they had a personal interaction alone. Mrs. Obama, she was sure, would not know her from Adam. Or more accurately Eve.

"Right. Let's see if that GPS has found its location." It was now showing 79% charged. She unplugged it, figuring she would get it all charged later. "Can you hand me the GoPro?"

Ceylan grabbed the small box and tossed it to Azunna.

"Ostensibly, this thing can transmit by satellite itself, but I think if use the phone to transmit, I can have a real-time exchange with Headquarters while I am on mission."

"Sounds like a good idea."

She pulled out her phone and made sure she could communicate with London. She opened the messaging app and selected the operational address for London.

Test.

Then three dots appeared. Then disappeared. Then reappeared.

Standing by.

Plugging the camera into the phone she powered the camera up and the two devices began syncing. She ensured the phone was only using satellite, not Wi-Fi or regular cell signals.

Another text.

> *Stand by for test transmission.*

Three dots. Then a UK flag emoji.

Azunna cracked a little grin.

"What?"

"It's nothing."

Azunna could then see what the camera lens saw. She swiped the control left till it said video and pressed the red button.

Another text.

> *Are you seeing this?*

Another three dots. A thumbs up emoji.

> *Can you hear us?*

> *Loud and clear.*

> *Shutting down.*

> TTYL.

Azunna attached the camera to the helmet which already had a mount fixed to it. The wizards in logistics had devised an additional locking piece to keep it secure.

Putting the helmet on, Azunna plugged the phone into the helmet's communication system. She should now be able to transmit video and audio from the field.

She opened the video chat function and once again connected to London.

"Test, test," she said.

Three dots appeared.

"Oh, bloody hell, London. Talk to me. I won't be able to text bouncing across the desert."

"Fine," came back Mills' voice. "We read you loud and clear here in London."

Azunna aimed the camera at the bike.

"What are you seeing?"

"We have a good view of your motorbike."

"And now?" Ceylan waved.

"Someone waving at us."

"That's Ceylan. She's helping us out here. Let's try IR mode."

Azunna closed the garage door, and Ceylan killed the lights. A small amount of ambient flowed in.

"It's sort of a green mash-up."

"Ok, but it works. Good. All right, London. Azunna signing off. Cheers." She turned back to Ceylan. "I think that about does it. All we need to do is get it loaded in the back of that Fiat and head south."

"My father will be here for dinner and then we can go over the detailed plan for tomorrow."

"Sounds good."

"I'm off to do some other work. We have plenty of food, so help yourself. There is big satellite TV on the main floor, and it looks like you found the gym. I'd recommend staying close. Everything has been normal, but still. No reason to invite scrutiny. I will be back at about half six. Ciao!"

It was almost 1300, time had flown by as they prepped the gear. It was the sort of work Azunna enjoyed. Mission prep, running through how it should be, how it would be used, making sure it was ready. Gear inspection was always part of mission rehearsal for her. Fifteen minutes later she had finished all her final inspections and tidied up the area. She closed the doors and secured them with sturdy brass locks.

On her way into the main building, she grabbed some water, more bread, and some goat cheese and decided to watch some BBC news in the main living space. One news report on the everchanging government and plans for the coronation, and she was sound asleep on the sofa. Like any good foot soldier, her body would sleep when it could.

Chapter Nineteen

Kemal arrived shortly after six. Azunna was still dozing on the oversized couch and stirred as he walked in.

"I thought we could go over the insertion plan over dinner. Ceylan will be here shortly, and Hamza is making dinner. He will bring it with him."

"Sounds like a plan," Azunna said, sitting up and stretching her body awake. "So, Ceylan was telling me about some of your operations here. How do you manage to do all that?"

"Ah, well my company, Tyrone Distribution . . ."

"Tyrone? Awfully Irish name, for a Turkish Company."

"Ah, yes see, when I was reshaping my father's operations for the 21st Century, we decided to create a new company and create a clean slate, as it were. My favourite thriller novel is *The Dogs of War* by Frederick Forsyth. It's an homage to that. Anyway, a distribution company is the perfect cover for moving people and goods around the country on a regular basis. The situation in Syria has made that cover doubly so. We have legitimate contracts with the UN and numerous NGOs to bring food and other life-saving necessities to people in Turkish-controlled and rebel-controlled Syria. Most of what is going into both of those areas has nothing to do with our actual *raison d'être*, but it's important work and allows us to fund the operation."

"But why do this? Why work for us?"

"It's been the family business I suppose. My grandfather worked with the British to do his part against the Nazis, and my father his part against the Soviets in the Cold War. I just see this as continuing that legacy. Turkey and Britain are both members of NATO. In the big picture, we really have more in common than not. While I am not some Turkish super-patriot, I have not worked against Turkish interests either. But as far as I can tell, you and I both have similar goals. Getting rid of bad people."

Just then Ceylan walked in.

"Hey there, Baba. Kiana. How's it going?"

"Do you know where your brother is?"

"He texted, Baba. He's bringing dinner."

"Good. Get the maps out."

The large kitchen had a huge island in the middle of it with bar stools pulled up under the counter portion of the island – perfect for eating, food prep, and, in this case, tactical planning.

Kemal began. "Ok, we leave here tomorrow at 1400. We need to get Kiana to the drop site no later than 2100. That's more than enough time but she needs to be well on her way shortly after dark. Movement during the day will be just too risky." Both Azunna and Ceylan gave a silent head bob in agreement.

"You two will be in the Land Rover and will take the lead. We can hide your weapons in the unit below the passenger seat, and no one will find them on examination. We really should avoid an inspection of the van."

"So, you want us to call if there are any thorough inspections or checkpoints, Baba?"

"Nothing in the van is *per se* forbidden, but a nearly brand-new motorbike like that will arouse suspicion. If asked it's a personal order for a Turkish-area army commander, but that story is not well backstopped at this point."

Azunna was irked. "What if you are stopped and detained? What if the bike is confiscated? What then?" She was not accustomed to risks that could not be overcome with fire support from a higher supporting echelon.

"Then depending on how much they have learned or how much we have been delayed we abort and try again another day. If worst case scenario, the bike is confiscated we come back here and develop another insertion plan."

"I don't like it."

"Well, we aren't even sure what your specific mission is. We were just told to get you to a certain location and support your insertion and extraction. I assume though that if HMG was willing to make a bigger splash, they have the tools to do that. But they have sent you, so this is what we have."

Azunna relented. "Ok. I get it."

"Both vehicles are properly registered in Turkey as work vehicles for Tyrone Distribution. They have been in this part of Turkish-controlled Syria numerous times. There is absolutely no reason for us to even be stopped. You are a representative of our British partner UXT, Ltd. All that is backstopped. There will be no problems."

"Hey there!" Hamza had arrived with the food.

"Hamza, this is Kiana," Ceylan introduced them. He was clearly younger than his sister, but another good-looking member of the family. Thick dark wavy hair, and eyes that were almost black. Not a bodybuilder, but the tight navy-blue T-shirt suggested that he worked out.

"Nice to meet you." He had nearly accent-less English, he *must* have spent time in the UK as well. Ceylan went to help with the door and see if her brother needed her to carry anything in. Brother and sister started to dish the food while Kemal and Azunna looked at the map.

"We are in the north centre of town. Getting to the ring road will be the hardest part of this until we enter Syria proper. Ceylan will be driving lead and will get us to the O-54, the ring road around Gaziantep. That will take us down here to the D-850. From there it is a straight shot to Syria." He had used air quotes around the word straight.

The food arrived.

"What do people want to drink? "

"Do we have any Pablo? asked Kemal.

"Of course," replied Hamza.

"Kiana, you should really try this," joined Ceylan. "Turkey

has a great craft beer movement. This is one of the best. It's called Pablo Bira."

"Sure, I'll have one, too."

Ceylan grabbed four bottles of the Turkish beer and popped the caps off all of them. They all clinked their bottles of beer and cheersed each other.

Hamza presented the food. It was a good, hearty Turkish meal. Roasted lamb, hummus, fresh bread, vegetables, nuts, and olives. And, of course, baklava which Hamza had evidently made just before bringing everything over. After digging into the food, they returned to planning the next day's mission. Kemal went back over the details.

"Hamza and I will be in the van and will try to stay in visual contact with you but being that it is Friday that might not be easy. In addition to the normal traffic, you will have people going places for the weekend. I will text you if we lose sight of you, but in any event, we will meet up here just short of what was the Turkish-Syrian border." He stabbed his long slender index finger at a point on the map. "Kemal Tir Parki is a rest stop just short of the old border. We will refuel there and stretch our legs and regroup. After that, we will get back on the road and head into Syria."

"What happens at the border?" queried Azunna.

"There should be absolutely nothing there. One of the open secrets of this whole mess is that Turkey had essentially annexed this part of Syria. But if we are stopped, at the border or anywhere else, we are simply there inspecting our distribution of humanitarian relief supplies."

"Got it."

Kemal continued. "Next up is Azaz. It's the largest functioning city in this part of Turkish-controlled Syria. I do not want to stop unless we must. We will drive through Azaz and then continue southwest out of the city. Follow the signs to Kafr Kalbin, then Kaljinbrin, and then Marera. Hamza and I will overtake you in Marera. At that point we are heading south. About five miles out of town there is a dirt road to the left. You should be in visual contact with us. We will pull off to the road, and this is where we will unload your motorbike."

"What's there?"

"It's mostly agricultural area. At one time it would have been reasonably busy but at this point you are close enough to the no-man's land separating the Turkish and Syrian Armies that no one wants to risk getting caught in the crossfire between those two sometimes trigger-happy organizations. Occasionally, they do exchange gunfire, but not very enthusiastically. Any casualties are merely a by-product."

"I see. Well, that sounds like a good launch point. I would doubt that anyone we run into would want to risk interfering in our affairs anyway."

"Precisely. The people there are just trying to survive. No need to bring anyone else. No upside. After Hamza and I get the bike and other gear out of the truck though, we are out of there. You and Ceylan are going to do the final prep and launch."

"Good. I am comfortable with that plan."

"Both vehicles will return to the rest stop in Turkey. It should be no more than a 90-minute drive. And we are only going that far out of an abundance of caution. We can stop in Azaz if we must, but I would prefer not to, mainly because I don't want people looking for you."

Azunna figured she could return to Turkey on the motorbike. She decided to keep that thought in the back of her mind.

"And after I am done?"

"Ceylan will pick you up at this location. Program the grid into the Garmin and you should get right there." Kemal had the quick answer. Clearly done this more than he was willing to let on.

"What about the motorbike?" Azunna asked.

"Leave it." Kemal had never been required to maintain accountability of now-His Majesties Government equipment.

"We should all be back here by Sunday noon and then you can be on your way." Ceylan ever the optimist.

"As long as everything goes to plan."

"Well, there are plenty of time contingencies. The thing is once you are south of the demarcation line there is very little we can do to help you. We can meet you in another location, if necessary, but that's about it. You are on your own down there."

"I gathered that."

"I think that does it. Ceylan? Hamza?"

"Nothing from me, Baba."

"Me neither," added Hamza.

"Another round of beers then?"

Everyone agreed that was a good idea.

Chapter Twenty

Azunna slept late. It was a challenge to sleep when the adrenaline of mission prep kicked in, but she had long learned to, if not control it, at least manage it. She stayed up later than normal and then did not pressure herself to drop off. Eventually she fell into a deep sleep, that while not perfect, would certainly get her through the next forty-eight to seventy-two hours.

The temperature was going to be all over the place. She needed sturdy clothing that would regulate her temperature and survive a beating travelling via motorbike across the Syrian desert. Dark iron prana cargo pants, a light grey henley, wool commando jumper, the Brady Belstaff jacket, and her black Crocket and Jones boots should get her through this mission.

Coming down to the kitchen at 1100, she found it empty. Once they hit the road it would just be water and she wanted to enjoy one last cup of the magnificent Turkish coffee, so she began to grind the beans. Even though no one was there she noticed the Fiat van and Land Rover Defender pickup were combat-parked side by side and ready to go.

She made herself a filling, early lunch of yoghurt, fruit, sliced meats, cheese, and some whole-grain bread. This would need to carry her for the next forty-eight or so hours. Finishing up, she returned to her mini-suite and arranged the luggage she was not taking. If something went wrong, they would not need to spend a lot of time packing. It was at times like this she felt like she should write Ngozi a letter, but she never knew what to say.

At 1400 they all met in the courtyard. Ceylan and Hamza had loaded the motorbike earlier. It was strapped down and ready to go. Azunna locked the MP7 in the securely hidden compartment of the Land Rover, her pistol in a high-ride holster on her hip and hidden by her jacket.

"The traffic all appears to be the normal busy Friday, nothing excessive and no noticeable Turkish Army movements," reported Hamza. The Turkish Government was repeatedly assuring the public that the millions of Syrian refugees the country was hosting would eventually return to Syria. Realistically that was not in any immediate future, but sometimes they would publicly move more forces into the area as if something was going to happen that might make it possible. Not this weekend, however.

"Great." Kemal was parsimonious with his words when it came to times like this. Azunna, too, was downright taciturn, her emotions inscrutable behind her flat expression and dark glasses. Ceylan on the hand was completely pumped up, excited to get out on the road and on mission. In the forty-eight hours they had been together, Azunna had grown to like her and she was pretty sure she would be a great mission partner.

Finally joining in, Ceylan said, "Are we ready? Let's do this!" Azunna related, getting on mission was exciting. The four of them then jumped in the two vehicles, Ceylan and Azunna in the silver quad cab Land Rover Defender pickup, with Kemal and Hamza in the Fiat.

Pulling out of the compound the Land Rover went left and the Fiat went right. They would link up on the beltway around Gaziantep. The compound was almost surely not under surveillance, and there was no reason to think any aspect of Tyrone Distribution or their visitor from London had been compromised. Still, there was no reason to be careless. They had plenty of time, and they would use it to maintain security.

Ceylan and Azunna drove in silence at first. Ceylan was careful to obey the traffic laws, at least to the extent they were obeyed in this part of Turkey. No need to stand out to local law enforcement. Being invisible in the crowd was the key here.

Finally, after forty minutes of both side streets and main boulevards, they merged onto the belt road around the city.

"So, what's the link-up plan?"

"Hamza and I agreed that I would get in the far-right lane and go as slow as the normal flow of traffic allows. He is going to get in the far left and go as fast as the flow of traffic allows. We should meet before the turn south, but if we don't, we will both have shaken or detected any tail and can safely stop if we have to."

"Sounds like a well-thought-out procedure."

"This is not the first time we have done this. Even on regular business trips, we do this to keep in practice. And if someone is observing us over a longer period, the behaviour is all the same. We have not altered what we are doing."

Traffic was crowded on the beltway road. People were heading to family homes for the weekend, moving fresh fruits and vegetables to weekend markets, and transporting live cows, sheep, and goats also destined for markets and a short lifespan. What struck Azunna was the seeming normalcy of all of it. Less than one hundred miles to the south was an active war zone, and her life just went on. The refugees who began flooding into Turkey from Syria a few years ago made good talking points for Turkish pols, but for the most part, they had simply become part of the texture of daily life. Even if some rabble-rousers in Istanbul wanted to complain that the Syrian refugees were living a life of luxury for the sin of eating bananas.

As the miles rolled past and the commercial suburbs started to give way to pistachio and almond trees, Azunna thought about her family, which meant she thought about Ngozi again.

Their parents had been the children of Biafran exiles. Their paternal grandfather was a key aide to Chukwuemeka "Emeka" Odumegwu-Ojukwu, the President of Biafra. Their grandfather, grandmother, and father, at the time just a boy, had all boarded a Super-Constellation on a remote airfield just outside of Owerri the night Biafra finally fell to forces of the central federal government. Even though the British government had not supported the bid for Igbo independence, plenty of them found refuge in the UK. Her grandfather being an Oxford man, as her father would be, was able to call upon friends and allies to secure residency back in the UK where their grandfather taught post-Colonial African politics at the School of Oriental and African Studies, now a part of the University of London.

He had stayed involved in what he thought of as Biafran affairs, mostly from afar. The war had brought such suffering to the people of southeast Nigeria. The entire strategy of the Nigerian government had been to starve the people of Biafra. And they had succeeded. The corruption that so many people saw as endemic in the Nigeria of today, from oil bunkering to the famous Nigerian prince email scams were all by-products of the Biafran War.

And her father had absorbed her grandfather's passion for justice and protecting the less fortunate. He had double majored at Oxford in philosophy and economics. It was his goal to bring an efficient business-like approach to humanitarian relief in old Biafra.

Alongside their mother, he ran an NGO that not only provided food and shelter to those in urgent need but was on the cutting edge of what were now known as "durable solutions." Large numbers of people were on the move across Africa due to climate change long before the Europeans and the Americans had noticed, and her parents tried to alleviate that.

Human trafficking was a particular scourge, with many Nigerians essentially selling themselves into bondage in the hope of money for their families today and a better life in the future. For the men, this generally meant back-breaking work in the hot sun of Southern Europe, but for the women, particularly young girls this meant sexual slavery. Years in brothels around the world with no end in sight. And the end was more often than not suicide or drug overdoses. Working to put an end to this had been her parents' life's work until that day in 1999 when they were killed that car accident while visiting Nigeria.

"Kiana, Kiana, hello." Azunna realized that Ceylan was speaking to her.

"Uh, sorry, I was just thinking about something."

"The mission I hope."

"Yes, of course."

"The truck is four vehicles behind us. We are making good time. Could you hand me a bottle of water please?"

Azunna leaned over the back of the seat and grabbed two bottles of sparkling water, opening one and handing it to Ceylan, and keeping one for herself. She twisted the cap on her bottle, first releasing the gas to make sure it did not spew all over the car, then removing the cap and taking a long pull. Suddenly she realized how thirsty she was and sucked down the whole thing, tossed the empty bottle into the back seat and grabbed another one repeating the opening ritual.

"We should be at the border in another thirty minutes. So, what's your life like back in London?"

"In flux." Azunna preferred the friendship and familiarity of another person by having a common mission experience, not disclosure of her past. Her comments were short and of course the truth. Officially she was on loan from the Royal Marines to the Service until what amounted to a probationary period was over with. A probationary period where she needed to kill two particularly bad people, who it had been decided needed to be eliminated. She had killed enough people as a Royal Marine to know it was a dirty business, but in this world it was unavoidable. There were nasty people out there doing nasty things to others and someone needed to do something.

A sign showed their destination just a few kilometres away. Time for a rest stop.

Somewhere between the quality of the latest rest areas along the M1 where you can charge your EV, buy a Hawaiian shirt, and get a Gregg's sausage roll, and the one pump stations in the middle of nowhere, they pulled over. They filled both vehicles with petrol, relieved themselves in a clean place, and stretched their legs. No one paid any attention to the anonymous vehicles or their occupants.

Kemal gazed at the traffic moving south at a steady pace. "Good, good," he said to himself, but Azunna heard him.

"What?"

"Oh, nothing really. But with the traffic moving at this pace the chance of any stoppage at the border is virtually non-existent. After everyone had stretched their legs, they huddled up for one last discussion before heading out.

"Everyone good on the route?" Head nods all around.

Azunna was accustomed to being in charge on missions like this, but one of the aspects of good leadership was good followership. She knew that once she threw her leg over that motorbike, she would be making all the decisions and dictating how the mission went. No reason to get into an exhausting decision cycle yet.

"Alright, let's go."

Back in the vehicles, they were soon crossing what was still officially the Turkish-Syrian border. Looking at it though, it was hard to imagine that was ever going to return in fact.

Driving through the Syrian countryside was almost no different than driving through the Turkish countryside, although there were more signs in Arabic, and it looked poorer. That said there was no sign that the current regime had ever exercised any control here.

The plan was to enter Azaz from the northeast and skirt the town exiting out through the southeast. The problem started just as they arrived at what should have been the entrance to the city. A vegetable truck and a truck full of goats had collided. The vegetable truck, being overloaded and top-heavy meant that tomatoes, onions, and cucumbers were strewn about the road and the goats, suddenly liberated from their rolling captivity were making their escape in all different directions. As is almost always the case at accident scenes like this around the world, every witness had come out of the woodwork to simultaneously gawk and offer up their opinions of what happened, who was at fault, and what should happen now.

The Turkish military police were trying to sort all of this out. An Army major was in charge, and he rubbed his temples. It was Friday late afternoon, and this was the sort of thing that was rife for use as cover for a terrorist attack. Between the

Kurds, HTS, and the Syrian regime someone was surely going to want to take advantage of this. He needed a beer.

The two-vehicle convoy was caught up in all of this before they realized what a mess it was. When Ceylan saw what was going on she tried to back up, and that's when the Turkish soldiers thought something was wrong.

"Durmak! Durmak!" The soldiers were screaming at her to stop. They had their MPT rifles up at their shoulders and were advancing thought the traffic to the Land Rover. Ceylan kept here wits enough to put the car in neutral and her foot on the brake. She and Azunna put their hands up. Kemal and Hamza in the van five cars back could only look on helplessly.

An NCO demanded papers from Ceylan while a private pointed his rifle at Azunna. The NCO was quizzing Ceylan when the major in charge of the scene arrived. The fact that Azunna was clearly not from Turkey quickly drew his attention.

"Documents," he demanded from her in Turkish.

"I'm sorry sir, but I don't speak Turkish." Her words were those of respect and submission, but her tone was anything but.

"Ah, you are English!" His tone softened. "Passport."

She handed him her passport. He flipped through it.

"What are you doing in this part of Turkey?"

She supressed a laugh. The soldiers on the ground knew the score. This part of Syria was functionally Turkey now.

"I am the Global Solutions Team Lead for UXT, Ltd. We are helping NGOs bring humanitarian relief to the area. I am just inspecting the work my company has performed."

"On a Friday afternoon?"

"Oh, you know, time and tide wait for no man, or woman." Then quickly, "When I was in the Royal Marines, we did some training down here with your Land Forces. Ever do any NATO exercises in the Med?"

As a matter of fact, he had, and those exercises had been far more fun than this current mission was. They quickly ascertained they had in fact both been part of the same large exercise a few years back. He thought for a minute. It was all rather plausible. The truck's papers were in order and the driver had a verifiable history. He had more important things to do.

"Let them go," he told the soldiers.

"Dotsum," Azunna had decided to be bold, using the Turkish phrase for 'friend.' "Could you please help us, and that vehicle get out of this mess?" She indicated to the Fiat van five cars back.

The Turkish Army major was as capable as any person of recognizing when someone was sweet-talking them. And even though women were not operating in the Turkish military the way they were in the UK, it was nice to be recognized as a professional by another professional. He had decided to let them go, getting them out of there quickly would only help. A few words to the NCO and the soldiers were moving the cars so the Land Rover and the Fiat could get moving again.

Finally, with a wave from Azunna to her new friend they were back on the road, but they were heading west and had lost an hour.

Working mostly on instinct with a little help from her GPS, Azunna began navigating. Ceylan was still new to this sort of work and the interruption to the plan had unnerved her. They were on side streets with fewer people, but they were also narrower. Azunna gave a series of left right, left turning commands. Then her phone started buzzing with text messages. It was Kemal.

Where are we going?

I've got this, she replied.

We should stop.

You are the one who said we shouldn't. Follow us. Three minutes.

"At the next street, you are going to want to make a hard left."

"Right." Fifty kmph seemed very fast in these side streets, and as Ceylan yanked the steering wheel hard, she clipped another car, shearing off the right-side rear-view mirror.

"That's alright, you weren't using it," remarked Azunna wryly.

Ceylan scowled at the remark and yanked the car to the left, smashing off the left side mirror as well.

"Wasn't using that one either." Azunna smiled. This one would do just fine.

The good news was they were now on the major east-west road through town, the bad news was they were still heading west. But then they entered what must have been the biggest street on the westside of town and a large roundabout.

"Go all the way around and let's go back the way we came."

Thirty seconds later they came back round with the Fiat in trail, and they were heading east through town. Azunna texted Kemal.

> If the main north-south corridor is not blocked, we will be out of town in five more minutes.

Roger.

They crossed the main street and two minutes later they were on the edge of town. Azunna looked to the left as they passed what looked like the last major street and saw the gas station that they had agreed was a possible stopping point, confirming they were in the correct place.

"Let's go."

Ceylan put her foot to the floor.

The sun was going down and there was no time to waste. Places like rural Syria were sketchy at the best of times. Even though they were still in Turkish-controlled territory, that didn't mean they wouldn't run into an errant Syrian patrol or one of the many militias the area had spawned. This Friday evening though there was no one moving about.

Back on track and through the last town, the Fiat suddenly sprinted past the Land Rover, Hamza at the wheel. He signalled a left turn with just one flash of the blinker, Ceylan slowing down to give them a little time to get into position.

Turning right at the same location there was just enough light they did not need to use the headlights. Back on the main roads, it was not a problem, but headlights in the middle of the field would attract the attention they were hoping to avoid.

Seeing the Fiat up ahead, Ceylan shifted down, giving them one more minute. By the time they rolled up, the Scrambler was coming down the makeshift ramp in the back. There was no time to waste, Kemal was just glad that he had built in enough time to cover for something like goats roaming all over the main road.

"Here we go. The motorbike and the other gear. Need anything else?" Kemal knew the answer, but he still he posed the question.

"Nope, we've got it from here." Fist bumps all around and then Kemal and Hamza were in the truck. Hamza rolled down the window of the driver's side.

"Ceylan, we will wait at that first gas station in Azaz."

She gave a silent thumbs up. Then the two men were gone.

It was beginning to get dark, but Ceylan was hoping enough ambient light would get her back to the main road.

Azunna retrieved the MP7 and magazines from the hidden compartment. She strapped the sub-machine gun to her chest and slid the magazines into cargo pockets. She put the satellite phone on the motorbike with the special mount and put the Garmin on her wrist, switching it on.

The GoPro was already on the helmet, and she turned that on. Finally, she put the helmet on, activating the Bluetooth system that would allow her to hear. She pulled the visor down, the Garmin, the phone, and the GoPro were all linked to the helmet by Bluetooth and the visor was a special heads-up unit display that allowed her to see the route and text messages in the visor.

She then used the phone to connect to the London Operations Centre.

"Regal Centre. This is Harrier, do you have me?"

"The is Regal Centre. Affirmative."

"Roger."

She turned to Ceylan. "Thanks. I'm all set. You need to get out of here."

"Right. Do be careful my sister."

"Always."

They bumped fists and Ceylan jogged to the Land Rover, now sans wing mirrors. A quick three-point turn, and she was down the road.

Azunna straddled the powerful bike and switched it on, the advanced electronic ignition bringing it immediately to life. The desert was now quite dark. She rolled on the throttle and was off into the danger and the darkness of the Syrian desert.

Chapter Twenty-One

Dr. Werner Gantz was not pleased to be heading into the Syrian desert. It was too dry. It was dirty. It was usually too warm. Nothing seemed to work. And he could not get his pear schnapps. If all went according to plan though, he would be back in his Austrian chalet within twenty-four hours. He might have to sleep on his plane, but that was better than some dingy Syrian villa.

Gantz had made a fortune organizing criminals, terrorists, and other bad actors for the sake of making a lot of money and sowing chaos throughout the world. In school, he had tested well above one hundred and forty on at least one IQ test and his parents, Alpine farmers, had really not known what to do with the boy. He excelled in maths and the sciences, being one of the few to not be squeamish at the dissections in biology class.

What the teachers and his father did not know was he liked to conduct his own experiments and dissections on small animals he would capture in the mountains. If a neighbour's dog or cat went missing the assumption was that a wolf had taken them, but that was not always the case. Had Gantz been examined by a psychoanalyst they would have found that in addition to being a genius, was also a sociopath and quite mad. While a student at the University of Innsbruck, his father had died in a mysterious combine accident and that was the end of any inquiry into the mental health of Werner Gantz.

After receiving his PhD in Chemistry, he had gone to work for IG Farben, but it was not long until he came to the notice of the KGB who employed him in making compounds designed to kill. By the time the USSR had collapsed he had begun to develop his own network of assassins and found that he was also effective at the management of terror and sowing chaos. That was when he created the Abigor Legion. He felt an organization named after a Grand Duke of Hell would attract just the sort of associates he wanted. People devoid of compassion, empathy, or ethics.

Unlike some though, he did not revel in the adulation, rather he enjoyed sitting in his alpine retreat watching the chaos unfold across TV news knowing that it was he who had created so many seemingly unconnected problems.

The downside to the criminal enterprise he had created was, well, dealing with the people who would do his bidding. They tended to have the same pathologies as Gantz thus they were all in competition for attention. What differentiated Gantz was his intelligence, and he knew it. He had little patience with his intellectual inferiors, but he knew he needed Al-Assad, someone the thought of as inferior, for his operations. It was the most distasteful part of his job.

Maher al-Assad was one of those people Gantz wished he had not brought into the Legion. Gantz viewed him as lazy and entitled, as many of the children of the wealthy can be. Maher thought his military experience and his willingness to have people tortured made him truly fearsome. And in Syria it did. He was responsible for the deaths of thousands. Some at the hands of his thugs and hundreds of others under a rain of artillery shells. But it is easy to make the powerless feel fear. It is usually a part of their daily condition. Gantz was irritated by al-Assad's unwillingness to make the *powerful* feel fear. If he had done that, Gantz would not have had to make this trip to the Syrian desert.

***

"Regal Centre, this is Harrier. On Mission."

"Got you Harrier. Good strong signal. Good video feed. Tally ho."

She was in open farm fields, nothing very difficult as far as terrain, but she did need to be on the lookout for irrigation ditches. This IR system did not reduce the view to the tunnel vision two dimensions of older tube-based systems, but it was still a huge challenge. If she could find a path running alongside a canal should be able to drive faster. She had about twenty miles to go.

The intelligence was that Major General Maher al-Assad ran his drug empire this far north to keep it out of the site of his brother and his brother's new Security Division. Yes, he was part of the inner circle, but Syria was becoming a last-rat-standing situation. Captagon manufacturing was off the charts when it came to money making. Some of the product they were sending across the border into Saudi, but the market was growing in Europe. Anywhere rich Saudis and other Gulfies went, the market grew. He imagined that the market would spread as far and wide as the UK and the US at some point. But that would be someone else's problem.

His role was clear, get as much of the product to embarkation points along what remained of the Syrian border, the port in Latakia, and Beirut for onward movement to Europe and points beyond. Beirut had become problematic since the port explosion, not because of reduced capacity, but the fact that ammonium nitrate fertilizer had sat there for so long unattended had alerted security forces around the region to the serious security flaws in Beirut. How could the Lebanese, and the Russians for that matter, be that stupid? It boggled his mind.

***

Azunna had made it out of the fields and was now ascending the large hills, small mountains representing the unofficial demarcation line between regime-controlled Syria and other areas of what had once been the Syrian Arab Republic. This was riding that she was more familiar with, having tackled different off-road courses in Wales and western England. She had to watch out for big rocks, but as long as she did not shoot off the side of the mountain, she was probably not going to find herself face-down in a ditch.

"Harrier. Regal Centre here. We are tracking a small convoy of three vehicles coming in your direction from the west. They appear to be headed for the same location you are."

"Roger, thanks."

Azunna stopped and looked hard out in the general direction Regal Centre had indicated but saw nothing.

"Regal Centre, I have nothing. Please keep me informed though."

"Roger."

Finally, after ninety minutes of hard riding Azunna saw the target compound right where it should be. She saw another compound not too far away from it that looked like a transportation hub, surrounded by trucks and lights. Then she saw the small convoy London had told her about; three Toyota Land Cruisers moving at high speed across the desert road, headlamps on, with the sand in the air creating a both beautiful and eerie effect. This was a wrinkle that had not been planned for.

Oh, well, Azunna thought. *It's not like this is the first mission where the unexpected showed up. Probably won't be the last.*

The compound she was headed to was several acres large. It consisted of the main building, a few outbuildings, at least one garage, maintenance facilities, and barracks of some sort. It was walled in for the most part, but aerial reconnaissance indicated it had few gates, possibly guarded, maybe with some sort of monitoring, but it seemed clear that al-Assad's principal security measure was isolation. Isolation also meant not having many, if any reserves for when things go wrong.

Azunna watched the three Land Cruisers make the last turn for the gate. They had maintained their high speed until the last possible moment and the guards had not reacted. These people were expected. In an era where the vehicle-borne improvised explosive device had become the weapon of choice, static guard posts did not wait long to open fire on unexpected vehicles approaching at high speed. A soldier approached the driver's side door and then signalled to another guard who opened the gate. With that, the three-vehicle convoy was in the compound.

Interesting.

She opened the texting app. Azunna sent a message.

> The convoy was admitted with nothing more than a cursory inspection of papers.

Can you find out what is going on?

> I will see what I can do.

Seeing if we can locate the origin of that convoy.

> Thanks.

Looking to her right, the other end of the compound was only partially lit in moonlight. Maybe she could find an entrance there. She was less than a kilometre away now. She gave the motorbike some gas but moved no more than ten metres before it went nose first into a wadi, sending Azunna sprawling.

She ran through a mental and physical checklist of her body – head, arms, torso, legs, all fine. The helmet had done its job, her jacket, and boots all protecting her. Her weapons appeared to be in order, GPS functioning. The phone on the mount had one message unread.

What happened?

Azunna pulled the bike back up and it immediately rocked forward. Popping the visor on her helmet up, she allowed her eyes to adjust to the dark. It'd didn't take long for her to see the front wheel was quite bent, bent enough that the bike was not going anywhere with it.

That's going to be a problem, she mused.

Motorbike is NMC.

?

Non-Mission Capable.

Do you need assistance?

Stand by.

Entrance into the compound was always going to be the tricky part. Unmanned Aerial Vehicle reconnaissance had seemed to indicate there was more than one entrance, but the schematic had proved impossible to obtain and its veracity would have been hard to check in any event.

The helmet was useless except as a mounting device for the camera, she removed the helmet and took the camera off the mount. Then she grabbed the phone off the bike, tossing the helmet on top of the now useless Scrambler. Azunna attached a wired earpiece to the phone and slid the phone into her jacket pocket after ensuring the Bluetooth connection between the camera and phone was still working.

"Regal Centre, Harrier here. I'm on foot. Leaving the bike and helmet."

"We have a UAV on station. What can we find for you?"

"How to get into this bloody place." She paused. "And a heads up if you see someone coming."

"Can do Harrier. You appear to be clear to close the last six hundred metres to the wall."

"Thanks."

As a former sniper team leader, she knew that movement is what attracts the eye. Slow and steady is what would get her to that wall a mere six hundred metres away, rather than an all-out sprint. With that, she commenced her stalk.

It was a light incline, hard-packed sand, rocks, and limited vegetation. Slowly she put one foot in front of the other. The hard rubber commando sole of her boot gripped the dirt. A misstep here would most likely not hurt her, but it would almost certainly attract attention.

The six hundred metres was the longest twenty minutes of this mission. But finally, she was nestled against the wall.

"Made it."

Tickner and Mills had joined the call from their homes in London. "There should be an entrance at the corner as you move away from the main gate. We are not detecting any movement right now."

Azunna started down along the wall until she reached the corner. "Not seeing anything here."

"I'm going to see if the UAV pilot can get a wider shot," said Mills.

"Right, thanks."

The UAV had been circling and observing the compound itself. The pilot took the aircraft up and created a wider circle to get a better angle on the outside wall. It probably took no more than three minutes, but alone outside the wall of an enemy outpost, it seemed like forever.

"Ah, alright." It was Tickner this time. "If you come round the corner, there should be a door. You should be able to gain access there."

This sounded crazy. At the very least it would be latched from the inside. How was she getting in? She decided to cross that bridge when she came to it. She eased herself around the corner and found herself in front of the door.

"Can you see anyone on the other side?"

"Wait, repositioning the UAV."

That was the thing with missions like this. Operations centres were always telling field operatives to wait. They could sure be demanding for information though.

After what, again, seemed like forever, "Looks clear."

"Great. Looks." Azunna just shook her head. She pulled out a small, red-lensed penlight. Going old school here, like when she was first in commando training.

She was standing in front of what looked like a ship's passageway doorway. It was about six inches off the ground and no more than two metres. It appeared to be for emergency egress. Starting at the far-left lower corner she worked her way up. The door looked to be metal plate, not hardened steel. About centimetres from the bottom was a hinge. Ok she thought, the door opens out. Another a metre up she was at the middle and another hinge. Finally, she reached a top hinge that mirrored the one on the bottom. Solid, but probably manageable. Running her hands and light across the top she could see it closed but did not create a seal. There were small gaps between the door and the frame. Now at the top right corner, she gently pulled on the door. It moved a fraction out and then stopped. She started to move down the right-side peering into the cap. Ten centimetres down and across from the hinge, she could see a latch. She continued her way down finding two more latches that mirrored the latches on the side.

This all looks manageable. In the red light, it looked like they were just bars that need to be pushed up. But how to keep them up while she worked on the other two?

Fortunately, the door was flush against the wall and not reset in a portal. This just reaffirmed her idea that this had been put in for exit. Maybe even by a previous owner.

Deciding to start with the top l-bar that latched the door she gently worked it up until it appeared to be free. The door started to open, and she realized the bars had all been connected. The door was open. Problem solved.

"I'm in."

Azunna was well past the point that she could bluff her way through any encounter. All her senses were on high alert. After entering the compound, she receded into a dark corner to gather her bearings. The main building was off-centre and closer to her than the far side of the compound. The three Land Cruisers were parked up on the far side with Syrian soldiers milling around them, as well as some civilians who were clearly not Syrians.

Having pocketed the camera to come through the door she pulled it out and made sure it was transmitting.

"Regal Centre, are you getting this?"

"Roger. Harrier, that convoy came from the Russian-controlled air base at Latakia. The passengers arrived on a private jet from Klagenfurt, Austria. Maybe they are involved in this too. Use extreme caution."

Azunna was always amused by the cautions given to operatives in the field. *Oh, now someone else was here she needed to be cautious. Please.*

Nearer to her was a one-story block building that had the appearance of a small barracks. Soldiers, something to be avoided. However, the arrival of the convoy from Latakia had proven to be fortuitous, attention had been drawn to other places.

Bringing her attention back to the main building, she saw light emanating from a large window on the main floor. It looked like the glass went floor to ceiling and the panes at both ends had been opened for airflow. Azunna inched her way along the wall, remaining in the shadows.

When the shadow ended it was about six metres in the light before the darkest shadows of the main building. Looking to her left now she decided the men were most distracted she took six quiet steps across the right and back to the shadow. She was next to the building and was able to move next to the window where she could hear voices.

***

The soldiers in the compound's operations had finally started paying some attention to their duties again. But night after night of monitoring cameras was monotonous. No one was foolish enough to try and breach and al-Assad compound in regime-controlled Syria were they? One manned by the Fourth Armoured Division? Madness. An NCO thought caught some quick movement on the camera looking down from the main gate.

"Sir," he called to the lieutenant on duty, "I think I saw something."

"Wait a minute. I'm busy." The thing about working security and service for an authoritarian was the constant need to balance their demand for protection from enemies real and imagined, as well as respond to their requests for personal service. The lieutenant's team was doing double duty tonight with these, unexpected to them visitors.

***

Azunna could not see inside the room, but she could hear everything. She pulled out the satellite phone and opened the text function.

> Next to the building.
> Meeting about to a occur.
> Can you hear?

Stand by.

Three dots appeared. Then disappeared. Then they appeared again. Then . . .

> Recording.

"Finally," she thought.

"General Assad. I will get straight to the point. Some people are not happy, specifically, the people who are expecting the Captagon.. The last thing I want, or need is your clients making their way to Austria to complain to me about your inability to provide product. I get that the Beirut port explosion slowed everything down. And the detection of the Captagon in the Lebanese fruit really put a dent in operations. But our organization wants its money."

Assad was still looking for the traitor who had given that shipment to the Lebanese authorities. No way some intelligence organization or police agency had detected the Lebanese warehouse up with that on their own.

"I really care not if people are unhappy, Dr. Gantz." Once again al-Assad found himself regretting joining the Abigor Legion. The money though had been too tempting Who did

Gantz think he was? One did not just come into Syria and make even veiled threats against an Assad.

"I'm aware. May I?" He gestured to the seat of the table where Assad was sitting. Assad nodded. "Thank you. The flight from Austria was long and the drive from Latakia tiresome. What you may care about though is if your brother was to find out about our little arrangement. By my calculations you have underreported your compensation in this scheme by almost a billion dollars. I am sure the President and his precious Asma, who we know misses shopping London, would be most unhappy with you. He would be doubly upset to find that you had pledged your loyalty to the Abigor Legion, would he not?"

> *Are you getting this London?*
> *Have we heard of the Abigor*
> *Legion?*
>
> *Roger, Harrier. Researching now.*
> *Nothing in the files so far.*

***

In the compound operations centre, the NCO responsible for monitoring the cameras had finally gotten the attention of the duty officer who was of course irate for not being alerted earlier even as he had asked for the officer to come look at the video.

***

"Are you threatening me? Here?" Assad laughed dubiously. Dr. Gantz was completely non-pulsed. He had been dealing with powerful figures his entire adult life, and as a somewhat portly academic, was accustomed to this sort of treatment by men who overestimated their ability to achieve long-term goals with nothing but extreme violence.

"I would not call it a threat, General. I am just bringing your attention back to our agreement. We are aware that some of the problems were not, well, *probably* were not of your making. The detection of the product in the Lebanese pomegranates was very odd, but we have been willing to overlook that. If you would have your men load my vehicles with product that would reassure my colleagues that all is well and that you are still operating within our original agreement."

Assad stared thoughtfully at Gantz for a moment. This would mean the next Saudi shipment would be light, but he had not been short for MBS before and figured he could manage him. And that relationship had none of the shadows this one did. He could have his brother deal with MBS if necessary.

"Fine." Assad snapped his fingers, an aid came, and Assad whispered in his ear.

Gantz stood. "And now I see our business is concluded." With no more pleasantries, he turned on his heels and left. Glad that in a few short hours he would be back in his private jet on the way home to Austria.

***

The Syrian Arab Army Lieutenant was finally excised enough to manage to lead four soldiers to investigate, but the ten minutes he had wasted had been just enough time for London to receive the information. Because later two private jets would leave Latakia. Dr. Gantz in one bound for Klagenfurt and the Captagon in the other bound for Cairo. At 15,000 feet ascending out of Latakia the plane carrying the Captagon would be destroyed by an Astra 30 missile fired from the Type 45 frigate, *HMS Dragon* operating in the eastern Mediterranean.

Azunna was preparing for her next move when five Syrian soldiers rounded the corner. She pushed herself as low as she could go and lay still. Not knowing what or who they were looking for they missed her and split up to search other parts of the compound.

> Regal Centre. I think they know
> I am here.

Azunna hoped that UAV they had used to help get her in would now be able to help get her out after she completed her mission. From the corner of the building, she could see a mini-car park with numerous SUVs and military vehicles, but she doubted the keys were in the cars. On balance, she decided that making her way out of the compound on foot was the best plan.

Keeping low she crept across the space between the main building and the outbuilding. She could hear soldiers running around, probably looking for her, but she could not make out what they were saying. Slowly she worked her way to the corner where she could see the portal she had entered through. She queried London.

Regal Centre. Can the UAV see what is going on?

But London had gone silent. She was on her own and she knew it. The soldiers seemed to be searching in other areas of the compound and she made a fast dash to the wall, pausing there long enough to ascertain whether she had drawn any attention. It seemed she had not, and she moved down the wall till she was back at the door she'd entered through. She slowly opened it, any small noise it made drifting into the dark and covered by the growing chaos behind her. She crawled through the door, dropping into a crouch. Too late, as she reoriented herself, she realized that a very large man was there.

And then everything went black.

Chapter Twenty-Two

Azunna started to stir when she felt something tugging at her legs. As she became more aware, she realized someone was trying to take her trousers off. Instinctively she started to struggle.

"Stop moving bitch!" A slap across her face momentarily stunned her. Not enough to put her out again, but enough that her struggles stopped long enough for them to get her clothes off. She knew she had pushed it too far, too fast, and now she was paying the price. With her head bobbing, she glanced around trying to take in her surroundings. The room was a concrete box, with water stains on the ceiling and cracks running down the walls. There was a solitary bulb hanging from the ceiling, almost like a low-budget movie or a dime store novel. There were blood stains on the concrete floor. It was cold and damp. It reminded her of that cell in Wales.

Azunna was suddenly exhausted, the long day combined with the lack of water and food and having been knocked out had sapped all the energy inside her. Semi-conscious she was limp, and the guards were still struggling to strip her of her clothing. Now naked she instinctively started to struggle.

Smack. An oversized hand hit her across the face. "Stop fighting bitch. You keep this up and you will wish you were dead even sooner." She passed out.

Azunna started to come around again when she felt cold water splashing across her face. At first, a bucket of water had been thrown at her, but quickly she realized there was a towel over her face, and they were pouring water over her nose and mouth while the subordinate thugs held her arms down. She struggled to breathe, the sensation of drowning and the attendant panic overcoming her. Then they suddenly stopped. Leaving her lying on the floor, gasping for air, struggling to remain conscious. The respite was brief though, as two of the thugs grabbed her shoulders and the third began the process all over again.

They weren't even asking her questions. The whole point of this process seemed to be the cruelty. They had not asked her who she was, why she was there, anything. It was apparently recreation for this group of people. They finished this round and threw her to the ground. She cut her head on rough concrete and some blood trickled down the side of her face. The copper taste of blood was in her mouth.

"Let's go." The thug-in-chief had decided to pause the session.

An hour ago, she had been a confident intelligence officer and battle-tested Royal Marine approaching a target, now she lay naked, barely conscious in a dank-smelling cell below ground in the Syrian desert. The combination of exhaustion and physical abuse made her feel as if she could not go on any longer. She drifted in and out of consciousness. She was going to die here, because of her own rash action once again, it was all going to have been for nothing. She began to hallucinate.

Ngozi appeared in her mind. It was just before the first time she had deployed to Afghanistan. Being alone had become such a state of reflex for Azunna that when her sister had thrown her arms around her that day and told her how much she admired her, Azunna did not know how to react. They were far enough apart in age that they were never playmates, but Azunna was not quite a parent either. It was complicated. She loved her younger sister dearly; she just did not know how to relate to her. But lying on that floor in a Syrian torture cell, she could feel how important that relationship was.

Then it was Tom Colley. She remembered their first work up for deployment. They had spent days on the range both at Warminster and then with the Americans at Fort Benning, Georgia. They were both in this profession for the same reason, to make this world a safer place. And she knew then that Colley had followed her that day in the Hindu Kush because he had the same belief that she did.

And Phoebe. What would Phoebe do if she were here?

Then, through the haze of pain, she saw it. All her clothing and gear had been tossed into the corner. They thought so little of her as a woman that they did not even bother to separate her from her kit. Were they right? Was she that ineffectual that they could run that risk?

The steel door slammed open and now in came four men. The original three plus another. The trio grabbed her again, but this time she knew what she had to do. Terror was rising inside her, but she knew she had to harness that emotion to fight. She soon found herself on one of those cheap injection moulded plastic seats so common on the streets of the Middle East, one thug on each arm zip-tying her to the chair. She immediately, instinctively flexed her wrists to create a loose attachment. The thug on the left smashed her wrist against the chair, making it secure, but the one on the right did not. She had a decent range of movement.

"I don't know who you are or what you are doing here or what you want, but we will find out."

Things were coming into clearer view. She tried to focus on the one who was speaking.

"And by the time I found out who you are, who sent you, and what exactly it is you want you will be begging me to kill you. But I won't, not at once, at least. I will make it last longer, until I have toyed with you long enough that when I do kill you and drop your body in the middle of no man's land to be found by a pathetic refugee, you will be unrecognizable."

As she continued to try and focus, she noticed that all four men were wearing the distinctive Syrian camouflage pattern with the 4th Armoured Division's combat tactical recognition flash on it. That at least meant she was probably in the right place. The two who secured her to the chair looked to be everyday soldiers simply on duty.

Next was a bigger, fitter man oozing of menace and cruelty.

Finally, she focused on the one who was speaking. As her eyes returned to full function, she realized it was Major General Maher al-Assad himself, her target. She was in exactly the right place. She came back to his verbal vomit.

"So, who are you?" He almost shouted. The quality of her equipment had told him she was not a nobody.

She spat, trying to get some saliva in her mouth. "My name is Kiana Azunna." Her mouth had never been this dry before. She coughed. "I represent His Majesty's Government." She drew in her breath, coughed again, and then took in another deep breath. "And I am here to kill you."

Stunned silence filled the concrete block room. Her mouth was beginning to get some moisture back in it. Assad knelt and looked into her eyes.

"You know, I think you might actually believe that. But my aide here will get to the truth. And whoever leaves here dead, I highly doubt that it will be me." He patted her on the cheek. And then he laughed. Condescending mother fucker that he was.

"This room? Concrete block. This door? Solid steel. No one will hear you scream Ms. Azunna. Not even these two, who will be outside the door. We won't meet again."

He stood, nodded at the hulking NCO, turned on his heels and left with the two soldiers in tow. The door slammed shut and a steel bar slipped into place, leaving her alone with a brut of a man. She had finally had the chance to take in the whole room, rectangular, shorter on the depth than the width. A plain plastic table at one end with what looked like crude torture implements on it. In a crumpled pile near the door, she could see her clothing. And her weapons. The thing about thugs wasn't that they were not smart, it was that that they were arrogant in their ability to bully and hurt people. That arrogance made them sloppy. The dark spots on the concrete floor attested to the blood, she was quite sure of many victims of these people or others similar.

The thug walked over to the table and considered his options. He picked up one broad-bladed knife that looked like a standard kitchen knife, but then opted for something else. He ran his hands over some smaller implements that seemed to come from a surgical kit, intended for small precise cutting. Finely though he grabbed what looked like a commando knife. He came over to her while she harnessed the terror inside her as weaponized energy. Running the sharp blade across her cheek, he made a small cut drawing just enough blood to make it glisten red on the blade. He did the same thing across the top of her chest, making a slightly longer, but superficial cut so that blood trickled down the top of her left breast.

Finally, he took the knife and cut off the zip tie on her left leg, pushing her knee aside. Now her left leg was free, and she slowly slipped her right wrist out of the zip tie, preparing for action. The smirk on his face was disgusting. His breath a vile mixture of cheap tobacco, bad coffee, and poor oral hygiene. He was play acting a soldier, but he was nothing of the sort. She had seen better men than him not make it through tough commando training. His touch revolted her. He unbuckled and then dropped his trousers down to his knees, pushed her left leg to the side and then he was suddenly on top of her.

Summoning all her energy, she focused it into her left knee slamming it into his testicles, stunning him. The arrogance of his brutality and his underestimation of women was about to be his undoing.

He came at her again, in a rage, but also in significant pain. This time she brought all of her upper body strength and smashed him in the nose with one open palms, breaking his nose and sending blood everywhere. The advantage she now had was that she understood this was a battle to the end. He had assumed the end was a forgone conclusion.

Simultaneously she freed her right hand, as he doubled over, and she sent her index and middle fingers into both eye sockets, drawing blood from the left one. He kicked at her, knocking the chair over breaking the right front leg. The plastic leg flopped around, strapped to her leg, but the bulk of the chair was now simply attached to her left wrist with the zip tie.

He clutched his left eye with one hand and his groin with the other, both in too much pain for him to worry about his nose and now Azunna swung the chair at his head. The pain he was in had him off balance and the chair struck him at just the right angle, knocking him down. He struck his head hard on the concrete floor and leaving him unconscious.

Grabbing the commando knife, she cut herself free of the remaining zip ties and the remnants of the chair. She could see his chest rise and fall, and she jabbed the knife into the side of his neck, blood started to trickle out and then became more of a steady flow, until his chest stopped moving. A poetic end for him she imagined.

Her clothes were largely intact, and she dressed quickly. Lastly pulling on and lacing the black Jane boots she bought the day they recruited her. She performed a functions check on her pistol, and then placed it back in her high-ride holster.

The MP7 also appeared undamaged, and with three full magazines.

"Sloppy, sloppy, sloppy," she thought. Activating the IR scope, she could see it worked, and the suppressor had no moving parts. From the door, she aimed it back at the body of her late tormentor.

She pulled the trigger twice. Pfft, Pfft. Two bullets went into the corpse with no sound. Yes, all in perfect working order. Now to get out of this room.

Outside the two guards had imagined their NCO having their way with this woman who, if they understood correctly, claimed to be a British intelligence officer. A woman? A *black* woman? Nothing in their experience led them to believe any of that could be true.

Not knowing if there was some sort of specific signal to open the door Azunna decided she would simply knock. She lined herself up next to the door opening, brought the MP7 to her shoulder aimed at what she judged to be about head height and then reached out and knocked loudly.

She heard the steel bar slide back, her heart beating quickly but under control. As the door started to open inwards, she exhaled, a head was suddenly in view, and she pulled the trigger twice.

Two 4.6x30mm bullets travelled through the first soldier's skull. At point blank range they did not slow down enough to shatter in his skull but shattered in the concrete wall behind him.

Azunna stepped over his body to see the other soldier fleeing down the hall. He was a good fifteen metres away from her when those two bullets impacted, the first striking his right shoulder and disintegrating bone and muscle. The second bullet struck him in the head with the upper right quadrant of the skull completely disappearing.

All the poured concrete that was intended to protect the tormentors had been nothing but the muffling of their own demise. Because nobody else in the building had heard a sound.

Chapter Twenty-Three

Stepping over the body of the second soldier who had almost made it to the staircase, Azunna looked up. The stairs made four right turns before emerging on the ground floor. She moved methodically but quickly, figuring if someone was on the staircase, they would have come down to investigate the noise. Slowly she opened the door and emerged in what she could only call a mud room. Looking to her right was a door leading to the outside. It was dark but she could see the glimmer of sunrise. Dawn was approaching.

Turning left she emerged into the kitchen. No one was there and it was too early for morning meal preparation. Azunna had neither the time nor the resources to conduct a complete sweep of the house. She had to locate al-Assad, finish it, and be on her way. Exiting the kitchen to the left there was a concrete back staircase. The MP7 held high and ready with the night vision scope activated she moved slowly up the stairs, slowly because slow is smooth and smooth is fast. The back stairs remerged into the hall she had been in when they found her the previous evening.

Had he gone to bed? Azunna dismissed that notion. Despite him seeming self-assured as he had walked out of the torture cell, she was sure her direct declaration of intent to kill him had unnerved him. Bullies and thugs were fundamentally insecure. She was sure she was in his head.

Looking to the far end of the hall, a door led to what she presumed was a study – it would be at the centre of the house looking down on the compound's courtyard. She could see a light emerging from underneath the door. Azunna turned off the night vision function on the scope, activated the red dot, and checked the Thuraya Satellite smartphone. She was down to 50% power but had a strong signal.

Chapter Twenty-Four

Maher al-Assad held a worldview typical of men. He was born and raised in a world designed for him. He was two years old when his father became dictator of Syria. No one would ever tell him no or lead him to think any of his desires should ever be unfulfilled. The only real disappointment in his life had been that when his brother Basel had been killed in a car crash in 1994, his other brother Bashir became the heir apparent. Despite Maher's extensive military training and connections, his father deemed his too much of a hot head to run the country. That is when Maher connected with and became an operative for Abigor Legion. And a lucrative endeavour it had been.

Running an army division in a combat zone while also managing a large drug distribution network was time intensive especially for micro-manager like Assad. He poured himself a cup of tea as she shuffled through the various reports he demanded every day. Everything from army patrol schedules to drug production and shipping plans. It was hard to tell where one endeavour ended an another began.

He took a sip of tea and lit a cigarette. He perused some of the interrogation reports. Those questioned ranged from simple farmers who were in the wrong place at the wrong time but made suitable examples as "enemies of the state" even though they had probably done nothing wrong. Terror works by keeping everyone off balance. Then there were those who were caught trying to steal from his drug smuggling operation. They were made a quick example of after all the information had been extracted from them.

Sitting back, he exhaled a stream of smoke and wondered about this woman they had captured. Surely she was some sort of lone wolf, he thought. He could not imagine that he had made himself the target of the British or any other government. No matter, he had his top integrator on it. She would tell all, Assad was quite sure, before she succumbed to the tortures.

Azunna moved to the left side of the hall so that the door would provide some cover as she entered the room.

Assad's bigger fear was not death, it was torture at the hand of his brother's forces after determining his treachery. He could conceive of people wanting information from him, he knew he was valuable. What he could not conceive was that he would be simply eliminated and that a woman had been sent to do it.

Now at the end of the hall, Azunna slowly turned the knob and allowed the door to slide gently open. She took three steps and was in the centre of the room, MP7 to her shoulder. The nice thing about concrete floors was that why did not squeak.

Time seemed to slow down – Maher started to rise from his chair and speak. A look of confusion on his face.

"How did you ge . . . "

Pfft. Pfft. Pfft.

Three 4.6x30mm rounds struck him in the upper chest. The bullets disintegrated, creating a huge wound cavity, disintegrating his heart, and lungs so quickly that nary a sound was heard. He fell back, the force making him hit the wall and then forward onto the desk, where his body slowly rolled onto the floor. Azunna pulled out the phone and opened the message function.

Dealer is dead. Photo to follow.

Assad's body had collapsed on the floor, face down. Azunna used her boot for leverage under his right shoulder or what remained of it, rolling him onto his back. She reached down and straightened his face, pulled the phone back out, opened the camera function, and snapped several quick photos. She was sure one would be good enough for the facial recognition software. She quickly added the best three to the chat. They seemed to take forever, and she stared at the phone waiting for the word "delivered" and then for the word "read."

Tickner was the first to respond.

Scanning now.

Tickner had linked his phone to his computer, so the photo was instantly there. It was fortunate that photo recognition software and the analysis did not need to be done on the secure systems.

C texted.

> *Report.*

>> *Green on ammo. Green on coms. Red on transportation.*

Mills chimed in.

> *Do you need extraction?*

>> *No.*

Three dots appeared. And then disappeared. Everyone was waiting. Tickner finally came back online.

> *Five-point match. Confirm Maher al-Assad is dead.*

> *Well done. Get out of there Azunna.*

>> *On my way.*

Chapter Twenty-Five

Azunna took a quick look around the room. Dawn was breaking and no one else was stirring, but she knew she did not have a lot of time. Spying a leather messenger bag, she grabbed the laptop and several sheaves of paper, shoved them in the bag and slung it over her left shoulder. She made for the exit.

As she came to the end of the office, she noticed a gun cabinet to the right.

Never too much firepower right now. Looking in she found an AKS-74U and several spare magazines. She put one magazine in the weapon and charged it, putting the three spares in the leather bag. She slung the carbine over her right shoulder and made her way back to the rear staircase.

Looking out the kitchen window she saw a row of vehicles, mostly Army vehicles and nondescript SUVs, and she saw a G-Wagon. *That must be Assad's.*

A key cabinet at the end of the kitchen revealed the keys for the cars and other rooms. The key fob for the G-Wagon also had a remote starter.

Assuming the car would not arouse much inspection until people knew Assad was dead, she decided to make a dash for it.

Matte black with gold accents, oversized tires, a large brush guard, and tinted windows all the way around, Azunna calculated she needed to stay just barely ahead of the news she had created. She slipped out the back door and down three steps. The sun had fully crested and was now an orange orb in the sky, rays bouncing off the lightly blowing sand. With daylight here, her time was up.

She pressed the remote start and the Mercedes 8-cylinder roared to life. She then unlocked the vehicle, and the lights blinked twice.

It was ten metres to the vehicle – she made it in four long bounds.

Popping the door open she tossed the bag and the AK in the passenger seat, keeping the MP7 strapped across her chest. She put the key in the ignition to keep it from going dead, locked the doors, and plugged her dying phone into the charger.

The starting of the car had alerted the gate guards. Usually, but not always, Assad travelled in a caravan. The guards may have been in the most elite unit in the Syrian Arab Army, but they were still privates on gate guard duty. Who were they to question the Division Commander as he drove out? It was his car, no one else would dare drive it without his permission.

The guards began to manually open the gate, the big steel swinging doors each requiring two men to open them.

Azunna drove quickly, but not erratically towards the gate trying to arouse no suspicion. The right gate was fully open but the left one was still opening.

"Come on, come on," she said to herself. "Open up." She could just about get through, but putting her foot down now would open her up to suspicion.

Inside the villa, a voice screamed. The cook had brought coffee to Assad's office and found what was left of him. She threw a window open.

"The General is dead! Someone killed the Chief!"

In the armoured SUV, Azunna could hear none of that. She did though see the left gate stop moving, and the right gate begin to close.

"Time to go."

She gunned the big German SUV. Threading the space between the gates she managed to clear the entrance, but in doing so she scraped the left side of the vehicle from bumper to bumper, shearing off the left side mirror.

"Wasn't going to use that anyway," she said to herself, thinking of Ceylan with a smile.

Two of the guards ran after her, raising their AK-105s and firing a fusillade, but the bullets that did hit the vehicle fell away uselessly as the armour did its job.

It was less than fifty kilometres to a place where she could cross back into Turkish-held territory. She still hoped to make it clandestinely but making it was the most important thing.

Azunna grabbed the phone, selected Messenger, and used the speech to text function.

"Ceylan. Mission complete. En route rendezvous."

The transmission time seemed interminable. Waiting, waiting, waiting. Finally, that disembodied voice came back with the information. "Delivered." Then the voice said, "Read."

Soon the voice said, "Ceylan has sent a message. Would you like to hear it?"

"Play message."

"Ceylan's message says, 'Acknowledged. Etta?' Would you like to reply?"

"Etta?" Azunna did not understand the word? Then it came to her, and she experienced a moment of frustration. "ETA? How the fuck am I supposed to know?" Here she was racing across the Syrian high desert in a stolen Syrian General's SUV, who by the way she had just killed, and her contact is acting like she can hang out at the local coffee spot until the last minute. She can bloody well wait there.

"One hour," she said into the phone.

Three dots. Then a thumbs up emoji.

Azunna kept cruising across the high desert at high speed.

In the distance, she could see what appeared to be a Syrian Arab Army make-shift checkpoint. She slowed down.

***

Just as the short-wave radio had given law enforcement the advantage over crooks fleeing the scene of a crime, so too had cell phone towers extended that range. The real controlling factor of course was the quality of the information provided.

The 4th Armoured Division patrol consisted of two Soviet-era UAZ-469 light jeeps and a total of eight soldiers – a lieutenant, an NCO, and six privates. The unit was considered an elite formation, but in the Syrian context, this simply meant their loyalty to the regime was unquestioned, and as a result, they received some perks, including some better equipment. In this case, they had better clothing, boots, and new carbines. They were not highly trained special operations forces.

The lieutenant had simply followed in this father's footsteps. Father had retired a lieutenant colonel and had a modest house near the coast south of Latakia. That is what the lieutenant aspired to as well.

He looked at his phone and could not wrap his mind around the series of text messages he had received.

> *General Maher al-Assad has been killed.*
>
> *The General's personal vehicle has been stolen by the killer.*
>
> *All units should use violent action against the vehicle as soon as it is located.*

The lieutenant was not looking to be a hero, and he was no fool. The constant power plays, assignations, and back-stabbings kept everyone in Syria on their toes. On the one hand, the text messages could be true, meaning he would be safe in following those orders.

On the other hand, unseen forces might be trying to use him to kill the general and foment a coup on behalf of someone else. The lieutenant did not even care, he would pledge fealty to whoever was running the show. The problem was he did not know what was true. The very last thing he wanted to be was on the wrong side of a power struggle.

Like all weak men, the Syrian Army lieutenant was indecisive. He decided to conduct a mini-parade formation, figuring that if al-Assad was driving their way he would appreciate the honour. If it was not Assad, then they could let the vehicle pass and hit as it drove away, hoping that whoever was driving would simply accept any rendered honours as their due. He contemplated telling his soldiers about the messages he had received but decided against it. The last thing he wanted was them thinking for themselves, because one might decide to do something they could not walk back from. He lined his soldiers up on the side of the road in two ranks, the NCO one pace in front, he in the middle of the road.

Azunna could not believe what she was seeing. "What the fuck is this? The bloody palace?"

A running gun battle up to the border was the last thing she needed. She reached across to the passenger seat as she slowed the lumbering G-Wagon and grabbed the Russian-made carbine, laying it across her lap, the barrel pointed at the driver's side door.

She rolled to a stop right in front of the formation, the tinted glass hiding everything. The six soldiers and the NCO were standing rigidly at attention. The lieutenant had been in the middle of the road waiving her down. As he trotted up to the car door, a big stupid grin on his face she shouldered the Russian-made carbine. Meanwhile, he came to attention and rendered a salute.

She hit the down button on the window.

"Major General al Assad, it is a great pleas . . ."

The carbine made two distinctive cracks, as the bullets left the weapon and entered the skull of the hapless Syrian Army officer.

The NCO and soldiers, here principally because of their loyalty to the regime, took time to process exactly what was happening. Of all the threats that could have come from a visit by a member of the inner circle that ran Syria, simply being gunned down was not one they expected.

Moving the selector lever to full auto, twenty rounds spat out, most of them finding targets in the seven men. Three were killed instantly, while the other four were so seriously injured they could not follow her. All would bleed to death before Azunna was back in Turkey. She rolled up the window, put a fresh magazine in the carbine and hit the gas.

Chapter Twenty-Six

Borders are porous. Despite what politicians might say, and what authoritarians might do stopping the flow of people across international borders is nearly impossible. The East Germans had tried to completely shut off a small internal city border and ultimately failed. North Koreans routinely flee to China, and despite the promises of populist politicians in the United Kingdom and the United States, people seeking a better life continued to flow across the English Channel and the U.S.-Mexico border. In comparison, the line between regime-held Syria and Turkish-controlled Syria was virtually non-existent.

    Azunna had covered the remaining twenty-five kilometres in less than an hour. The sun was well up on this Saturday morning, a normal workday in Syria, though of course, nothing had been normal in Syria in over ten years. She saw two battered trucks making some sort of delivery trip but nothing else. Her Garmin directed her to the right grid coordinate. She checked her satellite phone. A text from Ceylan.

In position.

Azunna turned off the road and stopped by the last ditch that was just too much for the gaudy German SUV.. She looked up at the low hill in the distance knowing Ceylan was just on the other side. She estimated it was going to be about a five-kilometres yomp – maybe forty minutes?

She grabbed the bag of papers and slung that again over her left shoulder. And then the AK over her right. She looked at the G-wagon in all its gaudiness. She was tempted to do something dramatic like torch it but decided that it would be her backup plan if she did not make it to the other side of this hill, but she was hoping that by abandoning the vehicle she would frustrate any attempts to find her.

It was warming up. She unzipped her jacket to try to get a little more air in. She was tired, bruised, and dehydrated.

Adjusting her sunglasses, she was off. "Tally ho."

She texted Ceylan.

On my way.

The rock-strewn desert was doubly dry. Climate change was really doing a number on the Fertile Crescent. Azunna focused on her pace, avoiding getting her ankle stuck in rocks. *Slow is smooth, smooth is fast.*

At this point, she was less concerned about the Syrians than she was the Turks. A British national with no documents and carrying two firearms would be hard to explain. She was not sure she could count on her NATO experience to talk her way past a random Turkish Army patrol. In fact, she was quite sure she would not. Best to avoid them altogether.

Everything was aching in her at this point. She needed water, sleep, some Motrin, and a damn good cup of coffee. The crest of the hill was a mere five-hundred metres away. She should be able to see Ceylan when she reached the top of the hill. She texted her again.

> Almost there. Let me know
> when you can see me.

Three dots. Then nothing. Three dots again. Then nothing.
Azunna became momentarily concerned.
Three more dots. The thumbs up emoji.
Finally.
Azunna crested the hill. She looked down and approximately a kilometre away was the silver quad cab Land Rover pickup. Ceylan waived.

Azunna decided to ditch the AK and the extra magazines. At this point, they would add to problems rather than solve them. Tossing those aside the weight in the bag was immediately lighter.

It was literally all downhill from here. She took it easy for the first eight-hundred metres or so, slipping and sliding in the dirt as much as she was walking until it finally levelled out. She broke into a trot for the last two-hundred metres stopping at the truck.

The women bumped each other's fists.

"How did it go?" asked Ceylan.

"Oh, you know how it is. A little bumped and bruised, but no worse for wear."

They threw the bag in the front seat and secured Azunna's pistol and the MP7 in a hidden compartment under the passenger seat.

Ceylan hopped in the driver's seat and Azunna in the passenger seat. Ceylan handed her a big bottle of sparkling water.

"Just what I need. Thanks."

"So glad to see you again Kiana."

"Not half as glad as I am to see you." To say that Azunna was relieved would have been an understatement. This mission had put everything she learned and experienced to the test. She thought of Phoebe, she had lived to fight another day. And Ngozi, she would be able to see her again, Azunna pulled out the phone and texted the group again.

> In contact with our Turkish
> friends. Mission complete.

Ceylan turned pushed in the clutch and turned the key and the truck sprang to life. She placed the vehicle in gear, released the clutch, pulled a tight turn, and they headed off to the proper Turkish border.

Chapter Twenty-seven

C began without preamble. "We have a new mission for you. Strictly speaking, this is not a Chrysalis mission, but we need someone in the room when a major intelligence debrief occurs in Poland. You will attend in your role as a Royal Marine Major, you should not advertise that you work with the Firm now."

C continued, leaning forward on his large mahogany desk. "A major cache of documents, computers, weapons, and other things were discovered by a Ukrainian Special Operations unit working with us and the cousins. Have you heard of the Zimmer Group?"

"Of course. Nasty group of Russian private military contractors. Really just an extension of the Russian government, I should think. Brutal in Syria and in a variety of places in Africa. I think they have been used in Ukraine as well."

"Quite. Glad to see you have the time to keep up on the latest intelligence. In any event the initial exploitation teams are almost done, and now a debrief has been scheduled. What we are specifically interested in is related to your Syria mission. Is the Zimmer Group working as part of the Abigor Legion? We think so, based on where some of their operations have been taking place, including with the Taliban from the before the fall of Kabul. Your job is to see if we can confirm and connect these organizations."

Azunna's discovery of the Abigor Legion while in Syria had been a major coup. Major in the sense that there appeared to be an international criminal or terrorist network that no one in western intelligence had ever heard of until Azunna's mission to Syria. All the Five Eyes nations had drawn a complete blank. Moreover, the analysts were starting to stich information indicating known bad actors were part of something even bigger and more nefarious than previously thought.

"An A400 is leaving Brize Norton tonight at 0700. You need to be on it. You will link up with a new case and support officer, former Army, served in the Royal Ghurkha', did Afghanistan as well. I believe you two have met. His name is Khumalo, Sam Khumalo."

***

Azunna took the air stairs two at a time climbing into the plane. She had just made it in time to RAF Brize Norton. Once she had started travelling to London on a regular basis she has stashed an extra set of uniforms at Ngozi's flat, so after leaving Vauxhall Cross she made a quick trip there on her way to the airfield.

Ever since the invasion of Ukraine in February the United Kingdom had been providing all sorts of support to the Ukrainians fighting off the Russian invasion. The A400 fleet particularly LXX Squadron had been in constant motion. Moving supplies such as artillery to Poland for further transport to the front and moving Ukrainian soldiers to the UK for training. They were joining a shipment of 155mm and 105mm artillery shells to feed the American-supplied M777 and British-supplied L119 howitzers the Ukrainians were using with deadly effect.

"Kiana. Bloody hell. It's good to see you again."

"Sam." Azunna was decidedly cooler. No one had talked with her about the kidnapping in Wales. Not Elisa, not Mills, not C. While she had concluded that had been part of the training evolution, it had never been confirmed. She was convinced that Sam had played some role in the whole thing even if it had been a training exercise. She put her bag in the overhead and took the seat next to him.

"I'm glad to see you are OK. I was worried about you."

"I'm sure."

"What? Don't you believe me?"

"Considering this is the first time I have seen you since that morning . . . well, call me sceptical."

Azunna was not sure what to think. They had got on well at dinner and the sex was great, but they had barely started on their spontaneous trip to the beach when the kidnapping happened.

"I will have you know that even as they dropped me off at the pub and warned me your life would be in danger if I called the police, I went straight to the local constabulary despite the threats. I even convinced the police to accompany me back to the site where they ambushed us, no mean feat. I only had your name and we had known each other less than twenty-four hours. What else did I have to go on?" Khumalo was very matter of fact, not pleading. He was still very much interested in Azunna, but if she wanted to think he had not done enough or was somehow involved, she could just sod off.

"It was only after I received a visit from someone in the office related to my application that it was made clear to me that you were safe."

It all made sense. Azunna would have done the same. Had the shoe been on the other foot, she would have had no information about him. She thought maybe she could consider another chance. She decided to see how this mission went.

They both settled into their seats. It was a three-hour flight to Poland, but the country was only one hour ahead of British Standard Time. They needed to be ready to go to work when they landed. The jump seats they had managed to secure where not going to be part of the solution.

Slowly they settled into getting to know one another a little more. Khumalo doing most of the talking at first. This was his first mission for the SIS, he had been entirely straightforward that night in Wales. He was brought on as a case officer with an emphasis on logistical support and a side of analysis.

Khumalo was from Manchester and read history there before heading off to Sandhurst. He had been commissioned a subaltern in the Duke of Lancaster's Regiment and honed his craft as an infantry officer. When he was promoted to captain, he volunteered for the Royal Ghurkha Rifles and sent to Nepal to learn Nepali. A tour in the British Forces Brunei with deployments to Afghanistan satisfied that itch in him and he returned to the UK looking for a slightly easier life than being an infantryman in the field.

Azunna shared her military career history as well, that she had been at Oxford, and her sister was studying law in London. She mentioned that her parents died when she was young and left it at that. She did not go into the details of the Afghanistan mission.

About an hour after take-off the cabin lights were dimmed, and they decided to get what sleep they could.

***

The Royal Air Force A400 touched down at Lask Air Base, four hundred kilometres from Ukraine at noon. Azunna and Khumalo grabbed their bags and made their way to the expeditionary terminal that processed hundreds of people per day. Forces personnel, contractors, diplomats, and spies, everyone needed to run a modern-day war.

At check-in, they were told the briefing would begin at 1400 and were directed to the secure auditorium. After inquiry, there were also told where they could get some chow, since neither of them had eaten since the evening before. They found the dining facility, ate their fill, and were seated in the back of the secure briefing room by 1400.

The building was like all the Sensitive Compartmented Information Facilities (or SCIFs) Azunna had been in before.

A series of specially constructed shipping containers designed to avoid electronic access or leakage. All electronics, phones, tablets, even some modern watches, were checked outside. The room was lit with a florescent light that was like nothing in nature, the walls were white, and the small tables with uncomfortable chairs had room for about fifty people. There were at least sixty in this room and the air conditioning was working overtime.

C had probably envisioned them looking at raw intelligence, but what they had in fact come to see was what appeared to be a one hundred-slide PowerPoint presentation. Azunna and Khumalo looked at each other as the first slide appeared. There were no handouts and all they could do was roll their eyes. This was going to make the flight here look thrilling.

One of the features of these Top-Secret presentations was that they always had a "water is wet" quality about them. By the time raw intelligence was gathered and distilled down for decision-makers, so much of it was overcome by events or seemed to be common knowledge.

That is why when slide seventeen went up, Azunna, who had been struggling to stay awake suddenly sat straight up and was all ears. Looking back out from the slide was a photograph of the Talib commander Colley had killed more than a year ago. The slide notes indicated he commanded a "Legion" that analysts had concluded was that was somehow connected to the Zimmer Group based on the documents. This was the first anyone had ever suggested that Zimmer was connected to the Taliban.

The next slide was even more interesting, if also more cryptic. The face was blank as they had no known photograph, but it was captioned "the Austrian" and mentioned the "Gantz Legion." This person appeared to be connected to the poppy smuggling business the Taliban used to fund much of their operations. It was assumed this mysterious "Austrian" was a foreign recruit or an Afghan who had returned from living in Europe. It also had references to Zimmer providing security for these shipments once they left Talib control. This would have been an easy money-making venture for Zimmer.

Finally, the third slide in this series identified several camps in Eastern Ukraine that Zimmer was using, allegedly for logistics operations. It was difficult to connect the dots at this point.

So, C had been correct. The Talib and Zimmer were connected to the Abigor Legion. Between al-Assad and the Taliban and who knows who else, they could not have chosen a more apt name than a Great Duke of Hell. This Austrian must be the Dr. Gantz she encountered in Syria.

Azunna's hand shot up. The briefer, an American Special Forces major, looked annoyed, he had asked people to save their questions till the end. But apparently in a one-hundred-slide deck that might be asking too much.

"Yes? Our British friend."

"Major Kiana Azunna, Royal Marines. Have any of those sites been raided? Or is there a plan to?"

"No. We don't think this information is definitive enough to warrant such a commitment of limited resources."

"Thank you."

Khumalo leaned over, very intrigued, and whispered, "What's going on?"

"The bloke on slide seventeen was the target on my last mission in Afghanistan. Those three slides are why we came, and the Americans aren't going to do anything about it."

"Are you sure? How can you be sure?"

"Let me bring you into the bigger picture."

"That might help."

"I went to Syria to terminate the command of Maher al-Assad. While doing that, I learned of the existence of the Abigor Legion. A criminal organization run from Austria by a Dr. Werner Gantz. It seems based on that briefing; this Legion is connected to the Taliban and the Zimmer group." Azunna took a long deep breath. "We need to connect with C and see if we can get to that site on slide twelve. Let's go."

Khumalo hesitated. He was new to this intelligence business and as an Army officer, he was accustomed to doing what he was told. And he had been told to sit through the briefing. But Azunna seemed certain.

Once outside the SCIF they retrieved their phones, and Azunna opened her secure messaging app, texting both C and Mills.

> The Legion is in Ukraine. The Zimmer Group is definitely involved, and it looks like they are also connected to the Taliban. A photo of my last

> target in Afghanistan was found in a cache. They are working with that Dr. Gantz. Sam and I need to visit a remote site here. Can you get us support?

Mills was the first to reply.

> *We really don't have the time or the assets to help. It's very high risk.*

Tickner with his usual cautiousness joined in.

> *Are you sure? Can't you return and we can sort it out?*

> No. We need to visit this site and soon.

> *You don't have the equipment. Is Sam going? He wasn't recruited for field work.*

> Time is critical here. We might not get this chance again and if Zimmer finds we are on to them they may burn the whole thing down. Sam will be fine.

Azunna had proven her mettle in Syria. She was halfway to being a confirmed Chrysalis Program Officer. C and Mills looked at each. Then C picked up the phone.

***

Azunna and Khumalo approached the Ukrainian Air Force Mi-8 Hip at a 45-degree angle from the nose. They were kitted out with some American body armour, a couple of standard issue Ukrainian AKSs-74s, and picked up an escort of Ukrainian special operation soldiers, both veterans of training with the British SAS and American Special Forces. C clearly had some pull with the right people when he needed it.

This was going to be a quick in-and-out mission. Azunna and Khumalo, along with their Ukrainian escorts, were going to hit the building she had noted on Slide twelve, gather up any intelligence, documents, computers, maybe even a member of the Legion they could, and then return to base. They should be on the ground no longer than twenty minutes. One of the Mi-8s would provide security from overhead while the other carried them to the site.

The lead helicopter with Azunna and Khumalo on board, were piloted by two experienced special operations professionals and as soon as all were aboard, they began the process of taxiing and taking off from Lask's heavy traffic pattern.

All four of them, Azunna, Khumalo, and the two Ukrainian shooters were wired into the communications system and Azunna briefed them on her plan to infiltrate the building and search it for information. A brief look at satellite imagery indicated the helicopter could set down less than one hundred metres from the building, just across a small road. One Mi-8 would orbit the site while the other would set the team down and then join the gunship in a security orbit. The Ukrainian soldiers would hold security at the front door.

The helicopter flight was longer than the flight to Poland. From Lask they flew to a base neat Lyiv for fuel, then on to Kyiv, before landing in Kharkiv. From here they would launch to the target. The multi-stage journey was arduous but necessary from the security perspective. Even though the Ukrainians had made significant progress repelling the Russian invasion on the ground, the air space was still contested. The long helicopter ride, low to the earth, reduced their risk of detection and intercept.

While they refuelled in Kharkiv, Azunna, Khumalo, and the two Ukrainians went into a small hut to review the overhead satellite imagery and walked through the plan. Each one was trusting the other's professionalism.

It was less than eighty kilometres to the site. They launched from Kharkiv and flew at less than one hundred metres and thirty minutes later as they arrived at their destination.

The pilot came over the intercom, "Ninety seconds."

Azunna tensed. Going into action that was an automatic reflex for her, but last time she had been in this situation her best mate had died in the extraction while her most trusted advisor had been killed because she changed the plan. In her mind everyone was getting back on this helicopter and back to Kharkiv. This was for Phoebe and Colley.

The crew chief slid the door open and took up a position behind the second machine gun.

"Sixty seconds."

The half-moon provided just enough light to see. Azunna could tell exactly which building they needed to hit. After a year of war, even those that were pro-Russian kept to their homes when helicopters landed. So, unless they were going into an armed camp, and the pilot would be able to determine that through the Forward-Looking Infrared Radar, there should be no resistance.

"Thirty seconds."

The helicopter was rapidly descending in the thin mountain air, the four unplugged from the comms system and prepared to exit the aircraft.

"Fifteen seconds." The pilot's words were lost to the noise of the engine.

The tires of the helicopter had just brushed the surface when Azunna leapt out the door and was at a full spring with the other three in pursuit. By the time the team was halfway to the building, the transport joined the gunship in the security orbit. It had taken them less than thirty seconds to cross the hard dirt ground and throw themselves against the concrete block wall of the target building. Except for the sounds of the orbiting helicopters, it was deathly quiet, and their arrival, while probably not unnoticed, was not motivating any response.

They waited a full minute before Azunna signalled Khumalo, they opened the door, sliced the room like a pie as experienced room clearers do, and then entered. Azunna pulled out her small, red-lensed flashlight and began a more thorough scan of the room.

It was a combined, living and working area. Opposite the door was a cooking and eating area, to the left she clocked some discarded carpets and pillows and a few rickety chairs, and to the right, a small wooden desk, piled with papers.

As she rifled through the papers, Khumalo swept through the rest of the room. She stuffed the laptop she found in her musette bag and flipped through the documents. Thank goodness English had become the lingua franca of international terrorists and criminals. This was the mother lode. There were references to quantities of poppies shipped, money transfers, references to "AL" or "The Legion", and an elusive Doctor Gantz.

One of the Ukrainian special ops troopers leaned in the door. "Car coming."

"Let's go. Get the helicopter down here."

The Ukrainian operative radioed the helicopter and prepared two moves to the landing point. Khumalo exited the building with Azunna in trail. It had started to gently rain and Azunna saw the bright lights of two small trucks racing up the road towards their position. Out of the corner of her eye, she saw a small child wandering towards the road. For a split second, she was blinded, back in a place of darkness and fear. As the Ukrainian soldiers and Khumalo made their way to the helicopter that was now less than one hundred metres from setting down, Azunna suddenly broke towards the child.

Azunna scooped the child up like a rugby ball, never breaking stride, cleared the road, and set the child down just as the trucks screeched to a halt. The child was crying and screaming, but Azunna had no time nor even an inclination to soothe her, she just knew that they would not be run over by a car, at least on this night.

She sprinted to the helicopter and the rest of the team pulled her in as the pilot applied full military power to the Klimov TV3-117MT turboshaft engines. The people in the trucks had started to fire their AKs at the landing transport, but the door gunner used the General-Purpose Machine Gun to suppress them as the Hip made tree height and departed the area. The passengers held on as the pilot flew nap-of-the-earth until he was sure he could avoid errant gunfire or RPGs.

Everything had happened so fast that only Khumalo was fully aware of Azunna's brief detour to pick up the child, and right now did not seem to be the right time to talk about it. The Ukrainians had done their job, they were glad to be heading back to Kharkiv with all their charges intact. The pilots, while not quite mission complete, they needed to analyse what they found, it would need something truly unusual to happen for the mission to fail on their account.

Azunna breathed a sigh of relief. They had done it. Even with the kid in the road, they executed the plan as briefed, and they escaped with their lives and more information. Phoebe and Colley would have been proud. She was quite sure.

The helicopters touched down in Kyiv just after 2300. A quick refuel and they were on the way to Lyiv. In Lyiv Azunna and Khumalo returned the borrowed hardware to the Ukrainians who assured them they would see it all back to their rightful owners. Another quick refuel and the bird was off for Lask.

Azunna let London know they had quite the intelligence haul and asked Mills to have a vehicle waiting for them when they arrived. The A400 was departing at 0500, which would put them in at Brize Norton a little after 0500 British Standard Time, a weird coincidence. They might even have time for a spot of breakfast on the way back to London.

Chapter Twenty-Eight

The mission to Ukraine, while not strictly a Chrysalis mission, had been more successful than anyone could have dreamed. The documents and computer she and Khumalo secured proved to be a treasure trove of information about the Abigor Legion, its structure, and purpose. There were plenty of clues as to its reach and the people who were being victimized by the Legionnaires. The analysts and targeters at the Firm were busy determining interdiction plans and nominating people for the Chrysalis list. The Abigor Legion were clearly guns for higher to the highest bidder but also intent on sowing chaos for their own purpose, because they could.

What they knew so far about the Legion was this: The group had a presence in Afghanistan, at least before the fall of Kabul; and it appeared to be headed by this Dr. W. Gantz, the mysterious Austrian Azunna had seen in Syria. The Syrian drug operation made sense alongside the Taliban drug smuggling, and it seemed like the Zimmer Group was being used for security and probably murder. To the extent the Abigor Legion had any goal other than making money and chaos, well, that still to be ascertained.

In the several months since returning from Ukraine, Azunna was splitting her time between her apartment in Poole and staying with Khumalo at his flat in Islington. She had left enough clothing at his place that she could ride her motorcycle from Poole to London on pleasant days and not worry about luggage. They had not defined their relationship with terms like boyfriend, girlfriend, lover, or partner, but she had her own key to the flat and they were exclusive.

Ngozi as closing in on graduation and wanted to take up the banner of the human rights questions in Nigeria. She wanted to travel back there, even though she had not been in the country since she was two years old and remembered none of it. The land of her ancestors intrigued her, and she wanted to get to know it. The Azunna daughters had both inherited their parents' desire to make the world a better place. It was just playing out differently for the two of them.

Azunna had been back to Nigeria as part of Royal Marine training teams working with the Nigerian Army and Navy but spent little time in the communities. For Azunna returning was a decidedly mixed experience. On the one hand, she had positive memories of the place such as visiting various relatives that doted on her and Ngozi; on the other hand, she could vividly recall the worried expression on her mother's face, the scent of Chanel No. 5, the sudden bright light – then it was all a blur. The crash. Being lifted out of the car and set on the side of the road in the rain, her baby sister placed in her arms. It all merged together.

She knew that Nigeria was not inherently dangerous, but one did need to have their wits about them and needed to know where they could reliably get assistance, if needed. She worried about Ngozi's experience in navigating the world in a place like that. Maybe she just needed to arrange a trip for the two of them.

Which all brought her back to the office in Vauxhall Cross. Azunna hoped this meeting was going to result in some mission. Now that she had started to create a semi-regular life with Sam here in London, but she was ambivalent about getting truly established with the Chrysalis program and spending time away.

"Kiana, well done, very well done indeed." C was in a very good mood.

"Yes, Kiana, between the Syria mission and the intelligence you brought back from Ukraine, we understand a good deal more of what is going on in the world right now." Mills was feeling particularly chuffed, she was the one who had spotted Azunna as suited to this work.

C digressed. "Your family is originally from Nigeria, correct?"

"Yes. My grandfather was one of the key advisors to the Biafran government in the Igbo people's attempt for independence. When the war ended, he fled with his family, settling here in London. My parents established an NGO that was doing poverty alleviation work, with a focus in the southeast. They were killed in a traffic accident on the Port Harcourt Road back in 1997."

"How do you feel about going back?"

"It's fine. I have been on training missions there. No problem."

C studied her for a good twenty seconds. Her face was inscrutable. C did not appear convinced. He looked at Mills. An unspoken language shared between the two long-term colleagues suggested they thought Azunna was the right person for the next job.

"You know my history. Several missions training Nigerian Navy in littoral interdiction operations. The Nigerian Navy has some old US Coast Guard cutters, not state-of-the-art but serviceable enough. Drug smuggling and oil bunkering keep them busy enough."

"Socially?"

"You mean to see family? No." Azunna's tone of voice had changed. She understood that scrutiny of your personal life came with the job, but she was anxious to cut this off. Silence suddenly filled C's office, but it was clear Azunna was going to say no more. C finally decided to move on.

"Excellent. We pulled a thread in the material you found, and it seems the Abigor Legion, in addition to being a large drug smuggling operation, also has a large human trafficking operation. No surprise really. The two often go hand in glove."

"Godswill Uche. Heard of him?"

"Nigerian businessman? Oil services tycoon, right? All too well, I am afraid. I remember my parents talking about him.

Their NGO had clashed with his business on several occasions. How could I forget that name?

"Right. Well in addition to his legitimate businesses, he is big into oil bunkering, and we know now, human and drug smuggling. All on behalf of the Abigor Legion. The computer you brought back from Ukraine indicated that he was using charter aircraft to move poppy out of Afghanistan and moving Captagon from Syria as well. As you know, for many reasons, people across northern Sub-Saharan Africa have been on the move north. Desperate people looking for a better life. There are organized networks that do this, but Uche has taken this to a whole different level. He is using the planes and ships of his business to do it on an industrial scale. He is stocking brothels across Spain, Italy, and even here in Britain with young girls and sometimes boys who think they are getting scholarships to schools. They also end up in agricultural work across those countries."

"Do we have any idea of how he is pulling this off?" Azunna frowned. This seemed to be a very large and sophisticated operation that was being executed under the nose of most major western intelligence agencies. Outside, she noticed that the light grey London day was giving way to much darker clouds. The clear cube of an office along the Thames was much susceptible to the change in the weather. The sky matched Azunna's outlook on this whole thing.

Mills went on to detail the drug smuggling. Uche had one old Nigerian Airways A310 that could fly from Syria to Nigeria. He also chartered, although that word seemed to lend legitimacy to the nefarious activity, planes that moved poppy from Afghanistan, usually to Syria to combine with the Captagon. The planes under Nigerian contract had no problem receiving permission to overfly Iran.

Once the drugs were in Nigeria, it was easy enough to then ship them to other destinations around the world. Given that primary consumers for Captagon were not European and that raw poppy was often smuggled to nations with corrupt or less-than-effective security services, Nigeria made great sense as a hub. Which then led to the human smuggling.

Mills continued, "As you know, climate change and poverty have combined to put many people from the Sahel on the move. Human smuggling across the Med is big business, as is human smuggling across the Channel."

Not a week went by when the news wasn't plastered with pictures of Border Force boats stopping dinghies full of people from all over the world trying to make it to Britain. They came from all over the world – Eastern Europe, Asia, the Middle East, Africa – driven by war, famine, and the lack of economic opportunities, generally caused by a dearth good leadership and good governance. All the sins of mankind. And of course, sometimes the pictures the *Daily Mail* ran were their bodies washed up on shore.

"Uche has been able to land charter planes at obscure airports in the UK, Spain, and Italy and unload one hundred people at a time. When later questioned, customs and immigration officials swear the passengers had EU passports or the proper visas, but the records are completely non-existent after they depart the airport. Extensive investigation into the background of the officials reveals nothing odd in their finances or personal lives. Obviously, they might have missed something, but on a human smuggling operation this large it seems odd."

It did seem odd. Britain and the EU had very extensive visa vetting and issuance programs, even for tourists. They also charged a pretty penny for the adjudication, regardless of whether the applicant received the visa. Someone had clearly found a way to bypass that requirement.

C picked it up from there. "Based on the information from Ukraine, we sent several business inquiries from one of our cover companies pitching our logistical expertise. One of their representatives finally got back to us and they want to meet. You will go to Nigeria as a logistics expert from UXT Ltd. and try to determine what sort of business they are running. Learn what you can about where the victims are coming from, but more importantly, how are they moving all these people into the UK past Border Force. When you have all that, you will terminate Uche." C started to rise and head back behind his desk. "I'll leave the rest to you and Mills."

The women stood up. "Sir." They turned on their heels and were out the door.

They sat themselves in Mills' smaller, yet still transparent, office. Azunna was not sure she would ever get used to this.

"You will be met in Port Harcourt by Sam Khumalo. You seemed to work well together in Ukraine. He has been sent to Abuja as a temporary political officer at the High Commission."

This was a pleasant surprise, and Azunna was suddenly excited at the thought of working with Sam again. It occurred to her that Mills probably did not know she and Sam were seeing each other socially. She decided to keep that private for now.

"Seems straightforward enough. Sam and I do get on well. It will be good to work with him again." And to share a bed sooner than she had anticipated.

"So, as C mentioned, we have reached out to Uche's company soliciting logistics expertise for companies like the oil services business. We have indicated that our research shows they have an increased need for transportation services, and we are offering collaborative end-to-end solutions. All very corporate speak."

"Well done us."

Like so many people who have spent a good deal of time in the forces or even just government service, the vocabulary and syntax of the corporate world always sounded too smooth, too smooth by half.

"So, you will meet Sam in Port Harcourt. He will be there simply to introduce a great British company to a Nigerian company in need of services. Everything there will seem to be completely transparent. One of the High Commission's strategic objectives is to continue to build bilateral trade between our countries. Your cover with UXT is well-backstopped to the office in Chelsea just as it was in Syria. Anyone digging finds a company with all the bona fides and you are a recently hired ex-Royal Marine officer. As you know the best covers have the most truth to them. Your passport has already been sent to the Nigerian Embassy for a visa. That will be the biggest slow down. Good luck, Kiana."

***

That night Azunna had dinner with Ngozi. The clouds that darkened the offices in Vauxhall Cross finally turned into a regular downpour. Azunna wore her sensible Burberry trench coat as well as rubber Hunter Chelsea boots in a pale grey, and she carried an umbrella. The boots were not the perfect complement to her Navy-blue sheath dress, but her feet were dry and as an experienced infantry soldier, Azunna knew that dry feet were not a luxury, but a necessity.

Azunna wanted to make sure that her younger sister did nothing rash before Azunna returned from her mission to Nigeria. They met at a small Nigerian restaurant down in Peckham, near where they had lived growing up. They had left detailed instructions about schooling. The firm of solicitors had been above reproach when it came to their fiduciary duty. But the family they had lived with had not been quite as warm.

Their mother's distant cousin took the girls in because the stipend she received from the solicitors helped pay her bills. She did the minimum for the Azunna sisters, not abusing them, but also not giving them the attention, they really needed. The girls depended on each other, their school friends, and their teachers.

The restaurant Azunna walked into was upscale. It seemed every cuisine had gone upscale in some way or another. The ceiling was high, but not too high. The walls were decorated with a mix of traditional African art and contemporary paintings. London was a second home to so many creatives from across Africa that places like this had the pick of some of the best contemporary artists on the market. Of course, the pieces were all for sale, so there was a constant turnover. It was good business for the restaurant and the artist.

Ngozi arrived after Azunna, who was already at a table with a drink. She sipped her Rob Roy, essentially a Manhattan made with Scotch. When Phoebe and her father had introduced Azunna to the world of single malt Scotch, it was the gateway to whisky at large and all the cocktails one could make with it. Azunna raised her glass and silently toasted the memory of her friend.

As usual, Ngozi was late. Azunna blamed herself because she had always tried to take care of everything and therefore had left her sister with not enough responsibility. But Ngozi had good news and she could not wait to share it. Her long Barbour coat and bucket hat had repelled the rain, but unlike her sister, she had not learned the value of keeping her feet dry. Her red Converse low tops were soaking. She spied Azunna at their normal table at the back of the room just as the waiter was serving her second cocktail.

She approached breathlessly, only pausing long enough to order a glass of red wine from the waiter. Azunna rose and they greeted each other as sisters do.

Still shedding her coat, Ngozi could hold the news in no longer.

"Kiana, the Delta Restoration Committee has offered me an internship!" She could not contain herself. "I will be responsible for looking at how the oil companies and the Nigerian Government have been criminally responsible for this ecological disaster in Delta and River States. I think I can make a real difference there!"

"That's wonderful. I am proud of you. Do they have offices here in the city?"

"They do, but I would be going to Nigeria to start collecting data. I would be interviewing people whose lands and livelihoods have been damaged or destroyed by the oil industry."

The waiter arrived with her Ngozi's wine. "I'm starved. Same as always?"

"Of course."

They ordered jollof rice and beef suya. A favourite of theirs when they were sitting down for Nigerian food. They also ordered a bottle of Thavlin Signature, a red wine blend from Morocco.

Ngozi was excited and proud of herself. Like her older sister, she excelled in sixth form, working hard to get accepted to SOAS, one of the best law schools in the world when it came to comparative and international law. The Delta Restoration Committee was a group of committed people ready to take on the oil industry and their Nigerian government partners. They were serious and Ngozi was serious, it was the perfect fit. Kiana had been around the world in all sorts of dangerous places, and Ngozi saw no reason she could not do the same thing.

Azunna had trouble articulating exactly what her opposition to Ngozi travelling to Nigeria. Your average Briton would certainly perceive a level of danger that was wholly inaccurate. And although Azunna did not know much about the Delta Restoration Committee, she made the reasonable assumption they were not going to drop young people into south-eastern Nigeria with no support. No, this was deeper and more visceral.

"I am happy for you Ngozi. More than that, I am proud of everything you have accomplished. I just want to make sure you are fully prepared for that sort of trip." She hoped these words would put off what she knew must eventually come, a return to Nigeria for Ngozi. "I need to go back overseas for a few weeks. Maybe we can talk about it then and can come up with a plan for you to go there."

Ngozi had had enough. She exploded. "Why are you always trying to restrain me? You have travelled all around the world! To far more dangerous places and in far more dangerous circumstances!" Ngozi was red hot. "You were hurt so badly in Afghanistan you spent nearly a year in rehabilitation for goodness' sake. Your closest friends were killed! Why do you get to save the world? And I must stay here in London! Are you telling me to turn down this opportunity?"

Azunna took a deep breath. She had always tried to protect Ngozi. And it was all unravelling in front of her. For a brief moment, she saw that blinding light.

Ngozi stood up and threw her napkin on the table. "I will have you know, Kiana, I'm going to Nigeria. With or without your blessing. Not only am I going to for the Committee, but I am going to find the family we have there. I even have a visa!"

"Ngozi, would you please sit down." Azunna was trying to be calming, but it was not working. The news she had a visa was surprising. The Nigerian Embassy could be very mercurial when it came to visa issuance, even more so when it came to people who wanted to shake up the status quo. This news concerned Azunna all the more given what she had learned today at Vauxhall Cross, whether she might be missing something.

"No! I won't sit down. I am tired of you holding me back! There are people, powerful people in Nigeria who actually want to see change, and some of them have made contact with the committee. I am going there for work, to *help*. And while I am there, I am going to find our family and I am going to find out exactly what happened to Mum and Dad." And with that she stormed out of the restaurant.

A few people looked at Azunna, but then quickly averted their gaze when she returned their stares. She sighed then reached for Ngozi's untouched glass of wine. She took a sip and rolled the tannins around in her mouth. Unaccustomed to rows with her sister, she was at a bit of a loss. Sam was gone, and she needed to head out on her own mission soon. She just had to hope that Ngozi would not do something rash. That last little bit of information concerned her too. Powerful people who wanted to help? Who was that? Looking out the big plate glass windows she noted the rain had increased. She crossed her legs, twisted her lips, and signalled the waiter for to bring the ordered bottle now.

Chapter Twentynine

Lufthansa Flight 594 touched down at Port Harcourt International twenty minutes early, precisely at 1900. Filled mostly with western oil rig workers who would transit to the Bight of Benin straight away via helicopter and who would work there for years without spending a night on Nigerian soil – twenty-eight days on, twenty-eight days off. Kiana was one of the few non-Nigerians to clear customs and collect her luggage. It was the wet season, and the humidity was extreme, but even in the dry season, West Africa can be very humid, especially near large bodies of water. The Bight of Bonny and the Niger Delta pumped enough water into the air that a dry season here meant merely a lack of rain.

Azunna's white linen blouse clung to her chest, the sudden change of temperature from the air-conditioned Lufthansa Airbus to the tarmac and the un-air-conditioned terminal kicking her body's cooling system into overdrive. She bloused her tan linen trousers into the black boots and slung her

Belstaff duffle over her shoulder. Her ubiquitous roller bag was once again in tow.

After clearing immigration and customs, she found herself on the curb, looking for her ride. This part of Nigeria was relatively prosperous, but that was all relative. The uber-rich and the crushingly poor were separated by a larger middle class that helped run the oil industry in conjunction with American and European technicians. Nonetheless, infrastructure construction still lagged here, and the airport was small, under-maintained and the street was dirty. Ride-hailing services had not made it to Port Harcourt, so once again Azunna found herself running the gauntlet of would-be taxi services. The offers of rides ranged from the purely business-like to the downright obscene. But like any serious woman on business in the world, she simply ignored them. That being said, her senses were on high alert, not expecting danger but being ready for it in any event.

She did not really know what she was looking for until a twenty-year-old white Land Rover Defender pulled up. The passenger window was down, and the driver leaned over and shouted, "Were you on the flight from Cairo?" Sam Khumalo was looking at her with a big smile on his face. The question a lame attempt at a joke regarding their field of work.

"No," she replied, "Frankfurt." Azunna was happy to play along, glad to see Sam again after several months. It was only after he had left London before her that she had come to see how he had worked his way into her life. For the first time in, well as long as she could remember, she felt like she could open her heart to someone.

"Get in."

"Gladly."

Azunna opened the door to the back seat, and tossed her duffle, roller bag, and jacket in, before hopping in the front and locking the door.

"Welcome to Port Harcourt. Let's get out of here."

Popping the clutch on the Defender and applying the gas, Khumalo soon had the reliable Land Rover pulling away from the airport and the mob of would-be drivers.

"How was the flight?"

"Fine, Lufthansa Business Class is always reliable. The stop in Abuja is a little weird, but I suppose hitting those two cities is what makes this a viable route for the international airlines."

"Abuja." Sam just shook his head. He had been living there for the last two months. "This place is a challenge, Kiana, not going to lie. The roads in this country are really something. In some places, they are in decent shape if not particularly wide, while in other places they are worse than dirt trails."

"How could they be worse than dirt trails?" This assertion struck Azunna as absurd for some reason. As an adult, her time in Nigeria had been almost all out in the field where she expected little development and rough living.

"I know right? Roads were built out of tarmac, but they were not made properly, with layers and beds and such. Then they were not maintained. Which means at various places the tarmac has been washed away or broken up. Quite the mess. Fortunately, this baby was up to the task." He patted the top of the dashboard.

"How long did it take you?" She thought the idea of driving across Nigeria was mad.

"Two days. One night on the road. Not bad really. The two dangers are being robbed or kidnapped for ransom, but when that happens it is mostly a random act. Or if the vehicle breaks down. There is simply no reliable way to get aid and the cell phone network is spotty at best."

The sun was well down by now. Sam was keeping the vehicle moving, even if it was slowly due to the Port Harcourt traffic. He wanted to get to the hotel so they could get some rest, as well as be inside a secure compound. Nigeria after dark was not anyone's friend.

It was just after 2030 when they pulled into the Swiss International Mabisel Hotel at No.9 Mabisel Avenue in Port Harcourt. Khumalo had checked in earlier in the day, so after they self-parked the Land Rover a good distance from the exterior wall and near a side exit, Sam helped tote her luggage to the front desk while Azunna checked in alone. She was greeted by a bell clerk in black and white livery.

"Good evening. Welcome to the Swiss International Mabisel in Port Harcourt. How can I help you, Madam?"

Azunna produced her passport and one of the credit cards Mills provided in London. "You have a reservation under Azunna. With UXT. I should be here a couple of nights."

The reception area was painted a bright white. As if that was going to clean the city up. The furniture was oversized and all dark greens and blues.

Unlike at other hotels she might have checked into, a British business executive here was completely normal. Brits, other Europeans, and Americans came not infrequently because of the oil. Oil anywhere meant money. Money meant the developed world paid attention, no matter how challenging it was for people to get there.

"Madam Azunna, here is your room key, the WIFI password, and a card for one complimentary drink in our bar. Breakfast service begins promptly at eight in the morning. Will there be anything else?"

"No, thank you. Good night."

Azunna, with Sam's assistance, grabbed her bags, and they headed towards the elevator. She was going to the fourth floor.

They both knew that one of the rooms would get very little use, but they knew that if they only turned in one receipt, the accountants back in London would notice. They were not quite sure they were ready to advertise their relationship to the world.

As soon as Azunna and Khumalo were in her room they dropped her bags and threw their arms around each other, meeting in a passionate kiss. It had been too long. Soon their clothes were coming off, both of them surprised by the desire to be entwined with the other. Azunna had dated both at Oxford and after she graduated, but her intensity could put some prospective suitors off. It hadn't helped that she was always protecting herself.

Eric Coulson

It wasn't long before the lovers found themselves naked with a night ahead of enjoying each other's physical charms.

Chapter Thirty

With there being no time change between London and Port Harcourt, Azunna rose at her habitual 0500. She looked over at Sam, sound asleep in the bed, his back to her. She could hear him breathing, but otherwise, he did not stir. The room was cold, they had cranked the air conditioning on too high when they came in the night before and had not bothered to turn it back down before they fell asleep. All their energy had been focused on being with one another again.

Even when deployed with the Royal Marines, she had always tried to keep her exercise routine going, balancing the need for sleep against odd mission hours, workouts, and recovery. She quietly got out of bed and on her way to the bathroom, tripped slightly on her duffle bag, which she grabbed. As quietly as she could, she dug through the bag and changed into her running gear.

Normally even in a new city that might have a less-than-ideal security situation, Azunna would hit the actual road, but Port Harcourt roads were dodgy enough and she was here on non-official cover. She decided that three miles on the treadmill would be a sufficient level of maintenance exercise for the day. Twenty-four minutes on the treadmill, and then another twenty-four with the kettlebells and she was back in the room a little after six.

Just as she came in Sam was beginning to stir. She plopped down on the bed next to him and kissed him. "Time to get up. We have work to do." And then she started scrolling through the email on her phone. She had given it a cursory look in the middle of the night. She knew she had an email from Ngozi.

"Dammit!" Azunna cursed loudly.

"Wait, what? I'm getting up," Khumalo said surprisedly. Khumalo had been slow to waken but the exasperated tone in Azunna's voice had his full attention. He started to heave himself up and off the bed. He was going to need to get back to his room for some clean clothes.

"Oh, not you love." She put her hand on his shoulder. "Take your time." She continued to read the email that had her agitated. Ngozi decided to come to Nigeria despite what Azunna had asked. Evidently her NGO internship convinced her that she needed to come to a meeting with potential donors. Something seemed off to Azunna. She knew her sister was smart and knowledgeable, she knew that she had a great deal of potential, but why did an NGO demand that one of its newest interns was needed at a donor meeting? That made no sense whatsoever. She decided to put it aside until she could make more sense of it.

"What is it?" Khumalo was now fully awake.

Azunna hesitated. She did not want a distraction from the mission ahead, and Khumalo was only vaguely aware of the sometimes-contentious nature of the relationship between the sisters. As far as he knew it was typical sibling conflict. "Nothing. It's just Ngozi. I will talk to her when I get back to London."

Khumalo nodded in acceptance and told her he should get back to his room to get ready for the day before there were too many people in the hallway. They agreed to meet for breakfast in an hour. Sam pulled on his trousers and shirt, and they kissed as he slipped out the door.

Azunna was angry. She rarely became angry at Ngozi, frustrated yes, but not angry. She felt like she had an agreement with her, but upon reflection realized that her request had not been actually agreed to. Maybe she should have been a little more direct. Or maybe she should have listened a little bit more. Finally, she set it aside. She would respond later.

Azunna went to the window and slid it open to see what the temperature was like; it was already warm, and the sun was just coming up – that time known as nautical twilight that would lead into sunrise, when someone could navigate without artificial light. The sky was so big in this part of the world. It was hard to not be taken in by the beauty of it all.

Closing the window, she popped the BBC World Service broadcast on. Another group of migrants had drowned in the Mediterranean seeking a better life in Europe. She had seen it in many places – Afghanistan, Syria, Nigeria, even the UAE and Singapore. Poor people affected by huge forces they could not begin to comprehend much less control. She wished the people sitting in their back kitchen in Essex, tutting over a pot of tea about immigrants taking jobs could understand.

Shaking off her thoughts about the generally decrepit state of the world, she stripped out of her workout clothes and took a shower, moderating her normal 4 minutes under steaming hot water and one minute of ice-cold water to mostly cold water as she hoped to get clean and then keep her pores closed long enough that she was not in a sweat all day.

Emerging from the bathroom in the cream-coloured hotel robe she attempted to make a cup of coffee. A kettle to warm water and some Nescafe sleeves were all they had. A luxury hotel in Nigeria was still in Nigeria, and the challenges of modern supply chains still impacted people regardless of the amount of money they had to spend. *Better than nothing, she thought.* But she had made better coffee in the field with her Jet-Boil.

Her weak coffee ready, she got dressed. Trying to balance stylish and practical was a skill set she had long mastered. Blue trousers in a lightweight technical fabric tucked into her brown Crocket and Jones boots, white linen shirt, and tan linen safari-style jacket. She tucked the H&K into her waistband, she was confident she would not be searched here due to that constant underestimation of women. Grabbing her Barton Pereira Domino sunglasses and JW Hulme cross body bag, a souvenir of a training mission in the US, and looked at her Bremont. That hour she had agreed to with Sam was almost up.

Port Harcourt owed the existence of luxury hotels in its midst to the oil industry. If everything in Nigeria had been optimal, it would still not be a tourist destination. That's why, among other things, the breakfast would be a buffet that was a mix of Nigerian and European foods.

Arriving in the restaurant, she immediately spotted him sitting at a table alone. "Everything good?"

"Great. Better than I expected to be honest."

A waiter approached. "Madam, anything to drink?"

"Bottle of water and coffee, black please."

"Sir?"

"I'll have the same." And the waiter departed.

"I'm afraid if you a hoping for proper coffee you will almost certainly be disappointed," Azunna warned, "it will probably be more Nescafe."

"Oh, well hope springs eternal. It's part of Nigeria's charm though." Khumalo gave Azunna a huge endearing grin.

"Shall we?"

"Let's."

As they perused the breakfast selection Azunna couldn't but think that at least the French had left her colonies with good bread. What had Britain done? Being back in the land of her parents and grandparents though made Azunna acutely aware that she was very British, whatever anyone thought about her name or skin colour.

"Down to business. We have a meeting this morning with Jayamma Ejiofor. He is the Director of Transportation for Uche's company. Of course, what he really does is manage the human trafficking program."

"What are we pitching to them as UXT?"

"It seems that they have many more people they want to move than they can do organically. Like all businesses these days, they want to outsource as much as possible. We know that Uche has one cargo plane that can reach Europe and several shorter-range ones that can reach North Africa. We think he might want to coordinate chartering on a larger scale."

"Hmm. Interesting. I guess we will find out." They spent the rest of their breakfast strategizing just how they would approach the meeting.

***

The Delta Recovery Committee was holding a general meeting as it readied to kick off its fund-raising year and its new initiative for educating the youth of Nigeria. Among the attendees was Ngozi Azunna. Officially an intern she had already attracted some high-level attention with her achievements in school. She was a great hire for any law firm or NGO, and she had her pick of positions post-graduation. But her passion for the homeland of her parents won out.

Of course, it did not hurt that the DRC had pursued her actively. The recruiting officer liked her, but it did bother him that he was told to hire before all of the applicants had a chance to submit their packets. He had even been told to woo her, something that was unprecedented in the history of the organization. When he asked the Executive Director *why* he was supposed to pursue her, he was simply told that it was important to a key donor. The recruiting officer understood that money talked in the NGO world, as in most places. If she had not been so highly qualified it might have concerned him more, but she was, and so he decided to make no more issue about it. Besides, it gave him more free time when he was in London.

The daylong conference was intended to motivate the staff for the program year ahead and motivate donors to give more money. It was programmed down to the minute with plenty of time set aside for networking.

After the plenary session, a large man approached Ngozi and asked her about how she had come to be at the conference. Her biography and CV were in the program so the fact that he knew a good deal about her was not a surprise. But his knowledge of her life history went much further than possible to glean from a CV or even a cursory view of her limited social media presence. Later she would think this should have been a clue that something was not right about the conversation, but in her youthful inexperience, she took most things at face value and assumed both his knowledge and probing questions were just about a mutual interest in helping the people of the Niger River Delta.

The man cornered her again at lunch and peppered her with questions about what she thought could be done to help the region, intermixed with more personal questions. Ngozi was unaccustomed to this sort of attention and it made her a little uncomfortable, but it also made her happy to be taken seriously by someone much older than herself. She could see a place for her emerging in this work environment. Finally, at the end of lunch, he excused himself, telling Ngozi he had work meetings to attend, but that he looked forward to seeing what sort of good work she could do. Once he left it only occurred to her that he had never introduced himself and she had not bothered to ask him his name.

The Executive Director and the recruiting officer had eaten lunch together. About halfway through the meal, the recruiting officer noted that Ngozi was being monopolized by the attention of one man. Finally, as Ngozi's interlocutor rose to leave, the recruiter commented on it to the Executive Director.

"Oh, him. He's one of our biggest and newest donors. His donation is why I told you to make sure we recruited her. Seems to know or have known her family before they left Nigeria. He was very keen that we give her this opportunity."

The recruiting officer did not think to ask the Executive Director what the donor's name was.

***

Jayamma Ejiofor, known to most people as Jay-Jay, had few advantages growing up. Coming from a poor family in the Niger River Delta meant that he had to make himself useful and maybe even invaluable to others. He found that position with Godswill Uche.

Uche was an up-and-coming entrepreneur when they first met and he was always looking for runners and assistants.

Jay-Jay had been one of many who had come through Uche's businesses, but he was the only one who had stayed. He tolerated Uche's mercurial and sometimes abusive behaviour and had been handsomely rewarded. When others decided the violence was too much, Jay-Jay had been willing to step in and do Uche's bidding. Others had, for some inexplicable reason, decided that trying to turn Uche into the authorities or deliver him to his enemies might earn them more money. As if Uche wasn't three steps ahead of them. The Niger River Delta was an easy place for bodies to disappear.

And when the Abigor Legion had reached out to Uche, Jay-Jay had been around long enough that he was the only one Uche would trust to manage the operation. His involvement in Uche's legitimate business operations was limited at best, and most definitely concealed from most of the inquiring world. Jay-Jay did the jobs that needed to be done outside the rules of conventional business.

Jay-Jay's strength was that he could sense when something was off. That's why this morning's meeting was troubling him so much. The British company had approached them out of nowhere. How did they know the company was looking to move more people? Then Uche had put him on this meeting specifically. Normally other representatives of the legitimate oil services business would take this sort of meeting and they would do it at the company offices in Owerri. But Uche had insisted that Jay-Jay take the meeting at their more discreet office in Port Harcourt. Finally, Uche had been particularly excited by the representative the British company had offered, one Kianna Azunna. He would not tell Jay-Jay why, but it was clear there was something going on. Something was going on that Jay-Jay did not understand and he did not like it.

Azunna and Khumalo arrived at the offices at ten sharp. These offices were in a four-story walk-up on a side street. Not exactly what you would expect from an international oil services company. Khumalo managed to wedge the Land Rover 110 between Land Cruisers, G-Wagons, and Range Rovers. Not a vehicle that was going to attract the attention of thieves around here.

If Azunna had known about the other meeting going on that day, she would have been even less confident about the direction of this mission than she already was. Nothing about this felt right to Azunna. This was one of the biggest businesses run by one of the wealthiest men in Nigeria, these offices were hardly befitting of a company of this stature. The stairs were at the centre front of the building. There was no lobby to walk into. The concrete stairs deposited people on the respective floors, and each office or shop had separate outside access. Even for a Nigerian side street, the felt extra dodgy. They climbed to the third floor drawing no attention from their fellow building guests who were visiting everything from veterinarians to beauty salons. On the third floor, they turned left and went all the way down to the end of the corridor. The sign on the door read, "Uche Oil Services, Ltd., regional office." Khumalo knocked twice and opened the door.

"Hello?" The room was almost empty. It was painted a pale blue that was already dirty and had three cheap plastic chairs in no apparent arrangement. He could see that the first room opened into an office and there was at least a desk. They heard a chair move.

"Ah. You are welcome!" Jay-Jay came out of the office, his hand already extended. "You must be Mr. Khumalo and Ms. Azunna. Welcome to Nigeria. Please come in."

He ushered them into his back office. It was the same pale blue as the front room, a tad larger with one desk, the sort that came out of an office warehouse catalogue with matching desk and side chairs. The one small window in the back looked like it led to almost nowhere and the whole room was lit in the harsh fluorescent light so common that also emphasized how cheap it all was.

"My name is Jayamma Ejiofor, but please call me Jay-Jay! Everyone does," the man laughed. "Please have a seat. How can I help."

Azunna withdrew a card from her interior breast pocket and pushed it across the table

Kiana Azunna
UXT, Ltd
London, United Kingdom NW8 9DE
Global Solutions Team Leader

Azunna could sense Jay-Jay's unease, it was clear the legitimate business world was not his bailiwick as he shifted uncomfortably in his chair, his body language and mannerisms betraying the smile and bonhomie he was attempting to project. Azunna was starting to put together the clues. Meeting with the representative of a multi-million-dollar business in a rarely used office made no sense. Someone knew something, but it was not the man in front of her. She needed to know what he knew and what he did not.

"Jay-Jay," Azunna began, she smiled as wide as she could in her effort to disarm him, "UXT is a global leader in transportation and logistics. We understand Uche Oil Services could use expert assistance in moving people and goods to Great Britain and Europe. We wanted to see if there were opportunities for us to work together. Our initial inquiry was met with some enthusiasm so we are a little surprised to be in what is obviously a rather, shall we say, out-of-the-way office."

In addition to being uncomfortable as the point man in non-criminal affairs, Jay-Jay was also taken aback by confident women. He understood that Uche's legitimate business fronted for the various smuggling operations, but Azunna clearly knew far too much about their operations for his comfort level. He did though, have his marching orders from Uche. He was here because he could follow orders. Rather than put a stop to all this as was his inclination he decided to deflect. He came back with the big laugh.

"My sister! You are so anxious to get down to business. You must be Igbo, too. Have you been here before?" Jay-Jay attempted to radiate confidence, again with the big wide grin, his efforts to open up his body language painfully obvious.

"I have as a matter of fact. I visited several times with my parents before they were killed in an auto accident on the Port

Harcourt Road. I have also been here when I was in the Royal Marines working with the Nigerian Navy's Special Boat Service."

All of this officialdom was almost too much for Jay-Jay to handle. A former Royal Marine who had also worked with the Nigerian government? Uche had asked a lot of him over the years, and he couldn't help but wonder if he was being set up. What he really needed was information and, for whatever reason, Uche had not provided it. He just needed to trust in the directions he *had* received. In for a penny, as it were.

Jay-Jay decided to seize on her admission of Nigerian heritage. Maybe he could learn something there and also steer the discussion away from the plane flights. Even as he thought of that, he understood that would not work. Uche had invited them here to have this very discussion. While Jay-Jay had little formal education, he understood how the world worked. He just wasn't accustomed to being on the poor side of information. What he did not know was that, on this issue, Azunna was of the same mind – she seemed accustomed to having the upper hand.

"How do you find your time here in Nigeria?"

"I enjoy coming here, but obviously it's difficult given what happened to my parents." She hoped what most people might consider "TMI" would keep him on his heels. And indeed, that information did.

"Look, Jay-Jay, our company research indicates Uche Oil only owns one aircraft, and all those flights are public information, at least the flights to Europe. Your company must be operating that old A310 to the max. Let us see your operation and then we can develop options to assist you. But this is clearly not the place to make that sort of assessment."

For a few moments, they just looked at each other. It was as if Khumalo was not even in the room. The silence hung like the humidity. Azunna looked at her nails, then returned her gaze to Jay-Jay. A thin smile on her face. If the silence was meant to unnerve her it was failing miserably. Finally, Jay-Jay decided to speak.

"You are quite right. We have a need to move many employees and contract workers between here and several points in Europe on a frequent basis. We have one plane that can do the job, but we need it for other work as well. We are hoping to arrange for a twice-a-week charter from Owerri to airports outside of London, Milan, and Valencia. We would be sending 250 people, more or less, on each flight. That's 500 people per week, to two of those three cities. Can you help?"

On its face the whole thing was absurd. Lufthansa had regular service out of Port Harcourt, Lagos, and Abuja. Air France serviced Lagos and Abuja and had serviced Port Harcourt in the past. British Airways had done the same and if there was that much legitimate travel to be had there were easier solutions.

"Of course, we can." Azunna smiled. "Charter airlift is one of our specialities at UXT. We supported Her Majesty's Government in operations in Iraq and Afghanistan as well on training operations around the world. Terms would need to be worked out, of course, based on distance and weight. But we can do this. "

"Excellent."

"Of course, customs and immigration clearance are completely up to you."

"We have that under control."

"Quite. Any costs associated with returning people would be borne by you as well."

"That won't be a problem."

"Right, then. Well, I need to see the operations. I need to see the airport to determine whether an aircraft can overnight there. What are the crew rest options? We prefer not to double-crew a plane. It's expensive because we need to create more than normal crew rest space. We would probably use an A330 for this. What do you think Sam?"

"Absolutely boss, A330 sounds perfect. After you make the assessment and we have an agreement, I can make the trip to Owerri for the actual flights to ensure they go smoothly."

"Excellent." Turning back to Jay-Jay, Azunna had a large smile. "So, when can we see this operation?"

Jay-Jay had not quite anticipated this. He was accustomed to making deals with shadier characters across the region. Uche had other people to handle the legitimate side of his operations. They had a flight going tomorrow. Uche was prickly about who he let see the more detailed part of his operations, both legitimate and criminal. Jay-Jay felt another prickle of pressure and unease. He was not accustomed to making decisions like this, that was the price of being someone's lackey, and he had his instructions. "Uh, er . . . how about tomorrow?" He grabbed his datebook, quickly thumbing through the dog-eared pages. Datebook was probably too fancy a name for the small notebook Jay-Jay wrote random things down in.

"Perfect." Azunna smiled. "It's about a two-hour drive from here, no? How about same time tomorrow? Ten AM at your offices in Owerri? I just need the address."

Jay-Jay was off his game for this entire meeting, and it was beginning to show. He did not know what to do. But his boss seemed to want this to happen. He had to agree. "Of course, ten is perfect. Godswill Tower is located on Olu Owerri Road, across from the Imo State High Court, the post code is F2VG+V7 Owerri, Nigeria. That might help with navigation."

Azunna rose quickly, Khumalo right behind her. Extending her hand, "Brilliant. See you tomorrow." Jay-Jay wanly shook it and then did the same with Khumalo.

She was out the door before either man knew it, and Khumalo had to double-time it just to catch up as she took the stairs quickly. On the street, she adjusted her sunglasses, looking left and right before heading to the Land Rover. Built before auto locks, Khumalo had to lean over and pull up the lock for her. She got in.

"Get us back to the hotel. We need a plan."

Chapter Thirty-one

It had been a long day in the DRC meeting. Ngozi had met many people and participated in numerous breakout groups. It was a new experience for her. She was moving into the professional world, beyond the classroom and it was both exciting and exhausting. When she returned to her hotel, she planned to skip dinner and have a nap. Entering the lobby, she began to glide past the reception desk when the clerk waived her down.

"Ms. Azunna, a gentleman left this note for you earlier today." The clerk handed her an envelope that was sealed and the size of a note card. She carefully opened it. Inside was a white note card with a gold, highly stylized letter "G" on the front.

Ms. Azunna - It was a pleasure to meet you today. I was hoping that tomorrow you would accompany me to the Owerri where I can show you some of the educational efforts I have been working on to empower the youth of Nigeria. I think you will find it inspiring and something you can bring DRC efforts in alignment with it. A car will call for you at 7 AM.

Regards,

Your Uncle G

Ngozi was confused because she was not 100% sure who "Uncle G" was, but finally concluded it could only be the donor who had monopolized her time at lunch that day in London.

Despite what her older sister sometimes thought, Ngozi was not completely devoid of common sense. She called the recruiter whom she had meet in London to ask him who this mysterious "Uncle G" was. The recruiter was surprised because he had assumed that if the person who was talking to her at lunch had wanted her to work for the DRC so badly, she must have known him.

"Let me call the Executive Director, and I will call you back."

He rang back as promised ten minutes later and confirmed that the man she now only knew by the moniker "Uncle G" was the person she had spent her lunch with. She thanked the recruiter and hung up. Thinking she had enough information now to feel safe, she decided to accompany him to Owerri the following day.

***

"Sam, nothing was right about that meeting," Azunna said as they drove back to the hotel.

"I agree. Can you tell though what the objective is here?" Khumalo was no fool. He had not been read in on the Chrysalis

Program, but he knew that Azunna was not a "regular" intelligence officer, whatever that might mean. She was clearly designated for special tasks. And the fact that nothing else had ever been said about the events in Wales meant she had some professional secrets.

"This finally makes sense." Azunna and Khumalo were both putting the pieces together.

"My last target in Afghanistan was, as far as we knew simply the senior leader of one of the Taliban special operations type units. It turns out that he was also a drug dealer. I did not get that until the briefing in Ukraine." Azunna mused at all of this coming together. And she felt the presence of Colley and Sparrow.

"And then your mission to Syria was tied to more drug smuggling right? Captagon? Was that it?" Khumalo had picked up on more details than she had realized.

"Right. That's where we first heard about the Legion. That information is what led C to send us to Ukraine."

"The Zimmer Group turns out to be the organization's heavies? Is that what we think? Security and probably murder?"

"What we found in Ukraine certainly indicates they are a part of the Legion. Given their history in Syria and here in West Africa, those are logical conclusions."

"And Uche Oil Services is the transportation part."

"Sam, I think that is absolutely on the money."

"Boy, this sounds like something straight out of a spy novel. An international group of criminals? This seems crazy." They both had been doing this long enough to that truth was stranger than fiction. No author was going to invent half the shit they had seen on deployments. "What is Abigor?"

"Some Grand Duke of Hell or some such nonsense. A military commander in Satan's realm. Some very bad people seem to take him as some sort of inspiration. Scary people."

When they arrived at the hotel, they parked the Land Rover and quickly made their way to Azunna's room. Jay-Jay's office had no air conditioning, and they were both feeling the effects of dehydration. Fortunately, their hotel stocked the room with several bottles of water and Azunna rang down for more.

"Can you get a faster vehicle with a driver?" Azunna did not want two Brits struggling to find parking or with directions on when crunch time came.

Sam thought for a second. "Sure. The High Commission has a small office here, and an armoured Range Rover. Since the High Commissioner is out of the country, I am sure we can get the vehicle and a driver."

"Perfect. Next question – do you have any contacts in Nigerian Intelligence? People that can be treated?"

Khumalo had not been in the country that long, but he had been working to develop a support network, although that was mainly in the exchange of information, not support in the field. He recalled a colleague in Abuja mentioning the Nigerian Intelligence Agency could be helpful. "I think so. Let me make a call," as he left Azunna's room.

While Khumalo worked his contacts, Azunna perused Google maps while thinking about what had transpired at the meeting. Jay-Jay was a weak link for Uche, that much was clear.

Azunna wondered if Uche knew that. Regardless, Azunna assessed that Jay-Jay would give them all the information they needed and would lead them right to Uche. It was just a matter of manipulating him and playing on his weaknesses.

Khumalo was back shortly from his room. He had spoken with a contact in the Nigerian Intelligence Agency, and he had agreed to meet them in Owerri the following morning. He had arranged with the High Commission to get the vehicle as well.

They packed their bags because they did not plan on coming back to the hotel. With an afternoon and evening to kill they decided to set work aside and enjoy each other's company for their last night in Port Harcourt. They had no idea when they would be able to do that again.

Chapter Thirty-two

Ngozi was in the hotel lobby at 0700 the following day, dressed for a day of adventure. Unlike her sister's short natural hair, Ngozi had grown her relaxed hair out long and had it pulled back in a low ponytail. She wore carbon coloured Kuhl outdoor trousers, a lightweight French blue linen shirt Kiana had bought for her, and some Aku hiking boots designed for warmer climates. She carried a grey waxed cotton backpack from The Cotswold Hipster and classic Ray-Ban Aviators with gunmetal frames with blue reflective lenses completed the outfit.

Just about a quarter past the hour, two Mercedes-Benz G-wagons pulled into the compound. Ngozi watched the hotel guard raise the white and blue barricade, so the vehicles did not need to stop. They were clearly known to whoever had briefed the security people.

The vehicles rolled to a stop with the second vehicle squarely in front of the hotel lobby door, and someone exited the front passenger side to open the backseat door. From the matte-black vehicle, a large man the colour of sard, with an olive undertone emerged. He was wearing a traditional Nigerian-style suit of royal blue made from a fine linen, and a matching short sleeve shirt. Black Gucci lizard slip-ons with no back, but a small heel completed the outfit.

The man who opened the car door rushed to beat the bellman to hold open the hotel lobby door with them reaching for the handle at the exact same time. The aide demurred and allowed the door to swing open from the lobby rather than make his boss need to stop.

Ngozi rose from the couch she was sitting on.

"Ah, Ngozi! I see you are ready for adventure." The big man laughed, the sort of deep laugh that accompanied almost all of his pronouncements even though there was little that was actually humorous about them. "I should have formally introduced myself yesterday! You can call me Uncle G!"

Ngozi felt that was hardly a name for a successful businessman to go by, but that seemed to be all he was willing to offer, and she did not know a polite way to ask him to elaborate on his identity. The large scar on his cheek seemed more pronounced today for some reason. She had seen it yesterday, but today it rang a distant bell.

"Come!" And he turned on his heels now with his aide racing to get to the door before the hotel staff.

They exited the hotel and Ngozi felt the hot, humid air hit her like a ton of bricks. The sweat started to pore off her immediately, and even though it was loose, the shirt started to cling to the bare skin. She got into the same G-wagon as Uncle G but behind the driver, and before she even had a chance to buckle her seatbelt, they were out of the hotel compound and working their way to the road north.

Uncle G began without preamble. "I have a scholarship program for the youth of Nigeria, and I want you to see it. Maybe you can even help with the administration and chaperoning of the children."

"Well, I am really here to work on the environmental issues plaguing the Delta. "I'm not sure I know or have the time . . ."

But he quickly interrupted, again with the big laugh that did not seem connected to anything remotely humorous. "Ngozi, I have big plans and those plans include you. You do know that I made my donation to the DRC contingent upon them hiring you."

This was, of course, a big, uncomfortable surprise to Ngozi.

"But how do you even know who I am?" She had gone from being proud of her accomplishments to being afraid in an instant.

He laughed again, but now the laugh had more of a sinister undertone. There was clearly nothing funny going on now.

"I knew your family!" He hoped this revelation would put her more at ease. And it did to a certain extent. "I just wanted to make sure you got what you wanted."

They made it out of the city and were on the road north heading to Imo State. The Mercedes was travelling fast, way too fast for Ngozi's comfort. They were weaving in and out of traffic using all the lanes, the drivers seemingly heedless of any danger. She noticed she was the only one wearing a seatbelt.

"Are we in a hurry?" Ngozi tried to not show the concern she felt for her safety.

"No. Why do you ask?" Uncle G seemed genuinely perplexed by the question.

"It just seems like we are taking a lot of chances here on the road."

"Slow down." G's words to his drive had drawn an immediate reaction. "Drive like you would if we were in Britain."

"But sir . . ."

"Just do it."

"The rules of the road are much different here. We will be fine. Now let me tell you about my program."

But Ngozi could only half listen. Having grown up in London, she did not ride in cars other than the occasional Uber. She was utterly outside her comfort zone. For the next ninety minutes, she hung on to the armrest and kept her eyes fixed on the horizon in an attempt to stave off the nausea that was creeping up in her.

Uncle G though, like most narcissists, was entertained by other's pain and he took a small pleasure in Ngozi's discomfort. He prattled on the entire drive to Owerri. When they arrived Ngozi struggled to quickly get her door open and she vomited on the ground, only just missing the vehicle interior.

***

Azunna and Khumalo arrived in Owerri a little after 0800. Johnson, the High Commissioner's normal driver when visiting south-eastern Nigeria, had picked them up at 0600 as they checked out of the hotel. Unlike Ngozi's wild ride, Johnson was accustomed to passengers who expected the driver to obey more conventional rules of the road.

Owerri did not have suburbs that you slowly rolled through before getting into town proper. Being the wet season, it was very green, and that vegetation hid many of the huts and small shops that did exist along the road. That did not mean it was a small village, far from it. Owerri was a city of over one million people. It was the capital of Imo State and once capital of Biafra. They approached the city from the southwest and crossed the River Otamri before turning left onto Owerri Orbu Road.

Their first meeting was with the counter-intelligence arm of the National Intelligence Agency. They found the anonymous office on Wehteral Bank Road, less than a block from the Imo Headquarters of the Nigerian Federal Police, which was right across the street from the State Police Headquarters. One of the challenges operating in an environment that was predicated on so much corruption was not that so many people were double-dealing, it was that it was very difficult for an outsider to understand the tricky array of alliances. Uche's legitimate business had many allies and was a source of pride for Nigeria and the Igbo nation. On the other hand, human trafficking was not something many people were going to turn a blind eye to.

Ahmed Achmed was waiting in front of the Owerri NIA office. "Sam Khumalo? Kiana Azunna? You are welcome," Ahmed said with a toothy grin. Ahmed was of medium height, fit but not someone who spent a good deal of time in the gym. He looked like a runner. The carbon-coloured uniform of the Intelligence Service was highly pressed and fit him like a glove. The silver buttons sparkled, and the green aiguillette set off the uniform nicely. Ahmed appeared the epitome of professionalism. Azunna hoped his skill matched his appearance.

"Thank you for meeting us."

"My pleasure, come with me." Putting his sunglasses back on, instead of going into the building he turned right, and they walked up the dirty little no-man's land between the street and various buildings because no one could bother to build a sidewalk in Owerri. Azunna and Khumalo staggered themselves behind him, more out of habitual caution than any real threat. The street was bustling with people hawking juices, suya, corn, and puff puff.

"Hey, pretty lady. Pretty lady, take a look at my shop!" Called a random voice.

Azunna rolled her eyes behind her Barton Perriera sunglasses. *This shit never stops.*

They walked two blocks before Ahmed crossed the street and entered another nondescript three-story side building, and they followed him up the stairs to the first floor. The nice thing about these concrete block buildings being laid out so simply is that they limited possible avenues of ambush.

At the top of the stairs, they turned right and found themselves in a plain office with a table in the middle of the room surround by half-a-dozen chairs, each one different. The filthy tiles had not seen the right side of a mop in three years, and a small refrigerator hummed in the corner. And of course, the ever-present overhead fluorescent light.

"I thought this place might be a little more suitable for our discussion. Fewer people to take note of visitors." Azunna approved of the precaution. Ahmed seemed to have a good head on his shoulders.

Extending his hand, Sam introduced himself properly. "Sam Khumalo with the High Commission, I believe my Head of Station called your boss."

"That's why I am here." Ahmed offered another broad grin. "And you are?"

"Azunna. Kiana Azunna. Pleasure." She extended her hand.

"What do you do with Sam here?"

"I solve problems," said Azunna with her classic wry smile.

Ahmed, thinking his charm offensive was working he decided to press on. "How can I help?"

Khumalo started. "We are investigating human smuggling using the Uche shipping networks. We think he may actually be part of a larger criminal conspiracy. Ms. Azunna and I met yesterday with the organization's supposed Transportation Director at an office in Port Harcourt. And we are supposed to meet him again at the company's Owerri offices in less than two hours."

"Jay-Jay?"

"You know him?" Khumalo asked surprisedly, giving Azunna a quick glance. *Uche's organization caught NIA's attention. We are on to something*, Azunna thought.

"We know *of* him." He laughed. "Director of Transportation? Jay-Jay seems to be moving up in the world."

"How so?" Khumalo pressed.

"Jay-Jay is one of those people that sort of gets dragged along with other's successes. He makes himself useful enough. In this case, he grew up with Uche. Now, he is more like a personal assistant, but I guess to be fair to him he does most of the management of Uche's criminal operations."

Azunna was taking this all in rather stone faced. While Khumalo and Ahmed sat opposite of each other, she had selected a seat further down the table where she could observe both them and the front door. It was interesting that the Nigerians knew about Uche's criminal activity but had done nothing about it. She joined the conversation.

"If you know there is a criminal portion to his operation, why have you done nothing about it?"

Ahmed bristled a bit. His first inclination was to be defensive because he and many other security professionals in Nigeria were making significant efforts to enforce the rule of law.

"Are people of power and wealth held to account readily in your country?" Ahmed knew perfectly well that the twin currencies of power and privilege save many people around the world, regardless of the supposed effectiveness of equality in a justice system. "The truth is we have tried and have made some progress, but when you want to bring down someone with large resources it is hard. If we could connect him to the human trafficking and have some of the victims testify, that might help."

Azunna, though, knew that ship had sailed. Prosecution was the least of Uche's worries at this point. He just did not know it. Ahmed had, however, given her some insight into how serious he was about helping her and Sam. She was heartened.

"We are supposed to meet him in a little more than an hour to 'see their operations,' as it were. What do you think is going on?" Azunna leaned forward trying to engage Ahmed.

"Well, really the company's operations here in Owerri are mostly administrative. That and the use of the airport, of course. It's hard to know exactly what they want to show you. He is known for his philanthropy, by the way, another obstacle to prosecution."

"What kind of support can you give us?" Azunna focused the conversation on the short term. If Ahmed had any doubt about who was really running this operation, it disappeared in her tone of voice.

"Not too much I'm afraid, that is if you were looking for technical support. I do, however, have five field officers and a couple of vehicles that might be of use to you."

It occurred to Azunna she should try and understand what was motivating Ahmed, what his background was. "Where are you from Ahmed?"

"Kano State. You?" Ah, the north, that makes sense, no tribal ties to the south as potential impediment to his service to federal Nigeria, thought Azunna.

"London. What does Uche ship out of here?"

"All sorts of things. But they are almost always trucked in directly from other locations. The trucks pull up and load onto the aircraft. Then both depart. When one of his 'scholarship' planes, the philanthropy I mentioned earlier, departs, the kids arrive on buses and go straight to the plane."

"Scholarship planes?"

"Yes, Uche runs, or allegedly runs, a scholarship program for young Nigerians. They allegedly go to unspecified European countries for education, with the goal of returning a more educated workforce. Of course, we have yet to see any evidence that this is happening. I would have to double-check, but I think one of those flights is scheduled for tonight."

"Interesting." But at this point, Azunna was mostly just thinking out loud. She looked at her Bremont. They had forty-five minutes. "How long is it going to take us to get to their office?"

"Ten minutes at most. Even in this chaos." Ahmed gestured vaguely in the direction of the street.

"Can you get us, maybe five armed officers and a couple of vehicles?"

"Absolutely. The CI team here is excellent. Follow directions but can also think on their feet."

"Excellent. How long to get to the airport from here?"

"Thirty minutes at most. Maybe less."

"Should we meet back here at 1430?" They all looked at their watches. Heads nodded.

There was nothing left to be said. Azunna and Sam left.

***

On the street Azunna quickly crossed, dodging the minivans, tuk-tuks, and overloaded lorries.

"Sam, have Johnson meet us at that corner." She indicated a corner one block up.

Khumalo was nervous. Even though he was no longer that new to intelligence work, the idea of charging into a mass of humanity like she had just done made him nervous. He knew she was there to gather information, but he still wasn't aware of the exact details of her mission. She was a blank slate to him and so, like most men, thought he needed to protect her.

"Why don't we go back to the building and wait?" Sam was breathless as he caught up to her.

"Ahmed did not see the vehicle. No reason for him to see it before absolutely necessary."

"He seems like a good guy."

"I agree, and from Kano. If he *is* on the take, or has one particular patron, he is not from down here so I don't think he will have mixed loyalties."

"On the take? That seems like a leap!"

Azunna turned and looked at him. Her glowing, amber-coloured eyes peering over her sunglasses. "Sam," she started, "we all work and live within a system. We don't create that system, and though we might want to change it, we must operate in it until we can make those changes. This is not a value judgement on Ahmed. We need a practical partner, not a saint."

Feeling chastised Sam said nothing, but summoned Johnson via text.

***

A bottle of water seemed to appear from nowhere. Ngozi rinsed her mouth out and then finished the water in several large gulps. What little food she had had in her stomach was now gone as was most of the water in her system. She did not feel hungry, but she was parched. The ride and the nausea had taken it out of her.

The sky was a leaden grey and even though there was no direct sunshine, the brightness of the UV bounced off everything, making her very glad that she had her sunglasses on.

Looking around Ngozi took in the location. They were in a small compound with high cream-coloured cement block walls. They looked dirtier than they should have, and the razor wire strung across the top seemed excessive. While Ngozi had become quickly accustomed to the fact that most places of substance had armed guards around them, the guard force here also seemed over-the-top.

She also noted two large coaches parked to the side of the compound. They appeared to be in good shape and ready to use. The main square of the compound was a poorly laid tarmac that had already broken up. The one building that dominated the space was L-shaped, with the short part of the L against the back wall of the compound, and one story tall. The long part of the L ran along the wall to her right and was two stories.

The man she now knew as Uncle G appeared at her elbow. "Come in, let me show you the children we are sending to Europe for schooling."

She had missed his entire explanation of where they were going because of the crazy driving. She decided to target any questions based on what he told her and try to fill in all the gaps. They walked across the main compound and entered the one-story building. An anaemic air conditioning unit was struggling to put out cold air, but unlike the hotels in Port Harcourt, this one was failing badly. The people working in the building had also conceded the fact and opened the windows. When they saw Uncle G enter the office all of the adults stopped what they were doing and immediately stood up. He laughed.

Again, with the laugh. Ngozi could only hope that he was going to show her something remotely useful or meaningful, because she had already decided that he was a bit of a twat.

They moved through the office and down a short hall, turned left and entered what was clearly the long part of an L-shaped building. What she saw astonished her. There were four rows of beds that went at least twenty-five deep into the hall. There were young boys and budding teenagers, many filthy and in various stages of undress.

"This is the boys' level. The girls are on the top level."

"Most of them look like could at least use a bath, maybe get the air conditioning working, and some clean sheets and clothes." Ngozi was nauseated. She had thought the program was to help these children. By any objective measure providing a clean, hygienic place to live should have been a top priority in Ngozi's mind. She'd had her doubts about this "Uncle G" and nothing she saw here alleviated any of that.

"They will get bath and clean clothes just before they head to Europe," Uncle G said arrogantly. His tone had changed, the obnoxious laugh was gone. He said it so matter of factly, with a hint of menace. Ngozi was not entirely sure if it was the tone or the way he had suddenly switched, but a chill ran down her spine, all the more noticeable with the sweat that had gathered over her.

His comments just reinforced what she was thinking. Spying the stairs, Ngozi felt an unaccustomed boldness. Fuelled by her desire to make the world a better place, she headed up the stairs without asking.

"No need to . . ." G tried to stop her with his words, but she was already halfway up the stairs. "Get her!" His command to one of the henchmen was quiet but emphatic. But it was too late. If the scene in the boys' hall was unsettling, the girls' was downright disturbing. They were ranging in ages from around ten to sixteen. There were another hundred beds with at least that many girls in the room. They were in various states of dress, and filthy, but what really caught Ngozi's attention was the one girl, older than most, maybe even seventeen. Her simple shift dress was a bright yellow, dulled by years of wear. She wore it pulled off the one shoulder in a way that tried to exhibit sex appeal, and the look in her eyes betrayed the fact she had seen too much at her age, and a resignation that was her future.

At that moment the guard grabbed Ngozi by the shoulder and quickly hustled her back down the stairs.

She started with Uncle G, "I don't know what you are doing, but . . ."

"Calm down. I know it is very distressing. The conditions these children come from, but we are here to make it better. We are sending them to school in Europe. We will make it better."

Instinctively Ngozi knew there was something very, very wrong with this situation, and she wondered for once if her older sister had been correct, maybe she should not have come on her own. What she would not do now for Kianna's advice. Whatever that young girl she had just seen needed for a better life, it was not a scholarship to even a barely competitive school in Europe. She was not prepared for it, Ngozi knew that.

"Let's go!" G had commanded his entourage, and she was escorted to the vehicle, much less gently than she had been beforehand. It began to dawn on Ngozi that she was one small fish swimming in a school of sharks, and about to be swallowed up whole.

***

Precisely at 1000, Johnson dropped them off in front Uche Tower. At fifteen stories it was big for Owerri. A symbol of financial success in a poor country. Jay-Jay was waiting eagerly in the lobby to meet them.

"My friends. You are welcome to Owerri." He laughed but this "hail fellow well met" schtick was annoying Azunna. She and her sister had the same instinct – the laugh was a cover. *Oh, well. It will all be done by the evening.*

They took the elevator to the fourteenth floor with Jay-Jay chattering about the building. Most of it went in one ear and out and the other for Azunna. She was focused on three things; what they were doing, how they were doing it, and terminating Uche.

Finally, they arrived at Jay-Jay's office. It was well appointed with a decent view, but he had no "secretary" or "executive assistant" or any of those other code words. Despite his company title and office, he was a fish out of water here. And doing badly at it. They sat.

Jay-Jay began with his hallmark laugh. "You wanted to see our operation! Here it is!" He gestured around the office.

Azunna sighed. It was all becoming rather tedious.

"Jay-Jay. Thank you for having us. We need to see your operations. The administrative portion. How are you processing these people for transportation? Where is it taking place? As we might say in Britain, from soup to nuts. Show us the entire process."

Jay-Jay was at a loss and his face showed his confusion on what to do and say. He was, at heart, a criminal. And even though he had done well in that environment, he only really had two tools in his bag: carrots and sticks. This company had come to them. The constant request for information was annoying to him and set off his alarm bells. The concept of due diligence was completely foreign to him. And right now, he realized he had no stick to use. But he had his marching orders, so he took a decision.

"I think, what is of concern to you, is the ability of our passengers to enter the countries in question legally, is it not?"

"Nothing slips by you, Jay-Jay," Azunna said with her wry smile. "I have three big concerns, and that tops the list." She hoped the flattery would put him a little bit more at ease and get him to open up.

"Ah, then let me take you down the hall to our immigration operations section." They set off down the relatively empty halls until they reached a door at the opposite end of the building. "This is it," he said proudly as he pushed the door open.

This office was almost exactly like Jay-Jay's except cheap blinds had been lowered to cover the windows, and in addition to the desk dominating the middle of the room, there were three more desks along the walls with people doing what appeared to be data entry.

"Please meet Fred. He is the head of our immigration operations."

Human nature is such that everyone, or at least almost everyone, wants credit for what they have done. Criminals confess, cheaters come clean, thieves tell stories of their hijinks. They want to be seen as clever, even at a cost of freedom, love, or their lives. Fred was no different.

The truth is that most leaders, managers, and whatever else companies and governments title the people at the top of their organizations, do not truly understand the capabilities and vulnerabilities of the various technology their organizations use. Improvements to it are seen mostly as a cost with little benefit. The U.S. State Department's Non-Immigrant Visa system is so famously outdated as to be the butt of jokes among all U.S. diplomats, except of course the people in Consular Affairs that take things like that very seriously, as serious people should.

Fred was a hacker extraordinaire. Had he been born in a different country; he would have been making a large salary at a tech hub. But he wasn't, he was born in Nigeria and was therefore destined to make his way in the world within those limitations.

Fred had managed to penetrate the visa systems of the United States, the United Kingdom, and the European Union collectively. The saddest part, to Fred, of having penetrated the U.S. system was that the system was so antiquated that it required the printing of a physical visa. However, he was sure that he would eventually figure out how to visit his favourite Auntie in Atlanta.

The UK and EU's E-visa systems, which had only recently come online, appeared strong in many respects but in others had serious problems. The absence of a physical visa meant that counterfeiters and forgers were out of work, they simply were not needed in order to board an aircraft and cross a border. The airlines wanted travellers' money, but they did not want them to take up unplanned space on a return visit or risk fines from the various immigration agencies around the world. However, there was an easy way to avoid that risk, only allow people with valid entry documents on the plane. If the relevant immigration agency's computer verified with the airline's computer that a person was permitted entry into the country of destination, then the problems were much more straightforward.

What was needed was for the would-be traveller's name to appear to have an E-visa when they checked in for their flight and when they arrived at border control. For the hacker, this simplified the problem, because, once they accessed the system and inserted the relevant traveller data, it could be withdrawn later. It is true that a detailed forensic analysis would be able to tell what had happened, but if the suspect traveller was absent from the system, the bureaucrats were unlikely to order a full analysis of the history. Fred had cracked this code and he spent close to the next hour explaining how he did this to Azunna and Khumalo. Both of whom took detailed notes in their heads. Finally, he offered to demonstrate.

"We have a flight leaving tonight, let me show you how it's done. Here, take a look at the manifest." He handed several pages to Azunna, who gave them a quick once over before returning to look in detail.

Wait! What?! She read the names again. There it was at the top.

Azunna, Ngozi.

It had her sister's date of birth and what she assumed to be her passport number. She felt a quick panic rising inside her but knew that any visible reaction would not help her sister right now.

"Can you show me?" She asked trying hard to show no change in her demeanour.

"Sure, we are just about to upload the information anyway."

Fred was proud of what he did in breaching these systems. He was not going to lose the chance to show someone, especially someone who would really appreciate the audacity of breaching the British visa system.

"Are we ready?" Fred was getting his hacking team ready to take over the system for a short time.

"It takes a team, or rather I prefer to use a team, so we have different eyes watching other activity on the net. We detected a maintenance back door in one of our probes for the British Visa system. It's ironic that all the IT specialists around the world preach about better passwords, multi-factor authentication, all sorts of different security measures, but at the end of the day we always leave at least one way in, in case all the other access mechanisms fall apart."

As a regular computer user, but no tech expert, she could sympathize. *I guess even the experts forget how they spelled their first pet's name sometimes.* She and Sam watched intently.

Fred continued, "As you may know the British non-immigrant visa system is principally paper based, that is a visa decision is made based on allegedly objective standards. The adjudicating officer decides and then submits the information for upload and visa issuance. Since the UK Government has gone to the E-visa system, they don't need a passport to print a visa. Just the data that matches the machine-readable visa data on the physical passport. When that is scanned into the system, the officer at immigration will know whether they have a visa. They have reduced it to a binary choice. Get the data in the system and the answer is yes."

"So, you don't think the standards for visa issuance are objective? I mean I know that is a side issue here, but is it that unfair?"

Fred looked at her out of the corner of his eye. "I'm sure you reached your point in your company with no obstacle, right, sister?"

She was going to tell him she was not his sister but resisted.

"The poorest American, as long as they can get a passport and a plane ticket can waltz right into London with next to no scrutiny".

Azunna had to concede that there were injustices she was also blind to.

"Anyway, now that we are in the system through the administrator's portal, we are looking for someone who is logged on to the visa upload system but is not active. They may be in a Teams meeting or something, but if we can use their portal for a few minutes that is all we need."

One of the junior hackers seemed to have a suitable user. "SmythJ001 is logged in but in a Teams meeting. She seems to be toggling back and forth between Facebook and her meeting. She has not touched the visa system for five minutes."

Fred quickly brought up that user's screen. "OK, SmythJ001, let's see what we have. OK, visa adjudication officer, fully authorized to issue visas. These are six-month visas so pretty low threshold for scrutiny and issuance." He hit a few keys. "Now I am copying the data out of an Excel spreadsheet, a comma delimited format. Any database can accept that format. OK, let's upload this. What's she doing?"

"She's liking her friend's kitten pictures."

"Good. I just need another ninety seconds."

Azunna, Sam, and Fred sat and watched the circle spin. And spin. And spin. And then . . . *Your file has been successfully uploaded.*

"OK, it should be good. Check it out." Azunna turned to the last hacker, who had a stack of passports in front of her. She started running the passports through the MRV scanner, verifying they now had valid visas in the system.

"Of course, the British passport holders are no problem. They have to be on the manifest, but we don't upload them to the system."

It took about fifteen minutes to run all the non-British passports through the system, mostly Nigerian, but a few other random West African ones as well. Then she announced, "All verified."

Fred then led the metaphorical retreat out of the system. "OK, given SmythJ001 control of her access again." Once that was done, they closed all their windows except for the security portal they had used. One by one they logged off till only Fred remained. He wiped all evidence that they had been in the system. The only little trace that was ever left on the system was his final exit.

Azunna was very impressed, and she let that show. "Amazing Fred. How long have you been doing this with the British system?"

"A little over a year."

"How have they not detected it?"

"Not sure really. The only evidence of a breach of a system is my final logoff. No way around that. A real forensic analysis would find those final logoffs, but they would need to be looking for that sort of anomaly."

"Why not erase those?"

"Well, I cannot erase the last one. I could go in and erase the others, but they would take time to find, and I run the risk of being detected doing that, or erasing too much data, causing an anomaly, and causing them to change their protocols. We spend a good deal of time attacking their systems, along with the US and the EU to both distract from what we have already found and to come up with alternatives in the event this method is detected."

The magnitude of the whole thing was astounding. Hackers in a small office in remote Owerri, Nigeria had secretly captured the visa systems of the US, the UK, and the EU. And no one had a clue. More importantly they had to stop Ngozi from getting on that plane.

Chapter Thirty-three

Uncle G had a timing problem. His key lieutenant was meeting with someone that he also needed to meet with if the plan was to come to fruition. But he could not bring Ngozi, he needed to put her on ice somewhere for a couple of hours. He also had to convince her that she was the person to shepherd these children to Europe. Or at least that was what he wanted her to think.

Back in the car and on the road, G returned to his previous always-laughing self. "I know what you saw in there was disturbing," he began, a look of concern coming over his face, "but I wanted you to see what conditions these children were coming from so you could help them. Now we are going to see the group of children who are flying tonight. I would like for you to go with them to help them get into their various schools."

Ngozi was noncommittal, making a low sound as she looked at her phone. One bar. She needed to send her sister an email but was not sure she could do anything to help. At least she would know where she was. The air conditioning in the Mercedes was on high. She shivered.

Their little convoy was on the road for no more than fifteen minutes before they pulled into another compound almost identical to the first one, however, this one was much tidier. High-quality slate replaced the dusty hard dirt square. The windows were closed and once the vehicle doors opened Ngozi could hear the whir of the air conditioning. Once again, the transition from the cold air conditioning to the humidity hit Ngozi hard.

When they entered the offices of this building, the staff once again stood as G entered but here, he greeted people warmly. Children and teenagers were clean and well-dressed in school-type uniforms.

"This is where we do the final preparation for the students before we send them to Europe. I have a meeting to go to, so I will leave you here to get to know the children. I hope you will decide to accompany them on their journey to Great Britain." And before she could say anything he was out the door and on his way.

With him gone, Ngozi was able to use her phone more freely. Noting she had more signal here, she opened her email and dashed off a quick note to her sister. All she knew for sure was that she was somewhere in Imo State, Nigeria and she needed Kiana's help. She hit send and hoped it would get to her sister in time to help these children, from what she was not sure, but she knew it was not good.

***

Jay-Jay led Azunna and Khumalo up one flight of stairs. He explained they would have spent more time waiting for the elevator.

The top floor was more well-appointed than the one below it. The floor here was marble as opposed to tile, and at the east-facing end of the hall was what would have been called in the UK the C-Suite. Glass doors led to a reception area with glass walls behind it. Some of the glass was frosted, but most was clear. Sunrise was probably amazing here. Glancing behind her Azunna noted that a less busy office mirrored the effect on the west end as well. Amazing sunsets too.

Just before they arrived at the office, Azunna's phone vibrated. She glanced at it to see an email from her sister. When she read it, things began to make more sense. She dashed off a quick response with some instructions and then told Jay-Jay she was ready.

Entering the east offices, the elegant woman behind the reception desk rose, "Mr. Uche is expecting you. Please follow me." The trio followed the woman down to the northeast corner of the building, then entered the corner office. It was glass from wall to ceiling all the way around. The marble floors were covered in excessively plush dark green rugs. At the end of the office was a sitting area with two big, overstuffed sofas, four matching chairs, and a low glass table in the middle. The sofas and chairs were all a mix of black, red, green, and yellow, and each had a rising sun in the middle of the backrest. The rising sun of Biafra. It was all a bit overdone. Mid-century modern had never made it to this part of Africa. Godswill Uche rose from his desk at the opposite end of the room.

Azunna momentarily froze. The imposing man with a scar across his face was not so much seared into her memory as it was etched on her heart. Fortunately, it was merely a moment's hesitation and seemed to go unnoticed.

"You must be Kiana Azunna! I am so happy to meet you. You are welcome! And you must be Mr. Khumalo from the British High Commission! Please." He gestured to the sitting area. "You are welcome, Mr. Khumalo." The mixed level of formality and familiarity had not escaped Azunna, she just assumed it was the normal sexism of any big business around the world. She and Khumalo selected the two overstuffed chairs with their backs to the east, where they could best observe their interlocutors and beyond. Views could wait.

Bottles of water already adorned the table, along with the fake flower centrepiece.

"So, Kiana, you are impressed with our operation. No? Does your company want to help us?"

The undue familiarity was burning her. It was clearly meant to throw her off her game, but to what end? Did he know who they worked for? The real purpose of her mission? She dismissed those ideas. She was sitting in his office with an H&K P30 strapped to her hip. She had not been searched once, if he thought she was here to kill him there would have been some security screening. This was all just weird. It had all been a little too easy. Her senses were on high alert.

"Mr. Uche. ...," began Azunna, but he interrupted.

"Call me Uncle G. All my friends do. You are here to be my friend." It was not a question. Quiet suddenly took over the room as Uche and Azunna looked at each other. The tension in the air hung for a few moments too long while they both digested the asymmetry of information. Azunna decided to seize the initiative.

"Of course, Uncle G." Using his self-proclaimed moniker felt dirty, but she knew that she could see this to the end. "If understand it correctly, you want us to move approximately five-hundred people every week from the airfield here in Owerri to various cargo airfields around the EU and the UK. It appears that you have resolved the entrance requirements. You need more aircraft. Does that about cover it?"

The oblique reference to the visa system hijacking scheme one floor down threw him off his guard. He had not told Jay-Jay to show them the visa operation and he was irritated at his lackey. His annoyance at having an outsider learn about his little operation merely flashed across his face as he returned to the role of jovial Oga. He was sure that he would soon have her in his pocket. Though something might need to be done about her partner.

"Kiana, my friend, you have captured it perfectly! Is that something you can and will do?"

"Well, I still need to see the airport operations, and maybe after that hotel facilities. I can take all that information with me back to London after I have finished my assessment, I think we can have something on offer for you."

Suddenly her phone started buzzing in her pocket. The buzzing that indicated a series of text messages. "Will you excuse me a minute?" She pulled out her phone.

> *Cover being checked.*
>
> *UXT received several phone calls asking for you.*
>
> *Told you were abroad, gave them your phone number and UXT email.*
>
> *All appears well.*
>
> *Tally ho.*

She checked her UXT, Ltd email. Yep, several random messages. She pocketed her phone.

"Sorry about that, clients around the world you know."

But it was time for Uche to return the favour as his phone started pinging loudly.

> *Kiana Azunna, mid-level executive at UXT, Ltd.*
>
> *Former Royal Marine left service last year.*
>
> *Lives alone in Poole.*
>
> *Sister at school in London.*
>
> *You can do business with her.*

"Great news Kiana! But before that, do you not know who I am?"

"I think I do. The CEO of one of the largest . . ."

"No, no, no. Not that!" He seemed overly excited, too happy, exceedingly jovial. She knew exactly who he was. Even though it had over twenty years since she had seen last. "I really *am* your Uncle G! My father was your grandfather's brother! I am his youngest, but most successful son. When your grandparents left with your father as Biafra collapsed, my father fled for the bush. We are family! I even knew your father and helped him out on the work he was doing here before he and your mother were tragically killed."

She gave her biggest smile, which was still too small. "Isn't that a wonderful coincidence." Azunna had overcome her initial surprise with a resolve to complete her mission. Not only was she going to achieve the mission objective, but she was also going to settle a personal score. It had now become clear why they had penetrated the organization so easily. Azunna's heart started to race at the prospect of revenge. She knew she had to take her ego out of the equation to the extent that was possible. Her professional accomplishment would now be a personal one as well.

"When Jay-Jay told me your name I knew it had to be you. I mean I had to do some checking, but I just knew it was my long-lost niece."

"I'm not sure I was ever lost." A thin smile crossed Azunna's face.

Jay-Jay and Khumalo were merely observers to this drama. Khumalo didn't know if his partner and lover had a problem, but his instincts told him to play it cool.

"Uncle G, how about this: we can meet later at the airport, go over all the operations, and then once the plane leaves, we can have dinner and discuss old times." Her tone indicated fond memories, even though she had none. In fact, quite the opposite. She stood, and Khumalo followed her lead.

Seeing the meeting was concluded Uche and Jay-Jay stood as well. "Jay-Jay, please get them the information needed for the meeting later and make a reservation for four at my favourite restaurant. It is so nice to see you again, Kiana."

Azunna looked straight into Uche's eyes, "it was a pleasant surprise for me as well." And she thought she'd have one for him as well. But she kept that to herself.

Back on the street Johnson pulled up in the Range Rover, and Azunna and Sam jumped in. "Let's go."

"Where?"

"Away from here. Fast."

"What the hell was that?" Sam was very confused and concerned.

"Uche killed my parents. I did not know that until I saw him, he had a face that I would never forget. But I don't think he knows I remember that night. And somehow, he has managed to get Ngozi here."

"Your sister? Fuck! Is she in danger?"

"Yes. As are we." Azunna was deadpan. Sam recognized that the woman he loved had that certain ice in her veins that made her very, very good at this work. She continued, "I was very impressed by that visa operation, weren't you?"

"Impressed? The whole visa system has been compromised!

Think of the implications for our social safety net. The security of the country is at stake."

Azunna just stared at him over her sunglasses. "Johnson, get us back to that office you picked us up from, then go find a place where you can wait for a while securely. Sam, have Ahmed meet us at the office."

They made the short drive back to where they met Ahmed. Sam and Azunna jumped out and Johnson sped away.

Ahmed showed up three minutes later and they followed him up the stairs.

"What have you got?" Ahmed began without preamble.

"Uche is running a human smuggling operation and looking to expand it. Two hundred more young people are going to be smuggled tonight. We can put a stop to that right now. Ahmed, can you get those five officers and two vehicles?"

"Yes. I have a squad of five armed officers. I can have two Land Rovers. What do you have in mind?"

"Ok – that makes eight of us, that should be more than enough. I don't get the sense that Uche worries too much about security."

"Once we arrest him, we might have to deal with the regular police, but I can probably manage that."

"Sure." No need to tell him there was not going to be an arrest. He was bringing armed officers. He understood things could go sideways. "Here's the plan. Uche is expecting us to see the operation anyway." She pulled out a Google Maps printout of the airport. "Now, Ahmed, tell me if any of this is out of date, but with this group of huts here, we can set up and observe what is going on. Before passengers board, we will drive across the airfield and grab Uche. Straight forward enough. Meet back here in an hour?"

"I will be here with my men."

"Excellent."

With that Ahmed left.

"That seems like a terrible plan Kiana. Won't Uche be able to respond?"

It was time to take Sam fully in. "Our arrival with armed Nigerian officers will provoke a violent response. That is exactly what we want. Uche is leaving that airfield in a body bag."

Chapter Thirty-four

Ngozi was at a bit of a loss. She had not agreed to specifically do anything for Uncle G. He had taken his entourage with him and left her with the staff of this facility. She was tempted to simply walk out of there, but she had no idea where she was or how she could get back to the hotel in Port Harcourt. She checked her phone. There it was an email from her sister with some fairly precise instructions. Her tone didn't even sound that angry.

The children started to gather. The effectiveness of air conditioning here had changed the entire environment. All of the supposed scholarship winners had bathed and been given new clothes – sensible black shoes, grey trousers for the boys and skirts for the girls, white shirts or blouses, and blue jumper vests. Too warm for Nigeria, but not for their destination. They each wore a small satchel with what Ngozi presumed were the sum total of their worldly possessions.

Ngozi was tempted to start talking to them but worried their stories would break her heart. After reading the message from Kiana, she guessed there would be plenty of time to learn those stories later. Ngozi still wasn't even sure what role she was supposed to be playing here. She asked a kindly-looking woman in a staff uniform, but she knew nothing other than that Ngozi was supposed to get on the coaches and travel to the airport with the children.

The older childcare seemed excited, hopeful. One teenage girl caught Ngozi's eye. She could have been the sister of the girl she had seen at the other facility, cleaned up, changed, and with a tentative smile on her face. But her eyes spoke volumes – whatever her future held, there was a good deal of trauma to deal with from her past.

After half an hour, the coaches Ngozi had seen at the first compound arrived. After they parked and the doors opened, the children were sent out to board. Ngozi walked with the woman she spoke to earlier; she had a clipboard, and they went to the door to the first bus, while another woman with matching clipboard and uniform went to the other bus.

The would-be students boarded as quietly as they could after their names were checked off the list. Some of them seemed to have made fast friends they tried to sit next to, while others kept to themselves, staring down at their new, smart shoes. Ngozi imagined that leaving their homes and families behind must have been very difficult, but even the youngest of this group must have realized they lived in crushing poverty and the opportunity to go to school in Europe represented not just help for them but for their families as well.

Finally, all one hundred passengers were loaded onto the buses. Ngozi and the staff boarded last, finding seats towards the front. Luckily the buses were air-conditioned, and it was on full blast. Ngozi was parched and wished she had asked for a bottle of water before they left but decided that maybe she would get one at the airport. It occurred to her too that the NGO staff might be looking for her back in Port Harcourt. She really needed to figure out how to contact them. But it might be too late for that now.

She looked at her phone again, to make sure she understood what Kiana wanted her to do. Feeling like she needed to conceal the contents of the email she turned at an angle so the matron she was sat next could not read it, but the woman seemed lost in her own concerns anyway. Ngozi put her phone in her pocket and looked out the windshield as the bus pulled out of the compound.

***

Azunna along with Khumalo, Ahmed, and five other field officers of the Nigerian National Intelligence Agency sat in two Land Rovers parked between two thatched roof huts on the far side of the Owerri International Cargo Airport. Ahmed and his team were all armed with Heckler and Koch MP5s. The sub-machine gun had been ubiquitous to most western Special Operations and Police Forces for fifty years. Nonetheless, in the Nigerian context, a team armed with high-quality German weapons meant that they knew something about firearms and tactics.

From here they had a full view of the airport, the runway, the aircraft, and the interior of the hangar. They were facing the west and it was a good two hours till sundown. The common grey ceiling of the wet season had broken up. Rain was predicted later, but the sun was still enough in the sky that shots of yellow and an emerging orange worked their way through the gaps in the cloud cover. It was humid as always, their clothing clung to their bodies.

The old Airbus A310-300, once a mainstay of Nigerian Airways, sat near the hangar closest to them, farthest away from the main terminal. This aircraft could take a light load of passengers and with extended-range tanks, make this an easy flight to any place south of Scotland.

Even with the cloud cover, Azunna felt beat down by the intensity of the heat and humidity, though this was being counterbalanced by the confrontation she knew was coming. The Land Rover was one of the old-school 110 Defenders. No top, and the windscreen folded down, in an aging safari-tan with white wheels. Probably a leftover Biafran Army vehicle. She sat in the front passenger seat, her right foot on the point where the windscreen met the bonnet, slouched down, ready for observation and preparing for action.

She found it difficult to determine how long the aircraft had been sitting there – it almost glistened with water droplets and humidity, but the fading paint might mask appearance of freshness. Azunna would have been surprised if it had overnighted there. With no apparent fences on this airstrip, one could hardly leave it unattended.

Several tankers had come in off the highway to provide fuel, presumably having made the trip from Port Harcourt. This airport was advertised as an "International Cargo Airport," but it was going to have trouble gassing up any aircraft that was going farther than Cameroon, Equatorial Guinea, or maybe Benin without outside help.

A small van approached, barely piquing Azunna's interest. Five people got out all wearing similar outfits. This must be the crew.

"Alright Sam, let's go." They got out of the trucks. "Ahmed, wait until Sam calls for you, unless of course something like shooting starts. Then we could use your assistance."

"Sounds good." In the brief hours together, Ahmed was impressed with the visitor from London. She was smart, dedicated, and tough. "Hey, Azunna." She turned. Ahmed started to pull his Browning Hi-Power out of his holster. "You might need this. Just in case."

She smiled. "Right." He re-holstered the weapon.

Azunna and Sam started across the tarmac. For some reason, they both broke into a jog. No plane was coming in for landing for the foreseeable future, as far as they knew and they were in no rush, but it just seemed strange to causally stroll across a large runway. They got to the aircraft just as the air-stair truck arrived. The crew seemed a little surprised by their arrival, probably because they had just walked up seemingly out of nowhere, but they didn't seem shocked.

The crew was attired in matching livery, grey trousers for the two men and grey skirts for the three women, all with matching white shirts, patch pockets and epaulettes. *Air Uche* was stitched in red over the left breast pocket and they all had name tags on the right. The pilots also had wings pinned on their right pocket flaps.

Azunna approached the group, sticking out her hand to no one in particular, "Kiana Azunna, UXT. Mr. Uche should have mentioned that I was coming along with my colleague Mr. Khumalo."

"Ah, yes," said one of the pilots extending his hand. "I understand your company might be able to give us some relief. Glad to meet you, you are welcome." Handshakes and names were exchanged all around. For Azunna these pleasantries went in one ear and out the other. She had come on this mission with one agenda point, but her sister's name on that manifest and the revelation of Uche's relationship with her parents had added another.

"So, tell me about your operation here." Azunna was throwing the most generic question out there to see what would happen.

"We have been running this flight about once a week. Sometimes the UK, sometimes Spain or Italy. Of course, that is in addition to all the other flying Mr. Uche has us do. We are quite busy, sometimes cargo and sometimes him and his entourage."

"Really? Where do you take him?"

"We have been to Cairo, Damascus, Tehran, Baghdad. Small airfield in Austria."

All the garden spots. Abigor Legion operations, Azunna thought.

"It's not that these scholarship flights are a bother per se. It's just the timing wears on you. The overnight flight from here to Europe so that the young people going on these scholarships can make bus, train, or flight connections to other places and arrive the same day. And we never know where we are off to next from Europe. We can be returning to Nigeria, or we can be off to someplace else. We are always pushing our work hours to the maximum and get the minimum required rest."

"How do the children seem on these flights."

"Oh, they are always so excited!" One of the female cabin crew spoke up. "What an opportunity for them! They are hoping to change not only their future but the futures of their families."

Azunna gave a half-hearted smile and a nod. She could not decide whether this flight crew had cynically absorbed the cover story for this human trafficking ring, or really believed it. She supposed that when hope was in short supply, any source of it would do.

"Sam, why don't you talk with the crew about what the operation here is like and what sort of services we would need to coordinate, hotels, fuel, et cetera. I am going to take look around."

With that Azunna left Khumalo to chat with the crew – she wanted to stake out the killing ground. She estimated that there was just enough room for any busses to travel from the main entrance to the hangar and pass between the hangar and the aircraft. With no proper lounge, the hangar would at least keep the passengers out of the rain or sun, keeping up the pretence of being cared for as opposed to being sent off into slavery.

There was not much else in the hangar. The floors were an aging concrete. They had never been smoothed out correctly and now had cracks. The aircraft-support equipment looked serviceable but minimal. Any aircraft that had major problems after landing here was going to be stuck for a long time.

The hangar itself was basic, made of concrete and sheet metal. If she was able to manoeuvre Uche so there was no one behind him, he should be the only casualty. That and the dreams of the people who thought they had received scholarships to a variety of British schools. That was the thing about human trafficking, it relies on the victims to believe that whatever system they are giving themselves over to will improve their lot in life. Azunna turned and looked out the hangar, down the runway. The sun had continued to descend, the orange hues grew darker, bolder. And the time was drawing closer.

***

The coaches were high quality, well made, comfortable and intended to be smooth, but no suspension was going to be able to completely erase the challenges of the Nigerian road network. The trip from the compound was a challenge. Ngozi was incredulous when they came to a point on a major road that was just completely washed away. The coaches, in a long line of cars and trucks, eased off the tarmac and onto the rocky ground, all the vehicles slowly making their way down into the shallow culvert, and then back up onto the tarmac.

Ngozi noted that neither the bus driver nor the woman she was with seemed phased at all. It was just another part of life. When things like this happened here in Nigeria, people simply got on with whatever they needed to do.

As it was later in the afternoon, the streets were beginning to fill up with people beginning their journeys home. As the bus passed through Owerri's Freedom Square, Ngozi took note of the city name, finally figuring out where she was. She had missed so much in the nauseating ride from Port Harcourt.

"How many people live Owerri?" She had finally engaged the woman sitting next to her.

"Oh, easily over a million people."

The two-coach convoy was now heading out of the city proper on the Owerri Omuvva Road. The coaches made a left turn by a gas station onto Airport Road. They had been driving for almost an hour. Google maps would tell you that it was only thirty minutes from Freedom Square to the airport, but the coaches were slow, and the computer algorithm could not account for the random overloaded truck that was coming to the end of its life as a road-going vehicle.

The coaches made another left turn and Ngozi could finally see the entrance to the airport. She could see no fences but did spy a red and white barrier on the road that police officers manning the gate raised as the coaches approached. Clearly, they were expected.

They pulled in through a small car park and went on to the access road, heading towards the tarmac. Ngozi could see the plane as well as a large hanger, evidently where the coaches were headed. She tried to estimate distances as she had been told to do, but even more so she tried to ready her mind for action. She needed to play her part. She noted that the cloud cover was building once again, the gaps that let the setting sun in were beginning to close. She stared out the windscreen, she took a deep breath, slowly released it and looked for her sister.

***

Azunna watched the two large coaches easing themselves into the hangar. Realizing that Ngozi was probably on one of them, Azunna worked her way towards the opposite side of the hangar, away from where the coaches were parking. She positioned herself so that Ngozi could not miss her standing on the other side of the building. The busses stopped, punctuated by the application of the vehicle airbrakes and a loud hiss.

As the coaches came to a stop, a small convoy of three Mercedes-Benz G63 SUVs, painted a flat black and with tinted windows all the way around, came speeding onto the tarmac. The sudden appearance of the convoy seemed to be expected as the aircrew continued about their businesses unphased.

Uche. *What the fuck is it with bad guys and G-Wagons. Always need to make an entrance.*

The doors on the middle vehicle were open almost as the vehicles rolled to a halt, with Uche and Jay-Jay exiting before their entourage could open the doors for them. The pilot trotted over to Uche and Jay-Jay. Azunna could see them exchanging words and then the pilot pointing over at her as Sam made his way back across the hangar.

"What's the plan?"

"I guess we will have to see how this plays out."

"Want me to call Ahmed?"

"Not yet." She was completely unfazed, while he was getting more anxious by the minute. Jay-Jay and Uche broke up, Uche heading over to the coaches while Jay-Jay made his way to Sam and Azunna.

"What do you think, Ms. Azunna? Can we make it work?"

Her expressionless face suddenly gave a big smile, mirroring the attitude Jay-Jay had been portraying all day.

"Absolutely, Jay-Jay! I think we have a plan that will work!"

"Excellent." Jay-Jay smiled back, thinking he had the upper hand and that he would deliver what his boss had demanded: the Azunna sisters on a plate. "Mr. Uche will be here in a minute."

"Brilliant."

As they now stood three abreast watching and waiting for Uche, the complete lack of expression returned to Azunna's face. She hoped her sister had read the email. More importantly, she hoped that she was ready for action.

***

As the coaches pulled into the hangar, Ngozi was half standing in her seat straining to see the layout of the area. She sat back down when she spied the lone figure standing, waiting across the building. At least she now had a fixed point to head to if things got out of hand.

The doors of the coaches opened, and the women-in-charge started having the would-be scholars unload the buses and prepare to board the planes for what they hoped would be a better life.

Uche, not normally a patient man, waited for the children to exit the coaches. He revelled in the power these children represented, and his power over their lives. He had the power to take them from families with the desperate hope that the separation would lead to a better life for the children, if not them all. Sometimes they were so grateful, he could barely contain the glee he got from manipulating them as he waved away their thanks. So, he was happy to patiently wait as the children slowly climbed down the stairs of the coaches and gathered, readying to board the plane.

He watched Ngozi as she emerged from the first coach. He imagined she had not noticed her sister, or he would have noticed some reaction.

The relative quiet of the scene was broken when the low roar of a Gulfstream 700 jet sounded as the plane broke through the low cloud ceiling at the far end of the runway. Good thought Uche, Ngozi's ride was here.

***

The Gulfstream jet was a new wrinkle for Azunna. She considered two possibilities, the first being that the plane's arrival was completely unrelated to the scene unfolding in front of her. She quickly dismissed that idea. A criminal like Uche would never leave anything like that to chance.

So, what or who was this plane bringing? Or maybe it was intended to take something or someone away. She considered that possibility as the plane taxied. She watched it park on the far end of the taxiway, the pilot turning it so the cabin door faced the hangar but so it was angled such that it would be easy to take off. The cabin door opens, but the engines remained on and idling. This plane was not going to be staying for very long.

***

Inside the Gulfstream, Dr. Werner Gantz wrinkled his nose. He hated leaving Austria. Travelling around parts of Europe was OK, but going further south than northern Italy offended his sense of orderliness. He was a portly man and the warmth of a place like Owerri was going to wear on him immediately. He had worn a tropical weight suit, but he knew the minute he stepped off the plane his shirt was going to be soaking wet from sweat.

He remained in his seat until the door opened, and once it did, he felt the hot air rush into the cabin, despite the air-conditioning working overtime to combat it. Normally, he would not have made this trip, trusting it to one of his many minions in the organization. But, with his transportation network, Uche had already made himself one of the most valuable members of the Legion and, when Uche had explained his plan, Dr. Gantz had reluctantly agreed.

Standing at the top of the stairs, he donned some black plastic-rimmed sunglasses, because even as the cloud cover continued to develop, there was still a glare, and his eyes were sensitive. He turned to the head cabin attendant. "I will not be long, be ready to go." He had one of those flat accents that made it impossible to tell where he was originally from when he spoke English. The only thing the listener could be certain of was that it was not his first language.

Despite his less-than-svelte figure, he used his long legs to make quick strides across the tarmac towards the waiting group of people in the hangar.

***

Seeing Dr. Gantz making his way towards Azunna, Khumalo, and Jay-Jay, Uche finally started to line the scholarship students up for boarding. Azunna spotted Ngozi, and they made eye contact for the first time then quickly broke it lest Uche or Jay-Jay notice. The last thing she wanted to do at this point was a hostage situation on an aircraft. That rarely went well.

Jay-Jay- moved over and Uche stood next to Azunna.

"When I saw that you were who UXT was sending I knew we could do business. What a happy coincidence that you worked for them."

"Mmmm," Azunna gave an untelling half-smile.

"Are you not excited to be in business with family?"

"Who's this?" Azunna changed the subject with the approach of the man in the blue suit who had arrived on the Gulfstream.

"Ah, this is one of my partners, Dr. Gantz

The connections were coming together more quickly now. This was the man who had been meeting with al-Assad just before she had killed him. The Abigor Legion connection was confirmed, but what was he doing *here*?

"I have a surprise for you, Kiana. Ngozi! Ngozi! Come here!" He waived her over. "Aren't you surprised to see your sister here? Three thousand miles from home! Sisters reunited in Africa! In Nigeria! Your real home!"

Azunna just continued to stare at the plane and would-be passengers. Ngozi started towards the group at a half-trot, trying to look surprised that her sister was there.

"I knew I could do business with you! Unlike your parents. Now I know your company can and *will* spend a good deal of effort making these flights several times a week. But I want to *ensure* that. So, Dr. Gantz here is going to take Ngozi with him back to Austria. To ensure your good behaviour, Kiana."

The humidity of the late day made Azunna's shirt cling to her body, and she suddenly became very aware of the moves she would need to draw her weapon. "I have to hand it to you Uncle G," the name hung in the air, dripping with sarcasm, "that visa breach is really quite something. Fred would be making millions of dollars a year based on his capability if he had been born in another country."

Now it was Uche that was surprised. He had expected fear and compliance from Azunna. Uche's face showed confusion, and he diverted his attention to Jay-Jay. He snapped at his erstwhile aide and number one sycophant. "You fool. Why did you show them the fourteenth floor?"

"Boss, they insisted on knowing how they were going to enter the UK legally. I didn't know what to do."

"Idiot!" Uche growled again at Jay-Jay. His demeanour changed and now he was clearly off balance in the dance he had so carefully tried to construct with Azunna.

Azunna continued to watch the children making their way to the aircraft, not meeting her sister's eye. "Ngozi, Mr. Uche would you like you to get on that plane with this gentleman and be his prisoner in Austria to ensure my good behaviour. What do you think about that?"

"I don't think that is a good idea," Ngozi said in a small voice.

Azunna looked at Uche. "Don't worry. The visa operation is the least of your sins. I know that this is a human trafficking operation, for instance. One that is only is the tip of the iceberg."

The iron grey of the clouds was now tending towards carbon, it was going to start raining. Azunna snickered. "It's over. You actually thought that you could *buy* Ngozi through the NGO, then hide her away in Austria, compelling me to do your bidding for who knows how long?" Her tone was questioning, but she was not expecting an answer. "You lack so much imagination. I know the whole story." She looked Uche dead in the eye. "And you don't know half of it."

There is a moment just before someone with great power loses that power, where they look into the future and realize it is all gone. They just have not accepted it yet. Whether it was Mubarak in Egypt, Ceausescu in the courtyard in Romania, or Pablo Escobar on a rooftop in Medellin. Uche did not recognize the feeling that was overcoming him as he was about to join them in the abyss of history.

"You know nothing, Kiana. I built a thriving business out of the wreckage of the Biafra War, a war caused by your grandfather's desire for 'democracy!' Then your father and mother tried to come back to "raise awareness!' God, how those do-gooders make me so fucking angry! The world is nothing but predator and prey. I even warned your father to stay out of my affairs, I gave him a chance. *I* didn't kill your parents. They killed themselves because they gave me no other choice. Besides, errant fuel tankers on roadkill hundreds in Nigeria every year. They were nothing but a statistic."

A look of horror crossed Ngozi's face. She looked at Uche with eyes that showed both fear and disgust. Everything was happening so fast she just knew she had to keep her wits about her if she was to survive.

"I know about the Abigor Legion," Azunna said flatly.

It was at this point that Dr. Gantz, who had so far said nothing turned on his heels and made his way back to the waiting Gulfstream.

Azunna ignored him, continuing to stare at Uche. "I am assuming that this aircraft has moved people as well as drugs for the al-Assads as well. Who knows, maybe you even brought people back here from Syria for them to disappear. And I don't think Dr. Gantz, who by the way you did not say goodbye to, or the other principals in the Legion are going to be happy with you, given how careless you or your buddy have been with information. But, after meeting your friend Maher, what I really want to know is this. What the *fuck* is it with men like you and the love of the G-Wagon?"

Uche and Jay-Jay, with all their flair and bluster, were not accustomed to real violence. They may have thrown a punch, pulled a trigger, or even ordered someone killed, but the true study and application of violence was reserved mostly for those employed on that basis. The repetitive training had made pulling the trigger for King and country pure muscle memory for Azunna. Thus, when Jay-Jay pulled out a knife and started at Ngozi, it was with one easy sweeping motion that Azunna drew the H&K P30 from her right side, brought the front sight post down pointed directly at his skull, lined up the rear notched site and pulled the trigger twice. Anyone watching would have been confused by how fast it had happened.

The two explosions that had propelled an equal number of 147 grain 9mm jacketed hollow point bullets into Jay-Jay's skull created several reactions. The first was that Jay-Jay's body now lay in an ever-expanding pool of blood. The second was that Dr. Gantz, who was about two-thirds of the way to his plane, broke into an awkward run as the Rolls-Royce Pearl 700 engines began to rev up.

Next, the young people who thought they were about to board an aeroplane and had been oblivious to the unfolding drama across the hangar, began scattering for cover, running in all different directions screaming and shrieking. Khumalo had the presence of mind to press send on a prewritten text to Ahmed calling for help. That action though was completely unnecessary, because Ahmed had been watching the whole scene play out through binoculars, and the minute the knife came out the two Land Rovers were on their way down the tarmac as the Gulfstream fled the unfolding fight. Khumalo also pulled out his own sidearm, keeping Azunna covered.

As Azunna moved her aim from Jay-Jay's body to Uche, he grabbed Ngozi. He was holding a gun to her head, and there was terror in her eyes. Azunna knew the only way to save her was to ignore her and focus on Uche. He was dead. He just did not know it yet.

"You should put the gun down. Killing more people in our family is not going to resolve anything here. You are just like your parents. They were interfering in our ability to raise money too. They were so naive!"

Who said irony was dead? She was already tired of his attempts at self-justification. While he rambled and shouted, she closed the distance to just five metres. Not ideal but his head was big and Ngozi, if not petite, was small enough. Azunna was just going to trust in her training and skill.

"Do you even know what time it is!" Uche shouted in his West African lilt. His face was red with rage. His empire had crumbled in a matter of minutes, and at the hands of the child of someone he thought he had eliminated twenty years ago. And to top it all off, a woman.

"Yes, it is time to die."

Time seemed to be moving slowly as Azunna put her plan in motion, but what happened next occurred so quickly that no one had time to process all of it until much later. Azunna nodded to Ngozi. Suddenly Ngozi's right fist shot straight out and with all the power she could muster she brought her right elbow back into Uche's solar plexus. He released his left arm as he doubled over in pain, but as his right arm fell away his gun fired. The round struck Ngozi in the side of the head, and she collapsed to the floor in her own blood.

With time moving so quickly it was a simultaneous action that as Uche's gun went off Azunna exhaled. And pulled the trigger twice.

Boom. Boom.

Two rounds from the H&K sent Uche sprawling backwards, releasing his grip on Ngozi. Two bullets had entered his head, one in the forehead and the other just underneath his right eye. Azunna was now on autopilot. As the blood pooled around his Uche's head, Azunna reached for her Thuraya satellite smartphone and opened the text function.

Stand by for photo.

Fortunately, at least for identification purposes, the bullets had entered Uche's head so quickly and at such short range, that they had done relatively little damage to his face, although he did have a certain grey balm about him now. She moved his head just enough to get a square-on shot, snapped the photo and hit upload.

Sending . . .
Delivered.
Read.

Three dots. Then nothing. Three dots again.

Stand by for confirmation.

Three dots. Three dots again.

Identity confirmed. Godswill Uche has been terminated.

Mission complete. Return to base.

Roger.

***

Khumalo rushed over to Ngozi to provide what first aid he could. Azunna was quickly by his side, her professional demeanour having been washed away in the seconds it had taken to complete her assignment before beginning to grieve her sister.

She settled on her knee, next to Sam and reached out to touch Ngozi's body. Suddenly Azunna was back in time, but at a place not too far from where they were right then. It seemed no matter how hard she tried tragedy was destined to follow her and she was going to lose the ones she loves most.

"Ngozi, I . . ." and tears started to flow down Azunna's cheeks. Then they heard a low moan. Ngozi stirred and Sam was able to get a closer look at her wound. He used the sleeve on his shirt to wipe away a good deal of the blood. When the gun went off, the pistol had fallen away enough that the bullet had travelled across her scalp, leaving a long wound. Sam found that, despite the amount of blood, the wound was only superficial, though she had been knocked out when her head hit the concrete.

In the time it had taken the drama to play out in the hangar, Ahmed and his team had raced down the runway and were deploying practically before the hand brakes were applied.

This was where the team from the National Intelligence Agency proved their worth. Once the shooting started the Nigerian Federal Police arrived a few minutes later, the small contingent at the airport having called for back-up. The NIA team quickly made contact, and since it was such a small organization, that worked to their advantage. The local police commander was content to wait and see what happened. He knew that the shooting had stopped. He was going to need some interactions from his commander here in Owerri. And if the scene commander knew his boss, he would need direction from Abuja. The situation was contained. No need to stick his neck out here. Being circumspect might even get him a promotion.

Khumalo grabbed his phone to text Johnson.

> We need you. The police have us cut off. Their response unit sealed the entrance to the airport.

On my way boss.

> Can you get to us?

Trust me.

Johnson rolled up to the checkpoint in the High Commissioner's Black Range Rover. He was immediately stopped at the entrance.

"Where you go, bra?" queried the Nigerian police officer.

"My boss is in the terminal on the odder side. What happened here?"

"Wait."

The Nigerian police officer quickly returned with someone more senior.

As the NCO perused Johnson's identification that showed him to be an employee of the British High Commission in Abuja, Johnson continued, "My boss flew down from Abuja. He has an important meeting tomorrow with Mr. Uche." The diplomatic plates meant the police couldn't search the vehicle. The nature of the police force made everyone so risk-averse that they were afraid of the wrong decision. Let him in with a British diplomat possible waiting in the car? Deciding to let him in would at least buy time, the NCO allowed the officer to open the gate. The Range Rover shot across the tarmac to the last hangar.

As Johnson pulled up, Khumalo was finishing tending to Ngozi's wound. He was able to get in cleaned up enough, although he was going to need a new shirt. The three of them piled into the Ranger Rover, Sam in front with Ngozi and Azunna in the back.

They had another choice to make. Try and get back through the gate or attempt to make it out the side they had come in earlier. There was no fence between the airport tarmac and the road from the south. Azunna decided they were not going to press their luck with the police.

"Johnson kill the lights. We need to get out of here, and we can't use any of the exits. We are going to slowly drive offroad, merge into the traffic on that road over there, and then you can turn your lights on. The Lufthansa flight leaves in three hours. Ngozi and I need to be on that plane."

The rain was starting. The low grey ceiling that had hung over the tarmac for most of the afternoon had finally given way to the downpour. The inky blue hues of the darker iroko tree forests mixed with the falling rain, creating contrasts, and playing tricks of movement on the eyes.

They were in the well-lit hangar at dusk, turning the lights off on the Range Rover drew absolutely no attention from the police officers on the far side of the airfield. Putting the SUV in gear, Johnson pulled the vehicle out of the hangar and turned right instead of left. He maintained an easy twenty-five mph and when the road met the runway he turned right again, heading south towards the main road that would take them away from Owerri and south to Port Harcourt.

Ensuring the all-wheel drive system was engaged, Johnson readied for the transition from tarmac to . . . well he did not know. He hoped that the ground would not be so muddy that they would have a problem with traction. Additionally, the possibility of fencing was also a concern. A Range Rover racing down the Port Harcourt Road with a chain-link fence clinging to the front would draw a great deal of unwanted attention.

There was nothing but silence in the vehicle except the sound of the air-conditioning pumping. It was a mere sixty metres from the runway to the road, but all sorts of unseen trouble could lie in those metres.

If everything went well it would only take five seconds to cross the unpaved area. The front two tires came off the tarmac and all four occupants inhaled.

One.

The grass was tall, but the brush guard handled it with ease, creating a two-metre-wide path.

Two.

The vehicle descended into a shallow drainage area.

Three.

The drainage was a small stream, and it was muddy, but there was enough vegetation that it was not a pit. Johnson's skill behind the wheel meant he knew exactly when to apply gas and when to take it off. He had timed this just right, the vehicle had enough forward momentum to keep moving forward without getting the wheels stuck and spinning.

Four.

The Supercharged V8 engine built by the expert hands at Solihull propelled the big vehicle back up the embankment.

Five.

No fence. The Range Rover drew parallel to the Port Harcourt Road, Johnson turned on the lights, put on the left turn signal, and merged into the light traffic.

They were in a dip-plated Range Rover, and if Johnson kept the speed reasonable there was no reason for anyone to stop them.

"The Lufthansa flight leaves at 2130. We should have plenty of time to make it."

"We need tickets. Ngozi give me your passport."

Ngozi rummaged around in her purse looking for her new blue passport, finally finding it in the bottom of her bag. She handed it to Azunna.

Azunna had her Thuraya open and was on the Lufthansa app.

Departure City? Port Harcourt.

Arrival City? London, Heathrow.

One way or round trip? One way.

Number of travellers? 2

Departure date? Today

Class? Business.

Traveller information.

Azunna's data had already pre-populated, and she carefully input Ngozi's information.

Use saved credit card? Yes.

Are you ready to purchase? Yes

Processing.

Under the best of circumstances, this always seemed like a pain and now with the very short timeline, Azunna's innate impatience was tried to its limits.

Approved. Enjoy your flight.

"We have our tickets. Let's go." Johnson pressed a little harder on the gas pedal.

The sun was well down, and the Range Rover was as comfortable as could be possible on Nigerian roads. At least the oil money kept some infrastructure in Imo and Rivers states somewhat better than the rest of the country. The road between Abuja and Lagos, the political and financial capitals, was washed out at points with no hope or plan of repair.

Azunna allowed herself to breath a small sigh of relief. The rain started to fall harder.

Chapter Thirty-Five

The traffic had increased. The sun had gone down and it was still raining hard. Another West African downpour. Some drivers used their lights, but others did not. To the extent there was a speed limit, no one obeyed.

Emotions were running high in the Range Rover. Ngozi, her wound quickly dressed and cleaned, was quickly passing from the fear of death to the elation of being alive. Although she did notice that she probably needed to change her blood-soaked shirt before they boarded the plane.

Azunna was reasserting control over her emotions. She briefly had flashes of guilt about the fact she had focused on confirming Uche's death with London before checking on her sister, but also reminded herself that if it had been the worst case, then there was nothing she could have done. Ngozi was going to be fine, and it was time to move on.

Khumalo was somewhere between euphoric and determined. It was an odd mix, to say the least. The adrenaline of the action had gone straight to his head. Watching Azunna, watching Kiana, confirmed what he had been feeling since that road trip in Wales was so bizarrely interrupted. He was in love with her. And even though she had been spending all her London time in his flat in Fulham, they had not actually used those words.

"Johnson, could you slow down a tad please?" Azunna asked. The speed, the rain, and the bright lights had created a sense of worry in Azunna that she could not identify.

"Yes, ma'am. Just trying to get to the airport on time."

The conversation in the vehicle was subdued, it was mostly everyone fussing over Ngozi. Making sure she was alright. Wiping the blood away. Azunna trying to get her bag so Ngozi would not walk into the airport in a blood-soaked shirt.

"Sam, are you set to return to Abuja?"

"I'll catch the first flight in the morning and then onto London the next day after I warp things up at the High Commission. No problem."

"Good."

The bright lights and the rain were becoming very disorienting for Azunna, and she was feeling at her emotional end. She settled in her seat and tried to close her eyes.

Sam unclipped his seatbelt and turned around as best he could in the front seat of the Range Rover. He wanted to look at Azunna, full on. His heart was full, and he could not keep quiet any longer.

"Kiana?"

"Yes?" She had an almost bored lilt to her voice, her head rolling back and forth on the headrest, eyes still closed.

"Kiana, look at me." She opened her eyes and saw Sam staring at her earnestly."

As they looked into each other's eyes, Sam struggled to say something appropriate. Suddenly a bright light suddenly appeared as if a stagehand had thrown the main switch at a climactic scene in a play. It was followed by the sickening sounds of metal-on-metal colliding and glass shattering.

Being a relatively new vehicle, the Range Rover did well. The airbags deployed, and the frame held. Afterwards people who viewed the wreck would remark that the Range Rover had gotten the better of the forty-year-old Mercedes semi-truck.

Johnson was the first one to come around, having been momentarily stunned by the airbag deployment. He helped Ngozi out of the back and they circled around to help Azunna out of the vehicle.

She was coming around as they yanked the door open, she was still trying to make sense of it all when she finally looked at Sam. Sam in his desire to open his heart to Kiana had taken off his seatbelt and was at an odd angle in the car when the collision occurred. Unrestrained he had been thrown forward and then back, snapping his neck and killing him instantly. Sam lay there in the vehicle awkwardly his eyes looking out now at nothing. Kiana Azunna collapsed into her sister's arms, and they sat in the pouring rain waiting for help.

***

Azunna and Ngozi spent two nights in a Nigerian hospital, mostly because there was no immediate place for them to go. Johnson contacted the High Commission and a representative worked with their contacts to make sure they were well cared for and that the fee would be paid. Another High Commission driver transported them to the Port Harcourt International Airport.

A subdued Azunna still needed to navigate her and her sister back to London. Ahmed covered for them in Owerri, so the Nigerian authorities were not on the lookout for them. Kiana bought two new tickets.

"Kiana, are you ok?" Ngozi had her turn to comfort her sister.

"I'm fine, I'm fine." She didn't really believe it herself.

The sisters got in the line for the security screening to get into the airport. They put their bags on the conveyer and emptied their pockets. The first screening was cursory, and they drew no attention.

Next was check-in. Business class and Azunna's long history of travel with the airline made this easy. Seats 4 D and G, near the front of the plane. The middle of the aircraft meant they could both get up without disturbing the other. And they would remain anonymous to most of the other passengers.

Next up was immigration. Azunna pushed the two blue British passports though the opening in the booth.

"You need to leave on your Nigerian passports," the officer stated without opening them.

"Sir, if you open our passports and look, you will see that we were both born in London. We are British citizens." Azunna was using all her energy to not challenge the bureaucrat behind the glass unnecessarily. He grunted and opened the passports, flipped the passports over and scanned them, tapped a few buttons, and then gave them their exit stamps. He handed them back without another word and waved them forward.

Azunna grabbed her bag and Ngozi's hand. The next security check was like the first one except for that it was intended to comply with the standards set in Europe. Even when the plane arrived in Frankfurt it would park at the far end of the terminal and be met by many Polizei, mostly looking for illegal immigrants. The important thing here was that they did not check any identity documents.

Security screenings in airports around the world seemed to have been interminably slowed, both by changing rules, or interpretations thereof, and passengers who at least acted like it was the first time boarding a plane. Although it seemed to take forever, the sisters were through security a few minutes later and on their way to the gate.

Lufthansa Flight 595 from Port Harcourt to Frankfurt via Abuja, was boarding when they arrived at the gate, which suited Azunna just fine. No waiting in the terminal.

The contract gate agent scanned their boarding cards, and they made their way down the jet way. It was connected to the aircraft about a third of the way down. In larger, more well-equipped airports, two would have been connected to the aircraft – one for economy passengers and one for those in premium classes, but here all shared the same. When they stepped onto the plane, they were greeted by the German aircrew and directed to turn left while most people turned right.

Seated, the cabin crew brought them sparkling wine, unbidden. It was a Champagne Duval-Leroy Brut Reserve and for an airline, quite excellent. Normally this was one of the perks of international travel Azunna relished, but she took a few sips and set it down. Ngozi on the other hand quickly downed hers.

***

It seemed like forever, but the German crew was efficient. The Germans spent the night and day in Port Harcourt, essentially confined to their hotels. They want to get going as well. Twenty minutes after the sisters boarded, the door shut, and the Airbus was taxiing. With no long line up of international flights, they were cleared to take off and the German flight crew wasted no time in getting airborne.

The flight was just about an hour and the sisters passed it mostly in silence. It touched down ten minutes past 2200. The onwards flight to Frankfurt was not scheduled to depart Abuja until 2330 but they would depart as soon as everyone was on board. The airport was far enough outside of the city that many of the diplomatic missions had policies that required their people to be at the airport before sundown. The airport was small enough that no one wanted to kill time there, unlike Frankfurt, De Gaulle, or Heathrow where there were plenty of distractions.

The plane pulled up to one of the two jet bridges. With no one disembarking once the door opened, it should be a quick turnaround. It had been less than two days since the shootout in Owerri and Sam Khumalo's death, but to Azunna it felt like a lifetime ago. A change of location and a glass of sparkling wine could do that.

Even as others got up to stretch, the sisters remained firmly in their seats. The Lufthansa cabin crew closed the door, and the aircraft backed away. The cabin crew brought them two more glasses of sparkling wine and now Azunna was little more relaxed she followed her sister's lead and knocked it back in one.

The Abuja airport has one runway. Remarkable for a capital city, it runs on the 04/22 access. That night Lufthansa 595 took off from runway 04. The big Airbus 330 gained altitude quickly, the German pilot giving the Rolls Royce engines all the gas they could consume, banked left towards Niger, Algeria, the Mediterranean and home to Europe. They would all see the sunrise in Frankfurt.

Ngozi gazed at her sister who was seemingly lost in her own thoughts. Kiana Azunna was realising that all of her efforts to protect her sister had just sheltered her from the reality of the world. She was going to need to work on that. Maybe later.

***

They sat in silence for a few minutes. The cabin crew was preparing to serve a late dinner. Maybe some good food and a few glasses of wine would help. Azunna asked for the wine list, and after careful consideration decided on the 2016 Gran Reserva from the Alta Palma Vineyard in Estampa, Chile. It was a Cabernet Malbec Syrah blend and was excellent.

Azunna savoured the taste as the tannins rolled around in her mouth, and after a few moments, the intense blackcurrant and oak flavours allowed her to think of something other than the last several days. She finished that glass as their meals arrived and asked for another.

Dinner was grilled tenderloin of beef with balsamic onion sauce, almond crusted vegetable and potato patty, green beans ragout and turned carrot and, while it was never going to be the fastest thing on a SoHo menu, it was quite good. If she had not known better, Azunna might have believed a chef had just grilled the meat in the forward galley.

"Kiana?" Ngozi spoke up uncertainly. "I'm so sorry. About Sam. I did not know you and him were that close."

Azunna mulled Sam's last words. "Neither did I. I mean I guess I thought we might be going that way, but he had never said that before."

"Did . . . do you love him?"

Azunna appreciated Ngozi's keeping him in the present. One of the things she had learned whether it was her parents, Tom, Phoebe, and now Sam is that even after they died they never really left. Azunna thought for a while, letting the question hang in the air.

"What were you doing there? I thought you were in the Royal Marines." Maybe she needed a different route of conversation.

Azunna signalled a member of the cabin crew and asked for two whiskies. It was Dewars. Not her first choice, but it would do.

The drinks arrived, and Azunna handed one to Ngozi. Ngozi had never drank much in the way of spirits, but she sensed this was a serious occasion and did not mention it. Azunna raised her glass. "To Sam Khumalo. The man I love." They clinked glasses.

"I am in the Royal Marines, my love. In fact, I was promoted, I'm a major now. We were chasing down that human smuggling operation. Sam and I had been working on it for several months."

"Oh, wow, that's amazing." This was the first time Ngozi had worked through complicated things like death as an adult. Someone important to her sister had just died in front of her and yet life had to go on. "I guess I had no idea that Royal Marines did spy-like things."

Azunna said nothing, allowing the silence and Ngozi's imagination to fill in the gaps. Ngozi was already accustomed to vague answers about Azunna's work and this seemed to satisfy her.

"You know Uche donated money to the DRC and told them to hire me. That's why I got the internship."

"Really?" This did interest Azunna mildly. "I guess he thought he was one step ahead of us." She saw no reason to get into her cover story with Ngozi.

Ngozi leaned across the wide business class armrest and put her head on Kiana's shoulder. Kiana patted her forearm, stroking it briefly.

The cabin crew cleared the dishes, and Azunna called for another round of drinks.

"You know, Kiana, I am still an intern with the DRC. Maybe we could do something together? You know, work on the environmental issues, but also, we could work on the human trafficking problems. I know he cannot be the only person doing that. Maybe we can reactivate Mum and Dad's work."

It was something that Azunna had never thought about. It intrigued her. The whiskies arrived and the sisters sipped them in silence. Ngozi was not in the habit of making toasts, but Azunna saw a glimmer of the future and silently clinked glasses with her sister.

"Now, that's an interesting idea, love. Let's sleep on it."

The cabin lights dimmed; they both transformed their wide recliner-like seats into fully lie-flat beds. Azunna thought about Sam and the pain of hearing those three words just to lose him seconds later. They adjusted their pillows and blankets as the big German plane banked northeast towards Frankfurt, and somewhere over Algeria, Azunna fell asleep thinking about Sam and how to honour the man she loved, and what the future might hold.

Chapter Thirty-Six

The two sisters arrived on the first flight from Frankfurt into Heathrow, deplaning at the Queen Elizabeth II Terminal. They cleared immigration easily, and with next to no luggage, customs simply waved them on through. Normally, Azunna would have hailed a black cab for the ride into Central London but given the early morning hour she knew they would be caught up in the commuter traffic and the last thing she wanted was to be stuck on the A40 heading into the city. They opted for the Heathrow Express into Paddington. Ngozi, accustomed to pinching pennies, had only travelled out to the airport on the Tube, so the quick clean express train seemed quite novel.

"What are you going to do?" They had kicked about of ideas around Ngozi's suggestion but had arrived at nothing concrete.

"I don't know."

They parted at Paddington Station. Ngozi splurging for an Uber home after the long trip, Azunna opting for a black cab to Vauxhall Cross. Though, not until they agreed to meet in the not-too-distant future at Hawksmoor in Knightsbridge.

It was an unusually sunny day in London. Azunna remarked to the driver on the large number of people enjoying the day in Hyde Park as the cab inched through the traffic down Park Lane. The traffic was slowed by the number of people crossing the street at Wellington Arch, walking down through Green Park towards the Palace. The cab was able to speed up as the driver skilfully manoeuvred it down Grosvenor Place, effectively the back side of the Palace.

One of the advantages of a licensed proper London cab driver is their absolute knowledge of London street geography. With a licensing program that predates the use of GPS and driving apps, they know all the backstreets. With the traffic bunching up around Victoria Station the driver put that knowledge to work, finally emerging on Vauxhall Bridge Road just past Pimlico Station. Crossing the bridge, the sun reflected off the glass of MI6 headquarters and the Thames River flowed quickly at its highest tide.

The taxi stopped where the road becomes the Albert Embankment and Azunna got out, waiting for the driver to move on before she went in the side entrance that Mills had shown her the first time she came into the building.

Riding the elevator to C's suite Azunna thought about everything that had happened that had brought her to this building once again.

Mills and C were effusive, she was surprised that they had not broken out the champagne the way they were carrying on.

Syria, Ukraine, and Nigeria. Nothing but success from their point of view. So much so that Azunna barely had a chance to get a word in, but she did what she needed to do.

It was early afternoon when she emerged from the main entrance. She was not sure where she was going to go. She still had the key to Sam's apartment but was not sure she was ready to face that. She thought maybe she would get a coffee and wander down the Thames. She had turned right and at the corner crossed the street, dodging the London traffic.

As she made the curb and looked at her designation, Pret, she saw Ngozi stand up and come towards her.

"What are you doing here?"

"I had hoped to catch up with you."

"But how did you know where . . .?" This was the first time Ngozi had really flummoxed Azunna.

"I put together a couple of clues and then hoped to get lucky. More importantly though, what happened?"

Azunna inhaled deeply. She was stepping out into the great unknown. "I quit."

"What's next then?"

"I guess we will figure that out together."

The sisters linked arms and headed back north, across the Vauxhall Bridge and enjoyed the unseasonable sun warming their faces.

* * *

Kianna Azunna will return.

Acknowledgements

This book has been a labour of love since the morning I started almost two years ago. It is an ode to a style of novel from a by-gone era. I would think fans of Fleming and Forsyth will recognize their influence.

This story is also a love letter to London and the United Kingdom. I was fortunate enough to live there for two years and it was a truly spectacular. It was during the time of COVID, and I was physically separated from my wife due to work requirements, so it was a tremendously difficult time, but made easier by living in such a fantastic city and country.

Thank you to my beta readers, Bekah Kitterman, Ian Kitterman, Carolyn Parker, and James Scott.

Members of the Royal Air Force, Royal Navy, and Royal Marines all helped me understand the services cultures much better. Any technical or cultural errors are surely my own.

Thank you to Sean Langrish for helping me understand the African diaspora in the UK better and contributing name suggestions.

Thank you to the people of Nigeria. It was a privilege to travel around your country. It is a nation of great potential.

Most of all thank you to Karen Coulson, my wife and partner in crime for over twenty-five years. She has read this book in at least three versions three times, including one complete edit. I knew I could rely on her because she would always want me to put my best foot forward. Her support in this project has been unwavering. I love you.

About the Author

Eric Coulson is a retired US Army and Foreign Service Officer. He has worked in Iraq, Egypt, Nigeria, the Dominican Republic, and the United Kingdom. He, his wife Karen, and their Egyptian street rescue Angel, split their time between Alexandria, Virginia, and various places overseas.

Made in the USA
Las Vegas, NV
08 May 2025